Good Mothers Don't

Laura Best

Vagrant Press is an imprint of Nimbus Publishing Limited
3660 Strawberry Hill Street, Halifax, NS, B3K 5A9
(902) 455-4286 nimbus.ca

Printed and bound in Canada
NB1462

Editor: Penelope Jackson
Editor for the press: Whitney Moran
Cover design: Heather Bryan
Interior design: Jenn Embree

This story is a work of fiction. Names characters, incidents, and places, including organizations and institutions, either are the product of the author's imagination or are used fictitiously.

Library and Archives Canada Cataloguing in Publication

Title: Good mothers don't / Laura Best.
Other titles: Good mothers do not
Names: Best, Laura (Laura A.), author.
Identifiers: Canadiana (print) 20200159429 |
Canadiana (ebook) 20200159437 | ISBN 9781771088282 (softcover) |
ISBN 9781771088299 (HTML)
Classification: LCC PS8603.E777 G66 2020 |
DDC C813/.6—dc23

Nimbus Publishing acknowledges the financial support for its publishing activities from the Government of Canada, the Canada Council for the Arts, and from the Province of Nova Scotia. We are pleased to work in partnership with the Province of Nova Scotia to develop and promote our creative industries for the benefit of all Nova Scotians.

For Brian

Harmony House

1975

I am well now.

When the pink dawn draws near to my bedroom window I take comfort in those words. For a long time I wouldn't have been able to make that claim, but now, if someone were to ask, "How are you, Elizabeth?" I could reply, "I'm very well, thank you," and I'd be right, and could show proof if need be. Still, there are times when I'm uncertain about that claim—when I fail to remember something so simple, or when a kernel of fear sprouts in my chest, sending out gnarly vines that spread far and wide, or when a whispered thought comes into my head when I hadn't been thinking of anything in particular at the time. The hospital says I'm well and so does the doctor who signed my release forms. They said that more than five years ago, and no one in their right mind would argue their own wellness when it's been clearly stated as fact, and neither should I.

They released me—the same authorities who declared me well—when dandelion seeds were blowing in the wind. There was a field of them along the route we took the day I came to Harmony House. I hadn't seen a dandelion for years, let alone a field full of them; soft grey balls of fluff trembling in the wind, their downy pips flying out across the air. I smiled and imagined that I might like to chase after them had we not been going at such a speed that I couldn't cry out for the car to be stopped.

That would not be the behaviour of someone who is well.

Wellness brings with it a certain responsibility, a promise not to act in a particular way or to say things of an inappropriate nature. So I watched and imagined and smiled until we were well past the field of dandelions, with Mrs. Weaver none the wiser.

"You can go home," the doctor said the day I was declared well. He was smiling as if this suggestion would have me leaping for joy. *Home* was a word I hadn't uttered in years; I feared for the longest while no such word existed for me. Or maybe it did exist in some strange, out-of-the-way place, one no one would tell me about. For sure it was some closely guarded secret and, somehow, intended for my own good.

"Where is home?" I said, sitting across from the doctor. I looked down and stopped myself from fiddling with the hem of my dress. I wondered if he knew more than he was letting on. He was a young man, too young to be in charge of my life, yet I accepted what he said even with the reservations I felt inside. They would send me home no matter where that home was. It was time to release the secret they'd been keeping from me for all these years.

"You're ready to re-enter the world, Elizabeth. That's all you need to know at this point."

His words caused my knees to tremble, and I crossed my legs to tame the uneasiness hammering away inside me. I didn't want the doctor to see how jumpy this made me in case he reversed his declaration of my wellness. His smile didn't wane, but neither did he look directly at me, as if he didn't want to see that far into the future—my future. The future that suddenly seemed murky and undefined. What was waiting for me in this future he spoke of? Even he didn't seem to have the answer to that.

"Someone will make all the arrangements. No need for you to worry about any of it," he said before he left me that day. I spent the next few weeks wondering about this someone and the arrangements they were making for me to go home.

Home. I had a home one time, one that hadn't been arranged. I must have. Everyone does. Step by step we build our lives with every choice we make, every thought we think, everything we feel and all the people we encounter. But that life, my life, was gone. I had no idea where. Places cannot stop existing. Yet it seemed that home, or at least my home, had done just that. Now there was nothing but a vague sense of familiarity lurking deep within me, a tangle of stale memories that I fought hard to remember. Flashes and flickers, small bits of the past, moved like static in my brain as I waited to start my life over again. And I began to wonder just how important those flashes and flickers might eventually prove to be. Some nights I couldn't shut them off. I'd toss and turn and wrestle the unknown, certain that something, or someone, would prevent me from ever seeing home.

This home the doctor spoke of became Harmony House, on a quiet back street in a little town not far from Halifax; a new start with freedoms I could only have dreamt about from inside the hospital walls. Home was a place to eat and sleep and watch TV, a place to breathe in the wide-open spaces, with trips into town and some money in my purse. And there was an old woman, the occupant of the bed on the other side of the room, who had been there for several years before my arrival.

"Mrs. Zimmer has her ways, but you'll get used to her soon enough," said Mrs. Weaver as we pulled up the driveway to Harmony House. "She means well." She left me standing in the middle of the room without a clue as to what I should do next. Setting my suitcase on the empty bed, I looked toward my roommate.

"Hello," I said with a smile she didn't return. Her mouth was pulled into a scowl and her flabby arms were folded in front of her. She turned her head and stared directly at me. I felt like an alien from a distant planet, a being with three eyes and a pair of horns sticking out from my head.

"Sal croaked just the other night," she said as I put my things in the dresser that had my name on it. "Stiff as a poker in the morning when they came to wake her. They just changed the sheets before you got here. The bed's probably still warm. We shared this room for four long years," she said, stretching out those last three words to indicate how miserable those years had been for her. She finished her speech by adding, with what seemed like a fair bit of satisfaction, "She always had a lot of gas." Raising a bushy eyebrow, she added, "You're not gassy, are you?"

Since the declaration of my wellness, I've contemplated my illness as many times as one can consider something they have little memory of. I'm uncertain as to when I became ill, what time of year, or even the year itself; whether dandelions were blooming or coloured leaves were hanging on the trees. I like to imagine it might have been in the cold of winter, a time when nature pulls back her hand, tired of making the flowers bloom and the grass grow; a time of rest. Certainly not in spring, with small shoots popping up from the ground, new life emerging. Perhaps I went to sleep one night fully aware of my life, but then entered a whole new realm of existence, a corridor that led me into a world different from the one I'd known all along. Or I might have been put under a fairy spell, transported to another land, stripped bare of my life, my memories stolen.

But I am well now, and all that is childlike thinking, hardly plausible explanations for the life I've lost.

So much of my life is now made up of uncertainties. But I've been told there is nothing unique in that. The only certainty in life *is* life's uncertainty. Sometimes in order for us to get to that place of wellness, things must be sacrificed. Life is a trade-off, a juggling of people, places, and events, maybe even the disappearance of time and memory if I were to make a guess. Isn't it only right that we lose some things along the way? I'm told even the most experienced juggler will drop a ball or two; I, who knows nothing about juggling, have managed to drop them all.

All these years and I still fight to push back the fear I sometimes feel, even with the declaration of my wellness. For a time it works and the panic quells for weeks, months, but eventually it floats to the top like a dead body at the rim of a lake. It's my own fault. I'll admit that much. An important aspect of wellness is the acceptance of the part we play in our own life's circumstance. *If this hadn't happened, or If only I had done things differently. Perhaps if I had been stronger.* I think all these things and wonder how much of it is true and how much is imagined, and it always comes back to the same irreversible thing.

A whispered thought as I drift into sleep.

The one thing that started it all.

You wouldn't have lost the life you had if you hadn't gone crazy.

Part I

1960

Jewel

"The roads aren't fit to be on, Cliff. You and your big ideas. How are you going to spare the gas for a joyride to Chester? You're not using the money from the steers you sold. You aren't."

"I know what I'm doing, Lizabeth," said Daddy. "Just get yourself ready."

We hadn't been to visit Aunt Joan and Uncle Dylan since Christmas. Mumma had been sulky that day. She let out a big sigh as Aunt Joan showed us the perfectly displayed gifts beneath the tree. On the way home, Daddy scolded her for acting out. "I suppose you think those fancy gadgets Dylan gave her aren't going back to the store next week. It's all for show," she'd said, turning toward the window of the truck.

When Mumma failed to move from her place at the kitchen table, Daddy looked at her and said, "Get around now, Lizabeth." She screwed up her face.

"Are we staying for dinner?" asked Jacob, gulping the last of his milk.

"We'll see," said Daddy, dipping the facecloth into a basin of warm water before wringing it out.

"And can we play down by the shore?" I asked.

"Possibly."

"No, you may *not* play by the shore," Mumma said, jumping to her feet. Jacob and I moaned our disappointment. Other than playing on the beach, there was little to do when we went to Chester. Ripping the washcloth from Daddy's hands, Mumma removed the milk from the corner of Jacob's mouth.

"Maybe some other time. The kids like playing on the sand, Lizabeth."

"Some other time is your answer for everything, and one day it's going to backfire on you, Cliff—on us all."

I looked out the kitchen window. Wet snow was spinning from the wheels of a passing car going at a snail's pace up the hill. I wondered why Daddy was so insistent that we go to Chester. Mumma was right: there would be better days for travelling.

"It's not fit to be on the road today, especially with the kids in the truck."

"You're exaggerating again, like you always do. Do you think I'd go out if it wasn't safe?"

"Go then, if you want. You don't need me."

"We're not going without you, and if you don't go Dylan and Joan will think something's wrong."

Mumma laughed. "They won't care. I could kick the bucket and they'd be happy as clams, the two of them."

"Now, that's just crazy talk, Lizabeth," said Daddy, steering Jacob's foot toward his boot. I looked quickly at Mumma, saw the peculiar look she was giving Daddy. There came a pause and I waited for what was to come.

"So you think I'm crazy, do you, Cliff?" Despite the smile that was now stretched across her face, Mumma didn't look the least bit happy. Tossing the damp washcloth at the counter, she threw her arms into the air and began to dance around in a little circle, breaking out into song.

"Crazed...crazy...crazy Elizabeth," she sang, stomping her feet as she moved around the kitchen.

"Look, I didn't mean...." Daddy's words fell flat as Mumma's voice grew louder.

"Crazy Elizabeth," she continued to sing as if it was the most delightful song in the world.

Grabbing mine and Jacob's hands, she pulled us along. Smiling, she continued to sing, "La...dee...dee...crazy Elizabeth...crazy Elizabeth." When Daddy demanded she stop, she sang even louder.

"Crazy Elizabeth...crazy Elizabeth."

We moved around in a circle, one foot over the other. Our feet gliding across the floor. We had no choice but to follow.

"La...dee...dee. Crazy...crazed...crazy Elizabeth."

"Lizabeth!" Daddy shouted, smacking his hand against the table. We all flinched.

"What's the matter? We were just having a little fun," she said, letting go of our hands.

"Can't you understand how important this is? The bank wants its money. We're barely scraping by. I've got to do something."

"And Dylan MacKay is our saviour? Well, hallelujah!"

Grabbing our coats from the hooks in the porch, Daddy began shoving Jacob's arm through one of the sleeves, nearly upsetting him off his feet. I zipped my coat and put on my cap and mitts while Jacob whined. I whispered, "Shush,

Jakey-boy," my lips trembling softly, as Daddy hastened us out the door.

"Hurry along, Lizabeth," said Daddy sternly. Pausing on the doorstep with his back to Mumma, he cleared his throat. "The sooner we get going, the sooner we'll get back."

A waft of April air blew past me. Taking Jacob's hand, I ran toward the truck. "If you make me do this, Cliff, you'll be sorry," shouted Mumma from the doorway. I was sure everyone in the Forties Settlement could hear. I turned back toward the house. The look on Mumma's face sent a chill through me.

"But Mumma," Jacob protested as we climbed into the truck.

"Don't worry about Mumma. She's coming," Daddy reassured him as he pressed the palm of his hand into the horn.

Honk. Honk. Honk. The sound echoed out across the Forties Settlement in the cold, damp air. *Honk. Honk. Honk.* It wouldn't go away. I shuddered, looking back toward the house. *Honk. Honk. Honk.* Daddy wouldn't stop blowing the horn, not until Mumma gave in. When the front door finally banged shut, the vibration reached us.

"Here she comes!" announced Jacob, sounding pleased. My heart fluttered when I saw Mumma step down off the doorstep, her bright red shoes a stark contrast to the snow.

"Where are your boots?" asked Daddy as she climbed into the truck.

"Bend over for a second, I'll give you a boot," she said, releasing a harsh laugh as she slammed the truck door shut.

"Suit yourself, but if the truck breaks down and we have to walk, you won't be laughing then."

"You got your way—isn't that enough?" she said, fold-ing her arms across her chest. She looked over at me and quickly winked. That's how I knew she wasn't going to tell.

"Stop it, Lizabeth. Just stop it," said Daddy as he started backing out of the driveway. "Do you have to do this today? Life isn't one big joke, you know."

A shot of guilt drew me to glance down at Mumma's feet as we pulled onto the road. Two days earlier, she'd given me her boots to wear. One of mine had gone missing from the closet at school.

"It has to be here somewhere," Mrs. Carver had said as she opened the closet door. I'd already assured her it was nowhere to be seen, but she seemed not to care about what I had to say.

"Did you check the shelf?" I caught sight of the white bloomers that reached down past her plump thighs as she climbed onto a chair to get a better look. I knew she wouldn't find it there either. This wasn't the first time something of mine had gone astray—a mitten, a toque, the wooden pencil box Poppy made me last year. I sometimes found the missing object trampled into the dirt on my way home from school. Sometimes it was lying in the ditch. The pencil box never did come back, but two days after it had gone missing, Jeff Peterson showed up at school with a shiny green pencil box. It wasn't hard to see it had been given a fresh coat of paint, but there was no way to prove it was mine.

"I don't expect your parents will want to replace a pair of boots this late in the season. You're a careless girl, Jewel MacKay. Maybe next time you'll take better care of your things." Mrs. Carver's mouth was tucked into a frown. I didn't tell her that Jeff Peterson was to blame for my missing boot. I knew it because of the pencil box and the things he said to me out on the playground, but if I told any of this to Mrs. Carver, Jeff Peterson would come after me. I walked home wearing a boot on one foot and a shoe on the other.

On top of all that, the sole of my shoe had a crack in it. I walked most of the way on my heel, with my left foot stuck up in the air so it wouldn't get wet. Mumma gave me a curious look when I came hobbling into the kitchen.

"Well, isn't that a stylish combination. You must have got your fashion sense from your mother," she said, wiping her hands on her apron. Tilting her head from one side to the other, she looked me over. "So, where did your boot run off to, or is it your shoe that ran off? There's one of each, so it could go either way."

I'd hoped to see the boot on my way home, had practised what I'd tell her if I didn't, but when Mumma pulled the boot from my foot, I burst into a blubbery mess.

"Stop your crying," she ordered. "Tears are a waste of time, and pity won't get you anywhere in life."

A strange noise escaped me and I snuffed back my tears. Taking my hand in hers, she marched me out to the porch to where her own boots sat on some old newspaper. Picking one up, she held it out and told me to shove my foot in.

"My sock," I said. "It got wet." There was a row of clean socks hanging from the line above the wood stove. She went into the kitchen and grabbed a pair. The socks warmed my feet as I tried on the first boot.

"Now the other one," she said, handing it to me. I took a few steps back and forth the porch. They were a bit big, but I was used to making do.

"Now, we can't leave any evidence behind. You know what your father gets like," she said, marching my lone boot back out to the kitchen. Removing one of the stove lids, she gazed down into the fire, watching the flames dance inside the firebox.

"Bye-bye, little boot. You're no good by yourself," she said, pushing it into the hole. I smiled as the flames devoured it up. Mumma was right. One boot was good for nothing and Daddy would never have to know.

"Now—what you need is a good pair of sensible rubber boots for this time of the year," continued Mumma. "Spring means mud. You can't wear winter boots all year long. Your father knows better than that. We'll have to check out the spring rummage sale the first chance we get." Next, she inspected my shoe. I wondered if it would meet the same fate as my boot. She bent the sole, revealing the deep crack that ran from one side to the other.

"No wonder your foot got wet. Look. That crack is bigger than the one in my head," she said, letting the sole snap back into place. "Hmm," she mused, "what to do with a cracked shoe? That's the question."

She thought for a few moments, then hurried to the closet. There was an empty shoebox on the shelf and she cut out a piece of cardboard to fit inside my shoe.

"A little trick I learned from Poppy," she said, looking pleased with herself. "There. As good as new, or darn close to it.... See, you were worried for nothing. Your shoe is fixed and you have a pair of boots for Monday morning. All's well that ends well."

"But what if these boots go missing too?" I imagined Jeff Peterson stealing one of them as well.

"Oh, bologna! If your boots go missing again, I'll march myself down to that schoolhouse and I won't leave until I find out where they went."

As I stood in the kitchen that day looking at Mumma, part of me feared that one day she'd make good on that threat and just what would happen to me if she did.

Elizabeth

The blinker clicked at a rapid rate as the truck slowed to a stop. I didn't have to open my eyes to know where we were. We sometimes stopped at this gas station to use the restrooms. The big thermometer had been on the side of the building for years. Winter or summer, the owner never took it down. The children and I sometimes made fun of it—Santa Claus tipping back a bottle of Coca-Cola in the heat of summer.

"Can we have potato chips, Daddy?" Jewel asked before the truck had time to stop. The jingling of change reached my ears as Cliff and the children climbed out. Moments later, the smell of gasoline found its way inside the cab of the truck. I didn't even care about the money it would take for the gas when I heard Cliff say, "Fill 'er up." I just wanted him to get back on the road, face Joan and Dylan's scrutiny, their disapproving looks, and get this miserable ordeal over with. But when two more vehicles pulled up, got gas, and drove off, I began to wonder what could be taking Cliff so long. There couldn't be a lineup of people inside the station, as ours was now the only vehicle in the yard.

An odd feeling descended over me, a feeling that rivalled the rational part of me as I weighed out the scenario I found myself in. There were no signs of anyone inside the garage that I could see through the narrow side window; not an attendant, not Cliff, not even a little head bobbing around. All I could make out was an array of fan belts hanging up on the wall inside the station, a cluttered counter, and a rack of potato chips in the corner. The place was deserted. Something had happened. I knew we should have stayed home. I was the only one in that godforsaken place. Something had reached down and snapped the children up. Kidnapped. Stolen. Lost—but not found. It was the only explanation.

Cliff wouldn't let that happen.

"He might if he wasn't paying attention."

No, he wouldn't.

I gripped the door handle.

Run into the station.

"No, I can't."

If I were wrong, Cliff would cart me off to Dr. Scott's office. He'd been threatening to do so for weeks now. I knew where that could lead—Roseland. I didn't plan on ever going back there. I could be rotting away in that place right now if Poppy hadn't brought me home the last time. And Jacob less than a year old—he wouldn't have remembered a thing about me. I tried to draw in a deep breath, but it got caught up in my chest and wouldn't let go.

Slow down. Slow down. And think.

There had to be some other explanation as to why Cliff and the children were taking so long. Inching toward the edge of my seat, I squeezed the door handle tighter. There was a strange beating in my chest, a fluttering of broken moth wings. My heart might explode if I didn't do something. As I pulled up on the handle, the truck door opened a crack—and at the same time a small bell tinkled somewhere; a door rattled shut. The sound of children's laughter expanded into the air. My hand squeezed fast to the door handle, the muscles in my arm trembling. Jewel in her pink coat scurried across the front of the truck. Cliff and Jacob were close behind. They were back from wherever it was they'd disappeared to. Quickly closing the door, I shuddered, completely spent. Hot blood flowed through me, flushing my face and neck, running down my arms and legs, finding a pathway to my fingertips and dripping out on the floor of the truck. I shook my hand to make it stop.

"Sit still, Lizabeth," Cliff commanded as he helped Jewel and Jacob back into the truck. Their chip bags crinkled as they settled in for the rest of the trip.

"The man had a nickel on the floor, Mumma," chirped Jacob, "but we couldn't pick it up."

"It was a trick," laughed Jewel, tearing open her bag of chips. "It was stuck right fast to the floor." There was a carefree ring in her voice, as if she hadn't a problem in this world. I looked over at her reaching into her chip bag and wondered, why hadn't I ever felt that way?

If I could be anything other than a farmer's wife, it would be a fish," said Mum as the sea wind blew through her auburn hair. Ordinarily, she would have tucked the loose strands behind her ears so as not to have them whipping about her face, but that day she didn't seem to mind. "No, wait! A dolphin! I'd rather be a dolphin than a fish," she mused.

"Why a dolphin?" Poppy asked, his eyes smiling as if he couldn't quite believe his ears.

"They're far more compassionate, Everett. I fancy being something warm-blooded." Her laughter climbed the air like a kite and I wanted to grab fast to it, soar up over the water, see us walking along the beach together, happy in that moment.

Mum used to say that because she was born under some sign called Aquarius, she craved water. Poppy would tell her she read too much and it was putting crazy ideas in her head. He would say it as though it were a bad thing, but his eyes always told a different story.

As a surprise, Poppy had taken us down to the water that day, and when Mum said perhaps we should stay home with all the work that needed to be done on the farm, Poppy said, "You won't be happy until you've dipped your big toe into the Atlantic, Marion," and he kept on driving. "I'd drive an entire week if that's how long it took us to get there."

"Lucky for you, you'll never have to prove that," Mum said, looking across the seat at him. I loved the look on her face as we drove up to the beach that day, and then she got out of the car and walked toward the water, not saying a word for the longest while. The sadness that had been following her seemed to have disappeared. I thought the fairies must have taken it away. I'd lain awake many nights listening to her and Poppy mumbling long into the hours of darkness and now the old Mum was finally back.

Gulls were swooping and calling out to us. The cool mist wetted my face, leaving a salty taste on my lips. In a quick moment, a shadow appeared to pinch Mum's cheek and I thought she was going to cry, but she didn't. We walked across the sand holding hands. The water lapped at the shoreline, and Mum pulled off her stockings and waded out into the water, bunching her dress up into a ball to keep the hem from getting soaked. I played at the water's edge, zigzagging through the waves. The sun winked at me through the clouds. The day couldn't have been more perfect.

With the truck in gear, Cliff pulled out onto the road. The children jabbered and ate their chips. I closed my eyes; my heart withered inside me. The radio snapped on. Static screeched across the airwaves and stopped on the local station. The song playing was about lonely hearts and lost love. I settled in for the rest of the trip, my head resting against the cold window. The vibration of the truck lulled me as we continue along. It was distracting, comforting, soothing. I drifted into one of Poppy's fairy tales, a world of queens and kings, once-upon-a-times and happy-ever-afters—my safe place and the only place where the dark prince couldn't reach me. I opened my eyes when Jacob cried out, "There's Uncle Dylan's place!"

And the dark prince slipped his hand in mine as he brought me back to the truth once more.

Jewel

All through dinner Mumma didn't say a word. She picked the bones from Jacob's herring and laid them on the edge of his plate. They looked like whiskers pulled from a cat, sticking straight up in the air. Aunt Joan babbled away about the work the church guild was doing and how they were busy raising money to send to the starving children in Africa. Every so often Daddy would ask her a question. He sounded interested, but I didn't believe he was. Uncle Dylan was too busy eating to pay much attention to what Aunt Joan was saying, asking for the pepper and salt and the bread, thanking her politely each time something was passed his way.

"Christian duty, that's what I say. We all have our Christian duty to perform." She was looking directly at me when she said "Christian duty." I glanced quickly down at my plate, stabbing some potato with my fork, wishing she'd take her eyes off me.

My cousin, Richard, was sitting across the table from

me. Every so often, he'd peek out from between strands of hair that were hanging down from his forehead, presenting a set of cold dark eyes. Scowling, he picked through his bony meal, his warty fingers rough from working on Uncle Dylan's boat. Reaching in front of Aunt Joan, he accidentally knocked over the salt shaker.

"Excuse me," Aunt Joan said, eyeing him with irritation as he dug around the potato pot unconcerned. Grabbing the shaker, she scattered salt grains over each shoulder before setting it back onto the table. Richard mashed up the potato with his fork and ate it like it was going out of style. When he was through, he stood up from the table, grabbed his glass of water, and drank it down in one gulp.

"You can all stop gawking," he said, pushing away what was left of his plate of herring and stomping away from the table.

We sat in awkward silence for a time before Aunt Joan bleated out, "Your good herring, Richard. You like herring! Come sit back down." She looked about the table as if searching for an answer. "Well, he always did like herring," she said. Her hand was shaking. I hoped she wouldn't start crying. I'd seen her cry once before, after Grammy MacKay's funeral. Just before she stuffed a date square in her mouth, she'd started to wail. Up until then she'd seemed fine.

"She's probably lamenting the cost of the dates in those squares she made," Mumma said. At the time it seemed funny and I struggled to keep from laughing, Aunt Joan bawling her eyes out in front of all of us. But as I sat at the dinner table that day, waiting to see if she was about to break out into tears, there didn't seem to be anything humorous about the situation at all.

Right after dinner, Aunt Joan scurried Mumma and Daddy and Uncle Dylan out of the kitchen and closed the door after them. "I'll find something to keep you occupied while the grown-ups have a talk," she said, cleaning off the table and quickly wiping it with a dishrag. She rooted through the kitchen drawers until she found a writing tablet and a pen.

"Now, you two stay put. Do some drawing or whatever. Your mother says you're a good little artist, Jewel."

I knew that was a lie. The last person Mumma would have mentioned my sketches to would have been Aunt Joan. Besides, Mumma had no interest in the things I drew. Whenever I showed her something she'd stare down at the paper. Sometimes she'd smile, but she never told me it was good.

"Your good herring," I mocked, opening the tablet. "He always did like my good herring." Jacob giggled and squirmed in his chair. Drawing for Jacob was always easy. If I sketched one of our farm animals, he'd be happy. I moved the pen across the paper quickly to keep Jacob interested.

"Look, Jakey, there's Bright and Lion!" I said, pointing down at the paper. It wasn't very good, but there was no way to change it. The look on his face told me right away that I shouldn't have drawn his steers. It had only been a few weeks since they'd climbed aboard Dell Jameson's old cattle truck and gone away. The empty stalls in the barn still ached for them to come home. I'd sometimes find him curled up in one of the mangers and make him come into the house to get warm.

Last summer he'd led them around the dooryard while Daddy kept an eye on him. "The smallest teamster in the land," Daddy said, laughing. Jacob had been planning to take them to the Bridgewater Exhibition this summer. Daddy had even promised. It was all Jacob talked about last winter, those frosty days when he'd hurry to the barn to help tend them.

"I can draw Dusty if you want," I said, flipping the page. I made a small, pointy ear on a clean piece of paper as I began to sketch again. The lines across the tablet spoiled the picture, but I hoped Jacob wouldn't notice. I continued to draw until a picture of Dusty materialized on the page. Jacob grinned.

"Look, Jakey, there's Dusty's long tail!" A troubled look crossed his face when the voices in the living room grew louder. I continued to draw Dusty running across our pasture, legs galloping, tail pointed outward. When the voices grew loud once again, I slipped out of my chair and crept toward the living room, pressing my ear to the door. I still couldn't make out what was being said. Jacob rolled his brown eyes up at me. When an odd sound came from Mumma, he jumped out of his chair. He hurried toward the porch and put on his boots. Jumping into the air, he grabbed hold of his coat and pulled it from the hanger in the closet. I helped him with the zipper and quickly put on my own. Shoving my feet into Mumma's winter boots, I opened the door. The snow was heavy and wet, melting now that the temperature was rising. Water dripped from the eaves and I ducked to escape the drops. As I closed the door, a gull screamed out at me. The ocean breeze touched my face and I was suddenly free.

Elizabeth

A mean fist hit me in the chest. It was all I could do to stop from calling out when I looked out at the ocean, swelling and rocking and slapping the shoreline.

Jacob. Down by the shore. Scrambling on top of a large boulder.

Jewel. I couldn't see her pink jacket anywhere.

Water struck the rocks, sending large waves into the air. Gulls cast shadows over the water; swoop high then low.

They were told to stay in the kitchen.

"Dylan could use the help. Couldn't you, Dylan? It would be a great opportunity for you. Richard's been talking about going back to school."

I pulled my breath in. A sharp pain jabbed me in the ribs as Jacob caught himself seconds before sliding off one of the rocks.

"And there are plenty of places to rent down here. You wouldn't even have to buy until later."

Wet, slippery April rocks. Jacob looked no bigger than a bug. Slip and fall. Slip and fall. Slip and fall. Broken bones and a cracked skull. I couldn't let it happen.

"I dare say a change of scenery might be good for Elizabeth."

In a second Jacob was in my arms, as I held fast to him on top of that rocky crag. Another second and we were sitting in the truck on our way back home. Still another second and I was tucking him into bed for the night, safe and sound.

"It's a big move, but it might be for the best. What do you think, Lizabeth?"

I had to get to the children. Jacob needed me. I had to catch up to all the places my mind had already been—Jacob safe and sound, and in my arms. Cliff touched me, and I shrugged him off. Jewel. I craned my neck. I still couldn't see Jewel. I went for the door. Cliff's hand tightened around my arm. "What are you doing, Lizabeth?"

Fighting to get away, there was only one thought on my mind. One final push and I managed to wrench free of his grip. Time was being wasted. It was sifting through my fingers like beach sand, and if Cliff didn't stop his foolish talk something bad was sure to happen. This time Joan was standing in front of me, blocking my entrance to the outside; to Jewel and Jacob.

"What's wrong with you, Elizabeth? You're acting crazy. Now, come sit down and let's talk this over like sensible people," she said, grabbing my arm.

"Get out of my way, you stupid bitch. You stupid, miserable bitch," I hissed. Pushing her aside, I threw open the front door. The wind coming up across the bay nearly blew me off my feet as I stepped down off the doorstep. Nothing was going to stop me. Sunlight fell through the clouds. The wind lamented and carried on. Trees rubbed their bare branches together, squeaked and complained. Gulls swooped and screeched. And I ran. The breeze pulled the words from my parted lips, scattering them like ocean mist as I screamed out to Jacob. Knowing there would be no reply, I kept going. Yet I hoped he'd hear. By some small miracle I hoped, the same way you come to hope, however foolishly, that at least once in your lifetime the rules will bend in your favour. That could have been my one time to bend all the rules. As I narrowed the distance between us I was struck by the realization that so much was depending on me; me—and only me.

If it hadn't been for me, Mum wouldn't have jumped into the water that day by the shore. If only I hadn't leaned too far over the edge of the wharf where I was playing. If I hadn't seen the tangle of lines and spinners, the red and white and sparkly gold, when she was talking to Poppy on the beach. But I did see it, and I reached out until my fingertips brushed against the bright gold spinner. Mum's laughter sounded like a lark song over the marsh. I kept stretching out my arm, my body, wiggling my fingers to make them as long as I could until I had the spinner in my hands. And then I was falling; screaming and falling. The sky pulled itself on top of me. I thrashed my arms and legs. And then I was going down, down, down into the salty water. It was cold, so cold I could barely move my arms and legs. And then Mum was in the water with me, telling me to calm down, to stop and be quiet. But I couldn't be quiet and I couldn't calm the monster struggling inside me to escape. I grabbed fast to Mum and then we were both going down.

"Don't worry. You'll be fine. Don't worry," someone whispered again and again. Somewhere between the whispers, Poppy pulled me out of the water. I kept screaming and crying for Mum, but she didn't come back. It was my fault she didn't come back.

With all the strength in me, I scrambled closer to the shore as something deep inside urged me onward.

Hurry, Elizabeth!

I slipped, not once but twice, into the wet snow, landing hard on my right knee both times. Yet I forced myself to keep moving.

"Can we play by the shore, Daddy?"

The ugly pile of rocks I'd always warned the children to stay away from loomed in the distance. Water and wind and wet, slushy April snow, it all cried of Jacob's imminent demise. It cried and wept inside me, this April snow and cold, slushy, wet wind, and the grey rocks Jacob was climbing as I lessened the gap between us.

Hurry, Elizabeth!

If I didn't get there soon, he'd be lost for good, swept into the sea. If only the snow would melt. If only it would rain hot water for even a few moments. I would stand a fighting chance.

"Can we play by the shore, Daddy?"

"Possibly."

Cliff's flippant answer from the morning filled me with rage.

And then, a fleck of bright pink flashed between the rocks not far from where Jacob was climbing. Jewel's blond head popped up over the rocks. I stood at the edge of the shoreline screaming until she finally turned my way.

"Stop him!" I cried, pointing to where Jacob was teetering on the rocks. Moments later, Jewel was helping her brother down to the shore. My heart throbbed, my lungs squeezed tight with relief.

"That's my girl. You did good, Elizabeth, you did real good."

Joan

"Good riddance to bad rubbish," I whispered as we watched Cliff drive off. No one should have to be insulted in their own home. Dylan slipped his arm around me and pulled me close.

"You did the right thing," he said. "You can't have her come in here and say those things. This is your house." I knew Dylan was right, but I still felt bad about the way it all happened. I was only trying to calm her down, stop her from racing out of the house like a madwoman, when she turned on me like a feral cat, swatting and hissing. I don't know what came over her. One minute we were in the living room discussing their future, and how we might be able to help, and the next thing she was heading out the door, screaming like a crazy woman.

To tell the truth, a part of me wasn't surprised. Things had been building between us for a while. I used to try and reason with her when she was being unreasonable, so protective of those children I swore she was going to suffocate them. She'd tell me to mind my own business, even had the audacity to tell me I hadn't done such a great job with Richard over the years.

"Children need structure. Richard's a boorish child," she said. I had to look the word up later to know what she was talking about. Elizabeth was someone I just couldn't warm up to, no matter how hard I tried. Yet, I did try—for Cliff's sake, I did—but we were like water and gasoline. *It takes two*, I used to tell Dylan. *It always takes two.*

As I watched the taillights of the truck disappear down the road, I couldn't help feeling like a failure. Elizabeth might be forbidden to step foot in our house, but she would always remain a footprint in our lives. Eleven years ago, I didn't believe we'd reach this point in time. Back then I made this family a promise to rid ourselves of Elizabeth one way or another, and it was a promise I still intended to keep.

"I showed her how we sort the clothes in the hamper and she couldn't even get that right. I mean, really, how hard is it to sort the sheets from the johnny shirts? She must have been brought up by a bunch of chimpanzees is all I can say."

It wasn't as if anyone had invited Doris Putman to our quilting bee. She showed up without an invitation, my guess bored to tears at her parents' house even though she insisted on coming home on her weekends off from the hospital.

I thought Sharon Fredericks was going to split a seam, of course Sharon was prone to laughing at anything that sounded the least bit humorous. And then, quite seriously, Abigail McMillan looked up from her quilt block and said it must be disappointing when they get in girls who don't know the ass end of a cow from the front, and that sent

Sharon over the edge, all of us, if I'm being truthful. Abigail wasn't one for making such comments about others, but she did that day. Pastor Hennigar would have said that poking fun like that wasn't a Christian thing to do, and I did feel a smidge guilty, really I did, seeing how we were in the church basement putting together a quilt to be raffled off at the spring bazaar, but Doris had such a comical way of putting things you couldn't help but laugh. And the faces she made while talking. Oh, the faces were something wicked.

"She can't be that bad, Doris," I said, wiping at the tears in my eyes.

"It's a good thing she's only working in the laundry. It's not like the health and welfare of the patients is in jeopardy. Most of the stuff I just keep my mouth shut about, but after a while it gets to you."

Now, Doris might be able to tell the other women that and have them believe her, but I knew better. Keeping her mouth shut was never Doris Puttman's strong suit in life. Knowing Doris, she was spreading stories to anyone who would listen, making this new girl's life miserable if I knew anything at all about Doris.

"I'd seen her around before, I knew I had, but do you suppose I could place her? No, sir. We worked all that first morning together until it finally came to me." Doris paused right about then, waiting for everyone to urge her on.

"And my dyin', you're just never going to guess who she is," she said, looking like the cat that swallowed the canary. The guild women took turns listing off names. Each time she'd shake her head and say, "Nope," like she was holding tight to some secret that the rest of world couldn't get their hands on. Finally, Birdie Davis told her to just spit it out because none of us were getting any younger waiting for her to tell. Doris inched her way out to the edge of her seat and lowered her voice. I'd like to know why she was whispering, since everyone there was obviously going to hear what she was about to say. It wasn't as if there were any spirits listening in.

"Well, you know Everett Brown?" she said, her eyes sparking like glass under water. Yes, yes, yes, everyone in that church basement either knew or had heard tell of Everett Brown, him being councillor for that area and well respected in the community. You'd have to be living in a small box all your life not to know who Everett Brown was. Even those of us living down here in Chester knew who he was.

"Well, it's his daughter. Nuttier 'n a bag of hammers, that one is. Although I heard that her father spoiled her rotten growing up."

I nearly jabbed myself with my quilting needle. Cliff's new girl was a Brown from the Forties. But it couldn't be. I mean, what were the odds? There were plenty of Browns around the country. She could be anyone's daughter—anyone's.

"Does this girl have a first name, or do we have to guess that too?" I said as casually as I could so as not to raise any suspicion. When Doris said, "Elizabeth," my heart plummeted into my stomach, hitting like a rock plunging into brackish water.

"Do you want to hear the best part?" said Doris, and of course everyone said, oh yes, they did. In fact, they were all ears by that time. "They caught her trying to crawl into one of the patients' bed—some young fellow with a broken leg."

The women shook their heads and made queer noises and Doris sat there with her mouth curled up into a satisfied grin.

"Let's just say that anyone crawling into some strange man's bed deserves whatever she gets." The rest of the women nodded in agreement. Even I had to go along on that one. But I kept my mouth shut. I didn't let on that Cliff had his eye on this girl Doris was going on about, because, really, I wasn't supposed to know any of that in the first place. Cliff had confided certain things to his brother, things I wasn't supposed to know. But when you're as close as what me and Dylan are, there's not a lot that doesn't get talked over in the dark after a long day.

Cliff had an eye for the ladies. Dylan wouldn't have said so, but it was the truth. *Playing the field,* Dylan called it each time Cliff showed up with a new girl snuggled up close to him in that old truck of his. He'd grin and rub the stubble on his chin like his younger brother was someone to be admired. It was nothing for Cliff to be driving around with a girl every other weekend. A few weeks down the road he'd be seeing someone else. So I kept my mouth shut. Why open a can of worms if you're not planning to go fishing? The guild ladies need never know. Besides, it wouldn't be long before Elizabeth Brown would be a thing of the past. I was certain of it.

"Elizabeth went funny in the head after her mother drowned, is what they say. I heard that she planned to drown them both. Everett got there but only in time to save Elizabeth." Doris was shaking her head as if she was sympathetic, but there was no kindness in her voice when she spoke.

"It would have to affect a child," I agreed, and really, what kind of person wouldn't feel sorry for a child whose mother tried to drown her?

"Oh, it's obviously affected her. Mrs. Hampton had to speak to her a few times for wandering around the corridors at night, sneaking into people's rooms. It's just too weird. They say those things run in families. I don't suppose she'll last long at the hospital—unless she gets herself thrown into one of their padded rooms."

I told Dylan what all Doris had to say on the subject of his brother's new girlfriend, and by my insistence he agreed to have a word with Cliff. Not that it did any good. Cliff as good as told him to mind his business, that it was gossip and for him to never mind. *You'll find out sooner or later, Cliff MacKay,* I thought to myself. *A leopard eventually shows its spots. You'll find out your older brother is right.* I didn't figure it would take too much time for that realization to hit Cliff, but how could I have figured on what would happen next?

Elizabeth

I see the moon; the moon sees me.
God bless the moon and God bless me:
There's grace in the cottage and grace in the hall,
And the grace of God is over us all.

I gazed at the sliver of moonlight touching the pillow mere inches from where my head was resting. That stupid nursery rhyme wouldn't stop repeating in my head. I couldn't get rid of it. The moon could see me—that part was true—but the rest of the rhyme was pure nonsense. God's grace wasn't over us and it wasn't in our cottage. If there was such a thing as God's grace, I had no idea where it was—on some mountaintop in the Swiss Alps for all I knew or cared. Earlier in the evening, Cliff stomped through the house like an ogre, snapping at the children when we got home from Chester. He tossed words at me as soon as he had them tucked in bed for the night. I was an embarrassment, he said, not only to him but to the children. I was no longer welcome in Dylan and Joan's house, and what's more, he couldn't much blame them. I'd accept my banishment willingly, not only if it meant Jacob's safety, but if it would end any further trips for me to the shore. As for the words I'd said to Joan, I couldn't even remember what they were. Words scatter like seeds in the wind as soon as they are spoken, and they mean nothing in the end. Thoughts are what count; the place where reality eventually takes form, a sacred place where mere mortals dare not tread.

Cliff's snoring was disturbing the night's silence. I couldn't think straight. Fists clenched, knees drawn to my chest, my arms tight against my body, if I made myself small enough the sound of his snoring wouldn't reach me. I hummed quietly to myself, trying to contain all the noise inside me. Like a cave hollowed out over the years, a conglomerate of thoughts and events rained down from the ceiling all at once. But then there came a sound from outside my cave that didn't belong to Cliff. I strained to hear. Something prodded me—Jacob and Jewel. Cliff had tucked them into bed hours ago, but with the commotion that followed, I'd forgotten to look in on them when I came upstairs to bed. My heart struggled inside my chest. *What if they've disappeared, the same way they did at the gas station earlier today?* I had to be sure.

Feet gliding across the floorboards, I hurried to their rooms. Relief barrelled through me, jolting me where I stood—they were both sleeping soundly. Jacob was holding fast to the paper that had crinkled in his hands all the way home from the shore. I tugged at it gently, and it came loose from his grip. Holding it up, I shifted it around so the moonlight caught it. The lines became visible. There was writing at the bottom: DUSTY—each letter crisp and perfectly formed in Jewel's handwriting. The picture was of Jacob's pony running across a field, the wind blowing through her mane. Free. Spirited. Light. I stared down at the picture. Running forever, forever running. I couldn't see where she was heading. There was no destination. Nothing showing in the distance. I crumpled the picture in my hand as Jacob stirred.

"Go back to sleep," I said, tucking the blankets around him.

"Dusty," he said, groping about in the dark, his eyes barely open.

"Never mind," I answered, squeezing the ball of paper tighter. "Shush now, Jakey-boy." His eyes closed. I kissed his forehead and left. There was no doubt in my mind, the picture had to go. It would only remind me of this awful day. And awful days never leave your head if you keep something of them around to remind you. The day was now over, already lived, already past, waiting to be tossed away and forgotten.

"There was never any danger, Lizabeth. The children were playing. They were only playing."

Moonbeams trickled through the south windows and shimmered on the hardwood floor in the living room. I moved about silently with the entire house sound asleep, stuck in time, placed under a magical fairy spell. I didn't need much sleep. I'd known that for quite some time now. An hour here and there. Sometimes two or three. Whatever sleep was granted me I gratefully accepted, never wanting or expecting more. Imagine handing your thoughts over and letting your dreams take control. I'd be a fool to give up control. Sleep is for cowards. I hadn't been a coward for a very long time. I'd been scared, but scared is not the same as cowardly. Cowardly stops you in your tracks. It sends you back the other way, tail stuck between your legs, while scared forces you to keep going. It propels you forward into this day and that day even when you're absolutely sure you can't go on. I proved as much with my miraculous courage today. Ridiculous to think any of the rest of them could have done what I did to save Jacob when they didn't even see the danger he was in.

After all the harsh words were said, by evening's end, I promised Cliff I'd go see Dr. Scott on Monday. There seemed no other choice. "I'm experiencing a metamorphosis," I said, "and these things take time."

"There was never any danger, Lizabeth, and now you're not even making sense," he said.

A small sliver of light is coming out from under the door. Poppy is talking but I can't make out what he's saying. Pushing on the door, it slowly swings open. His back is to the door and he doesn't see me come in. He's talking to Mum but she won't answer.

The women brought food today, and told us to eat. But I didn't want to eat. They hugged Poppy and asked, *"How's Elizabeth doing?"* He said, *"I'm not sure she understands."* I crawled inside the castle. In our game, Mum was always the queen and I was the princess trapped inside the tower waiting to be rescued. Poppy would show up moments before the dark prince arrived and release us from the cold dark tower we were imprisoned in. But today wasn't a game. Mum wasn't with me and Poppy didn't come rescue us. From inside the castle, I watched the people's feet trampling back and forth until someone found me. *"What are you doing beneath the table, Elizabeth?"* I screamed to be freed, but she pulled harder. I kicked and screamed, screamed and kicked and screamed.

At the end of the day, when the house was quiet, I rushed to Poppy's side and he put his arm around me. *"We'll get through this together,"* he said, squeezing me tight. I moved toward the box where Mum was lying. She had on a pretty blue dress and there was a white flower in her hair. Her cheeks and lips were unnaturally red. Turning toward Poppy, I asked, *"Why doesn't she open her eyes?"* But I already knew the answer. Reaching out to him, I stopped a tear from running down his cheek.

Toward morning, I climbed back up the steps. The night was becoming thinner. It would soon be gone, taking the beautiful enchanted moonlight with it. The sleep spell would vanish, the household would waken. My quest to find my knight in shining armour had come to an end. I would continue to search, at nighttime as well as during the day. There would come another time. That knowledge spurred me onward. Stopping beside the bedroom window, I whispered, "Goodbye, moon. Goodbye, enchantment." The words shimmered on my lips like morning frost. A flicker of movement from outside caught my attention in the moonlight. Stepping closer to the window, I wiped the water from my eyes. Jacob's pony was standing near the barn. Sensing me watching her, she looked up. Our eyes locked. I tried to turn away but was frozen in that moment, an empty shell incapable of movement. I wondered what would become of me if I remained motionless forever, a statue poised by my bedroom window for the remainder of time. It was not such an impossible thing to contemplate.

The pony let out a soft whinny, breaking the spell. Moving away from the window, I checked back over my shoulder. She was looking down at the ground, pretending not to have seen me. Dusk skipped on the horizon, smiling at me through the growth of trees across the road, but it couldn't dispel the feeling of dread that was gnawing away inside me. Cliff would take me to see Dr. Scott tomorrow. Already, this day was tomorrow, without anything separating it from yesterday. I was trapped between yesterday and tomorrow, and neither day was safe to be in.

Settling down in bed, I slowed my breathing, my heart, my thoughts, as I waited for sleep to capture me. From outside there came a noise. I strained to hear. It was the pony, her feet quietly crunching in the half-frozen ground. And then I heard her calling to me, inviting me to come with her.

"Wait for me," I whispered, drifting into sleep. I reached for her, my arms outstretched. There was nothing but air. As my body dissolved into the mattress, I could hear the pony running, racing off to a faraway kingdom, her feet pummelling the ground. I couldn't blame her for going. It wasn't her fault. She was moving forward all by herself. But then, so was I. And we both had to go alone.

Jewel

Poppy led the little chestnut pony up the driveway early one morning before Jacob was even out of bed. The moment I saw him coming up the hill, I ran out of the house, yelling for Jacob to come outside and see what Poppy had brought. Jumping and clapping in the dooryard, I could hardly wait for him to get here. The gold tooth in Poppy's mouth sparkled in the sun when he smiled and I thought maybe it had been a long time since I'd seen him look so happy. Jacob had been asking for a pony for months, and Poppy kept saying "We'll see," until I began to wonder if that *We'll see* would end up being forgotten the same way Daddy's *We'll sees* always did. For a long time, all Jacob had talked about was the pony he wanted, and I'd hoped really hard that he wouldn't end up crying over something he never got.

Sunlight flickered off the shiny brass buckles on the pony's halter as she trotted along with her head in the air, and I was scared to even think who that pony might belong to. What if Poppy had just brought her here to show us? What if she belonged to one of the neighbours? The pony snorted three times and moved her head up and down as she stepped along. Even *she* seemed to be happy. When I asked if I could touch her, Daddy lifted me up and set me on her back. When the pony made a few steps forward and back, I squealed, but Poppy said she wouldn't hurt me. "She's a gentle pony. Aren't you, girl?" he said, patting her neck.

Daddy moved in close beside me and told me not to be scared. I wrapped my fingers around the pony's mane, leaned over, and laid my cheek against her neck. She was soft and warm, and I thought she was even better than the Hereford calf that was born one cold afternoon in the winter, the one Daddy said would make a good mate to one James Redding already had.

Jacob came running out into the dooryard still wearing his pyjamas and started jumping up and down like he couldn't keep the happiness inside him. "Let me try, let me try," he was crying. Daddy helped him up on the pony's back with me. I wrapped my arms around his waist and held on tight while Poppy led us around and around the dooryard. I wanted someone to drive by just then and see us so that I could wave at them from way up high on the pony's back. I wanted to feel like someone special for even a tiny moment. The pony's hoofs clicked against the hard gravel in the driveway. She lifted her feet and tail as she walked, and I thought maybe one day she could march in the New Ross parade with us.

"Now, there's a boy's pony," Poppy said, and when he said that I suddenly wanted the pony just for me. I wanted her to be just as much a girl's pony as she was a boy's. It was my own fault for not looking any farther, for not setting my hopes on anything, for not planning for something more. Why hadn't I thought to ask for one? Except when Jacob asked I wasn't at all sure it would come into being. Good things happen to other people, I'd wanted to tell him.

When Mumma came out of the house, I stopped laughing because I didn't want to hear Jacob crying over the pony at night if she made Poppy take it back. Knowing Mumma, it was a good possibility. But I also knew if anyone could convince her to let the pony stay, it would be Poppy. Poppy never raised his voice when Mumma was upset. "No need to worry, Elizabeth," he used to say. "No need for you to worry." Poppy's voice was always smooth and sweet like chocolate pudding, and Mumma never stayed angry at him for very long. He had a way with her like no one else; even Daddy said so.

When Poppy said the pony was for Jacob, Mumma scrunched up her face. "Every boy should have a pony," he said, like he was waiting for her approval, and Jacob said, *Yes, yes, Mumma, they do!* She looked the pony over, walking around to see her from all sides, and finally said, "You already have a pair of steers to play with. Why does Poppy think you need a pony?" Jacob didn't answer, not with words he didn't, but I could see the look in his brown eyes, as if he'd never wanted anything so badly in all his life. And if I'd had the power to give him what he wanted, I'd have done so right then and there. As much as I wanted that pony for me, I would have given it to Jacob just to make him happy.

Poppy rubbed his hands together, raised his grey, bushy eyebrows at Mumma, and when she laughed I felt a small hiccough of joy leap inside me.

"Oh, Poppy," she said, smiling, "Just what we don't need. A chestnut pony." And in that smile she gave Poppy, I saw Mumma for the very first time.

"Where's Dusty...my picture of Dusty?" Jacob cried from upstairs. The sound of his bare feet hurrying down the steps brought an urgency to his question. There was a frantic look on his face when he entered the kitchen, as if he'd been told the world was soon coming to an end.

"The fairies must have taken it last night while you were sleeping. Now, sit up to the table and have something to eat," said Mumma, scattering cake decorations on top of his oatmeal and adding cream, telling him not to say anything to Daddy about the sprinkles. "You know what your father gets like."

"But my picture," Jacob continued. Thrusting a teaspoon into his cereal, she told him to stop whining and eat up.

I forced a mouthful of oatmeal down.

"But Mumma—," Jacob started to say.

When Mumma slapped her hand on the table hard, I jumped. "Can't you ever do what you're told?" she yelled. Marching over to the cupboard, she opened a drawer and took out a sheet of plain white paper. Jacob was sniffling. Nudging him with my foot, I tried to get his attention, to tell him to be quiet without using words, but he wouldn't look up at me. "Here," she said, forcefully placing the paper and pencil on the table in front of me. "Draw another picture for your brother." When I hesitated, she shouted, "Just draw the damn pony, Jewel!"

Gingerly reaching for the pencil, I started to sketch, steadying my hand as best I could. As the lines appeared across the paper, the joy I usually felt with a pencil in my fingers wasn't there. "Look, Jakey," I said, turning the paper for him to see, "there's Dusty's head. Want to see me draw her mane?" Jacob nodded and sniffed, and took a mouthful of oatmeal, swinging his legs back and forth. I looked up at Mumma. She was standing at the cupboard with her back to us.

Last night, when Mumma came out of Jacob's room, the moonlight had revealed something in her clenched fist. I followed her down the stairs, saw her place the crumpled-up paper on the cupboard and slip out the back door like a phantom. From the living-room window I watched her walk toward the fence in her nightdress, a pair of bedroom slippers on her feet. The moon, round and full, lit up the outdoors, mimicking daylight. As Mumma stretched out her hand, Dusty moved slowly toward her. I wasn't sure what she was about to do until she opened the gate and Dusty stepped quietly into freedom.

Looking up from my sketch, movement from outside caught my attention. Hurrying toward the kitchen window, I saw Daddy leading the pony toward the fence and back though the gate. I quickly looked over at Mumma. Her eyes were filled with tears.

Elizabeth

We arrived at Dr. Scott's office shortly after lunch.
Cliff pointed his finger at me to stay where I was, walked
into the adjoining room, and said something to the doctor's
secretary. Her answer was short. Leaning out from her desk,
she looked my way and flashed a quick smile, her bright eyes
bulging outward.

Curiosity killed the cat!
Pay a dollar for the privilege!

Cliff came back into the waiting room. "Sit still," he
said. I looked at the hanging plant in the corner of the room
and pretended to be interested; anything was better than
facing Cliff. We hadn't spoken on the way into town. There
wasn't much left to say. I set my mind on getting through
this appointment with Dr. Scott. At the moment, it was
all I cared about. A woman in a heavy wool coat coughed
into her hand. A toddler on the floor sucked on a squeaky
toy, drool running down his chin, while his mother flipped
through a magazine, unconcerned.

"Mr. MacKay, you can see the doctor now."

Cliff stopped me as I was about to get up. "I'm going in first, Lizabeth. You wait here." The secretary looked out at me again, but I refused to return her phoney smile. She was in on something with Cliff, all that whispering and nodding earlier with me not able to hear.

"I'm the one supposed to see the doctor," I stated. I couldn't let him undermine me to Dr. Scott.

"Never mind, Lizabeth," he whispered. "Just do what I say and wait here."

Wait here. Wait there. Where else would I wait? Cliff thought I couldn't see through his trickery. He'd planned everything out ahead of time; a meeting with the doctor first so he could fill him with lies. Anger ran jagged fingernails down my back. I wanted to strike back any way I could… but I had to tread carefully. Dr. Scott was the one with all the power.

The toddler crawled toward me, pulled his wet thumb from his mouth, and slapped my ankle. He gave me a strange look, as if he could tell I didn't belong here with the rest of them, as if trying to tell me I should hurry away before Dr. Scott had time to see me. Moving toward the edge of my chair, I swung my legs around so he couldn't reach me with his grubby little hands. His thin swatch of hair and round, droopy eyes angered me in a way that didn't seem quite reasonable. Babies are supposed to be cute, not slobbery and sad, and not spreading their germs over everyone. And certainly not knowing things about someone they've never met before. Tossing her magazine onto the floor, the mother scooped him up in her arms, cooing in his ear. "Come, Leo," she said, turning her back on me. The child squirmed in her arms, eyeing me suspiciously. I made a face at him when his mother wasn't looking and he began to cry. In that moment, satisfaction became mine. While my face didn't show it, I couldn't stop smiling inside.

And then it came my turn to see the doctor. Standing on wobbly legs, I took a deep breath. Cliff stood in the doorway behind Dr. Scott as I moved in the only direction I could. As much as I wanted to, I couldn't turn and go the other way.

Help wanted. Room and board provided. Poppy saw the job advertised in the morning paper. His eyebrows went up as he showed me what was printed on the page.

"I don't want to work at a hospital. Too many sick people and germs," I said, sipping my tea. I didn't expect he'd put much effort into this idea of finding me a job in town. It was something he thought was expected of him. Dell Jameson put this idea in his head. I'd overheard him out in the dooryard a few days earlier.

"Where's that girl of yours these days—still livin' at home?"

"Elizabeth helps with the farm," Poppy said.

"What she plan to do, live home all her life?"

Dell's prying kept me up half the night. He'd come to look at a steer Poppy wanted to sell and had no business asking about me. His question disturbed Poppy as well. I heard it in the way he'd answered Dell. I'd despised the animals since I was a child and couldn't bring myself to spend time in the barn.

"This will be good for you, Elizabeth. You'll see," said Poppy, folding the paper. "You'll soon be twenty-five. You can't stay with me forever. It's not right. It's not what your mother would have wanted. And you can come home on weekends. I promise."

The very next day he drove me into town. All the way

there I kept wondering, if I jumped out of the truck, would I break any bones, maybe hurt an arm or a leg, enough to keep me from taking this job at the hospital? Perhaps if I stayed in bed all day and refused to eat any meals, he'd take pity on me and tell me I didn't have to go.

He ignored my complaints of feeling unwell as we ate breakfast that morning. I hadn't wanted to get dressed. "It's butterflies, Elizabeth, everyone gets them," he said.

"I'm not everyone," I told him, but he didn't reply.

It was Sandra's day to clean, and she was in the kitchen clearing the table.

"Listen to your father," she said. "It'll be good for you." I would have believed anything Sandra said to me, but even then I had my reservations. Sandra was too optimistic for her own good.

"He's punishing me for some reason."

"Your father wouldn't harm a flea."

There had never been any talk about my doing anything other than staying at the house with Poppy. Sandra came two days a week to clean and cook. What if I learned how to bake bread and straightened up in the house? Sandra could help out on the farm. She was more than capable and well-suited for that kind of work. There was plenty to be done, and Sandra was crazy about animals. Daniel wouldn't mind what she did so long as she worked, I was sure of it. I quickly made plans of how it would all work out, tracing out all the details in my head, and it was a good plan, a reasonable one.

"Your father's right," Sandra finally said. "This will be good for you." She looked at Poppy and they smiled at one another, and I had no choice in the matter.

Staring at the road ahead, I went over everything in my mind: the yellow bedspread in my room, the quilt folded neatly at the foot of the bed. Poppy talked about the weather on the drive into Bridgewater, and the team of oxen he'd bought a few weeks back, how he thought they'd make a good team for hauling out logs in the woods. I counted the teacups hanging in the buffet, traced the delicate blue-flowered pattern on Mum's good china plates. I counted the number of steps out to the pasture, the mailbox, the barn. I counted all there was to count, traced it out in my mind, and then I did it all over again. Poppy's voice rambled on in the background. There was nothing he had to say that I wanted to hear.

I was going away. He was the one sending me away.

Authority rests upon those who wait. Wait. Wait. Wait. We squander one moment waiting for the next. They were likely no more than nonsense words plucked out of the thousands of words that circle around me daily, slipping and sliding into one another. But then suddenly the words made perfect sense. Dr. Scott was the authority, and he was waiting for me to answer his question. His pen clicked. Up. Down. Up. Down.

"Cliff tells me you've not been feeling so well, Elizabeth. Is that so?"

The tiny broken veins across his cheeks wouldn't have been visible if he hadn't been sitting with his face so close to mine. Cliff wouldn't stop clearing his throat. I looked directly into Dr. Scott's eyes, wielding both confidence and defiance. If I told him I was fine, he'd call me a liar; if I said I wasn't well, he'd send me to Roseland. He'd done it before, months after Jacob was born. Cliff would be more than willing to go along with that. I'd still be in Roseland if it hadn't been for Poppy, the way he showed up and rescued me one day. Pulling back my shoulders, I was determined to say all the right things. This appointment with Dr. Scott was far too important for me to make any mistakes.

I looked past Dr. Scott, at the diagram hanging on the wall—a shell of a man, head turned, organs exposed—the same chart that had fascinated me when I was a girl. Same chart, same office, same Dr. Scott, and not an ounce of comfort in any of that. I could smell what he'd eaten for lunch: a mixture of onion and some strange spice I couldn't readily identify. His jowls gave him a hound-dog look. The bags under his watery, red eyes were puffy. Pulling my fingers through my hair, I steadied the fine tremor I saw and quickly brought my hand down to my lap in case he noticed. The silence stretched on. I needed to say something more, something to prove Cliff's insistence that I come in for this appointment was unwarranted.

I smiled.

Dr. Scott smiled.

"Dr. Scott asked you a question, Lizabeth."

Already I'd forgotten what that question was. But I couldn't sit there completely mute, not with Dr. Scott and his authority waiting on me—that much I knew even without Cliff's interference.

"He asked how you're feeling—remember?" Cliff's voice was louder this time.

"Be patient, Cliff. Let Elizabeth answer for herself, in her own time."

"Aunt Helen used to say a cigarette was as good as a nerve pill. Her doctor even told her so. He's the one who got her started—smoking, that is."

Dr. Scott's face took on a peculiar expression as he looked at me and said, "Is that so?"

"We were alone in the house one day when I was a

girl. 'Here, take a puff,' she said. I knew Poppy wouldn't approve, but I took it from her anyway, Dr. Scott. What do you think of that? She's dead now, of course, some mysterious ailment the doctor couldn't pinpoint."

"Do you want a cigarette, Elizabeth?"

"I don't smoke, Dr. Scott."

Mrs. Hampton hired me and I started the very same day. When I came out to the truck to tell Poppy, there was a big grin on his face.

"It'll be fine," he said, touching my hand. "I promise. You'll be fine. I wouldn't lead you astray, my girl." Pulling my hand back, I grabbed my bag and marched into the hospital. Poppy had given me no choice. I was a kitten being tossed to the roadside and the driver was taking off as quickly as he could. Friday after work he picked me up and brought me back on Sunday evening. Sandra prepared a special meal on Saturday.

"For your homecoming," she said as a drizzle of gravy ran over my mashed potatoes. "Your father missed you.... We missed you." She smiled and Poppy smiled, even Daniel smiled, and not one of them remembered that I didn't eat gravy on my potatoes. I'd only been gone a week, but already they had forgotten. If I never came back, they wouldn't even notice. I didn't belong here anymore. I didn't belong at the hospital. I was neither here nor there, but some place in between.

Aunt Helen was smiling that day, the same way Dr. Scott was smiling now, as if they were both part of some deep, dark secret they were not about to share with me. And then it became crystal clear. Dr. Scott did know something about me, the same way Aunt Helen knew things. It was why she'd smiled that day. A secret was being dangled in front of me, threatening to tell on me if I said the wrong thing. I wanted to know what that secret was, but what if it turned into something even more frightening? I remember hearing once that ignorance is filled with blissful thoughts.

"I don't sleep very well some nights," I said, disguising the fragile spiderwebs that had formed inside me. My lips made a fine, thin line just wide enough for me to hide behind without being seen.

"So, sleeping has been a problem." He wrote something down.

I cleared my throat, hoping to bring new strength to my voice as I waited for the next question.

"Is there anything else troubling you, Elizabeth?"

"Unsettled." I repeated the word as soon as it came to me. "That is to say, I feel a little unsettled these days."

"And she overreacts to the smallest thing," said Cliff from the corner of the office.

Shut up, Cliff! Releasing daggers from my eyes, I glared across the room at him, piercing him in the forehead. Dr. Scott raised his hand.

"I want Elizabeth to answer for herself, Cliff. Is there something else you want to say, Elizabeth?"

Dr. Scott had the chart with all the secrets; secrets so dark even I didn't know what they were. He was the authority. My future was resting with him. I needed to convince him that I was okay if I didn't want to end up at Roseland. Home, as unbearable as it was by times, at least knew me for who I was. It was familiar and comfortable, and allowed me to wander about at night, to feel the silence, the enchantment, the magic. All Dr. Scott had was

Cliff's version of things. I'd seen Cliff's idea of the truth, the way he distorted facts and made things out to be my fault. Yet Dr. Scott hadn't a clue, didn't know a thing about any of that.

"You *do* know why you're here, don't you?" said Dr. Scott, his lips turned slightly upward.

"You're going to help," I answered dutifully, knowing he'd like that answer. He pulled my eyelids down and shone a light into my eyes, and I wondered what all he imagined he'll find in there.

"That I am, Elizabeth."

"I don't want to go away again." Gripping the arms of my chair, I pushed my feet into the floor, ready to bolt out of his office the moment he mentioned Roseland. He placed his hand on mine and told me not to worry, that there was no reason for me to go anywhere. I pulled in a jagged breath and glanced at Cliff.

"Have you had any thoughts of harming yourself?"

I resisted the urge to tell him that most all my thoughts harmed me. They churned inside and sent me off in so many directions and hardly ever allowed me to collect them properly. But then they weren't always my thoughts. The most sinister of thoughts came from the dark prince. Dr. Scott should have worded the question some other way: *Have your thoughts ever harmed you?* To that question I would have answered, yes, all the time. I straightened my back, held my head with fake confidence. "I'm not planning to kill myself, Dr. Scott, if that's what you mean."

He looked across the room at Cliff, then back at me, smiling awkwardly.

"I've got something that will help you, Elizabeth," he said, tapping his fingertips together and resting them thoughtfully against his lips. Cliff looked at the floor and

57

nodded. The dark prince reared his head. I didn't think any of this could possibly be real.

"Two a day," said Dr. Scott, as he came out of the adjourning room where he kept the medication. He was scribbling on the side of a little blue box. "These pills will relax you and level out your moods. You'll sleep better at night, too. It'll take a while for them to have an effect, at least a few weeks, so be patient."

Cliff reached for the pills and tucked them into his shirt pocket. "Two a day," he said. "You hear that now, don't you, Lizabeth? They won't do any good if you don't take them the right way."

Two a day. One a day. None a day. My triumph came as I left Dr. Scott's office without the mention of Roseland. It was all I cared about. At home I grabbed an apron and quickly tied it around my waist. Cliff took a pill from the box and put it in my hand. He filled a glass with water and handed it to me.

"These will help, Lizabeth. Things will be back to normal real soon. I promise."

Normal—the word vibrated like a lone violin string waiting for the music to start. But there would be no music in this house anytime soon. That was the one thing I was certain of.

Jewel

"Who could be writing me?" said Mumma when I handed
her the letter that afternoon. She studied the envelope as
if expecting to find some clue as to who it might be from.
"Looks to be a woman's handwriting. No perfumy smell,
though," she announced, giving it a quick sniff.

"Maybe it's from Aunt Joan," I said, although I doubted
that.

"Joan MacKay? The biggest gossip this side of Chester?
I hardly think," she said, studying the handwriting again.
"Besides, she hates me."

"Open it and find out," I said, my curiosity growing.
There was something exciting about this mystery. Mumma
seemed pleased, but then the smile suddenly left her face and
a dark shadow passed over her.

"What—and find out some bad news?" she said, tucking the letter into the cupboard alongside the dinner plates.
"No thank you, ma'am. I'd rather remain in ignorance."

"But Mumma..." I started to protest but quickly stopped.
I knew it would do no good to try and change her mind.

When I came home from school the next day, I found the letter ripped to bits and strewn over the floor outside her bedroom. "Burn it!" Mumma screamed when she saw me bent over the scattered pieces. I gathered them up and hurried down to the kitchen, fiddling with the stove lid before shoving the torn letter into my pocket. From upstairs I could hear her throwing things and banging doors.

"What's wrong with Mumma?" Jacob asked.

"I'm not sure," I said, promising I'd take him out to the barn to comb Dusty's mane. It was easy to distract Jacob. All I had to do was mention Dusty.

Later that evening, I laid the torn pieces of the letter out on my bed. When I saw that it was from Sandra Peterson, I swallowed hard. I had to know what she was writing to Mumma about. I moved the bits of paper around, trying to fit them together, but they were too small—a word here and there—and I wasn't able to make any sense of it. The pieces were gone from my dresser the next day and I worried that Mumma had found them and would be angry, but she didn't mention the letter again.

Weeks later, she started asking all sorts of questions about Jeff and Alice, who had been my friend for a brief time in second grade until Jeff forbade her to speak to me. "Are the Petersons acting differently toward you?" "Have they mentioned anything about me?" "The girl, the one you're friends with, has she said anything strange to you lately?" Sometimes she'd sound desperate for an answer, but I had nothing to tell. I hadn't seen anything different in the way they treated me. Jeff was still mean and Alice wouldn't look my way. At the end of each conversation, Mumma would warn me to stay as far away from the Petersons as I could get, and each time I promised I would. It was the letter; I was sure of it. Jeff had told his mother lies about me and that was why she'd written.

But the letter had come weeks ago. I thought that storm had passed.

Then one night Mumma woke me, whispering for me to get dressed.

"Where are we going?" I implored as we hurried down the road in the dark, ducking behind a clump of bushes at the sound of an approaching vehicle.

"The Petersons'. There are wrongs that need to be righted," she said as we waited for the vehicle to pass. Tears sprung to my eyes.

"Jeff's the one who took my boot," I spouted out, stopping myself from wailing like a baby, "and the pencil box Poppy made me—he took that too."

Headlights cast a bright light across her face. For a millisecond, the person in front of me didn't resemble Mumma at all but a sinister creature that had momentarily taken over her body. "I won't stand for this," she said, hurrying me along in the dark after the vehicle had passed. "I knew there was something you weren't saying. That boy needs to learn that there are consequences to his actions. His mother could stand a little educating too. Her, with all those uppity ways, you'd swear she *was* someone instead of an illegitimate bastard child the county helped raise."

We didn't stop until we reached the Petersons'. A dim light somewhere deep inside the house created an ominous effect. I imagined it was what a haunted house would look like after midnight on Halloween. Mumma paced the road out front, waiting for that dim light to fade. I didn't dare ask what she had planned. When the house was in darkness, we tiptoed up to the front door. I hadn't thought to bring my jacket and, complaining that I was cold, I begged to go home. Grabbing hold of me, she pushed her fingers into my left elbow. I twisted to get away.

"This is for you," she whispered in a raspy voice, and proceeded to write BASTARD across one of the windows with a bar of soap she'd pulled from her dress pocket. I feared being caught by her husband, a surly looking man with broad shoulders who worked at the feed store in town. When a dog whinged inside the house, Mumma hurried to the roadside and picked up two rocks. First she broke the attic window, and then she ordered me to throw the other rock. The dog started barking and a light came on inside the house. I squeezed the rock in my fist.

"Just throw the damn thing," she said, and because I didn't know how to disobey her, and because I hated Jeff more than anything in this world, I pitched the rock with all the strength in me. The sound of splintering glass sent us racing down the road. A man's voice echoed in the distance as we ran off into the night. The dog growled and bayed.

"There's nothing more gratifying than revenge, and nothing so sweet," Mumma said when we finally stopped running. In the moonlight, I could see that she was smiling. And I knew what she meant and why she was smiling, because I felt it too. Jeff Peterson deserved it and so did his mother. They were both liars.

As I crawled beneath my quilts that night, the euphoria I'd felt earlier quickly wore off, replaced by guilt as the possible consequences of what we'd done began to settle in. What if someone had seen us? I couldn't stop shivering. Mumma was in the living room sitting by the window. Her very presence in the house filled me with trepidation as I pulled the quilts around me. We were more alike than I wanted to admit. I tossed in bed, filled with the knowledge that when I woke in the morning things would never be the same—that I would never be the same.

Elizabeth

A thousand times I went to the kitchen window, Jacob trailing behind me.

"What are you looking for, Mumma?" Staring down at him, I clamped my teeth together. I didn't want to say, couldn't say. Speaking my fear might make it true. I couldn't live with myself if something were to happen, especially if I were the one responsible.

Especially then.

Most especially then.

"Shhhh!" I whispered, holding my finger to my lips.

I glanced at the clock. Looked away. Looked back.

I walked across the kitchen floor, Jacob now tugging at the bottom of my dress. Pushing his hands away, I kept moving. The clock vibrated in my ears.

Tick. Tick. Tick. Tock.

I went into the living room to get that incessant ticking

out of my head and to escape Jacob's question. Outside, there was shouting and laughter. I raced back to the kitchen window. Some children were coming down the hill—the Petersons—pushing and shoving one another along the road. I strained to see if Jewel was among them. She'd been told to avoid the Petersons like the plague. Yet I'd have been willing to let it pass if only I looked out and saw her there.

My heart sank.

I looked back at the clock. Fifteen minutes, now twenty.

I went over all the things that had happened that morning, searching for some clue as to why Jewel hadn't come home yet. If I found the right thought, I might figure it out. I fixed her porridge for breakfast. She complained, as always. I sprinkled it with cake decorations. She smiled and dug right in. I was on cloud nine. But then Cliff came into the kitchen and told me I was irresponsible. "She'll expect it every time now. Candy for breakfast," he said, shaking his head. "She ends up with a toothache, it'll be your fault, Lizabeth." Jewel set her bowl in the dishpan and gulped the last of her milk. I helped her with her jacket and pulled a cap down over her head. I sent her out the door. Her lunchbox was in her hand. Everything was fine.

Perfectly fine.

Except for the tiny bits of red and green in the corner of her mouth from the hundreds and thousands I'd sprinkled on her oatmeal. I grabbed a washcloth and wiped it away. It was an ordinary day, as ordinary as plain white bread. But I should have known. Ordinary days lull you into a false security, lure you into a place where you let down your guard. Those ordinary days are to be feared more than any other. Before you know it, the dark prince sneaks up from behind, taking all that is ordinary and twisting it into something dark and menacing.

I glanced at the clock: 3:47. She should be home by now, long before now.

Again, I traced out the morning.

Each time I hoped the dark prince wasn't waiting at the end of the story.

Each time he was.

Back and forth, forth and back.

From the kitchen to the living room.

Living room to the kitchen.

I sprinkled the oatmeal with cake decorations. There was a disapproving look on Cliff's face. I wiped the corners of Jewel's mouth. I helped her with her jacket. She walked away with her lunchbox. The only thing that had changed since the morning was the security I'd felt all day knowing she'd be home at 3:25. Now that was gone. The morning had started out as common as white bread, but the dark prince had taken my white-bread day and made it vanish. It was the only explanation that made any sense. Jewel had never been that late before. She was too young to have run away from home. The only place she would run off to would be Poppy's. But there was no reason for her to go off to Poppy's on her own.

I sprinkled the oatmeal with cake decorations. There was that disapproving look on Cliff's face. I wiped the corners of Jewel's mouth. I helped her with her jacket. She walked away with her lunchbox.

She might have cut through the woods.

There's a path we sometimes take.

No. The path is behind our house, at the end of the hayfield, where it's always been.

A wild animal jumped out and grabbed her.

No...no...no. I couldn't let my mind rest on that thought.

I wiped down the counter, the table and chairs. Opening the cupboard door, I looked for soda, salt, and flour, taking note that the salt was running low. I opened the door above the sink. There was barely any cinnamon in the can, but the nutmeg and ginger were fine. I pulled the notebook out of the drawer and wrote *cinnamon* and *salt* on my grocery list.

I sprinkled the oatmeal with cake decorations. There was that disapproving look on Cliff's face. I wiped the corners of Jewel's mouth. I helped her with her jacket. She walked away with her lunchbox.

Jacob wouldn't stop jabbering. He was standing behind me now, pulling on my dress again, interrupting my thoughts. His words ran together, overlapping each other like ocean waves, and I couldn't pick them apart and make sense of them. His voice grew louder. I closed my eyes and stopped what I was doing, finally demanding to know what he wanted, why he was interrupting me when Jewel was late and there wasn't enough cinnamon or salt in the house.

"A carrot, Mumma, can I have a carrot for Dusty?"

Reeling around, I grabbed him by the shoulders and stuck my face in close to his.

"There's more to life than that pony of yours! Now, go, Jacob. Stay away from me!"

That stupid pony was all Jacob talked about. Dusty in the pasture. Dusty in the barn. Dusty needing her coat groomed. And could he have a carrot, or an apple, or a sugar cube, for Dusty?

Without another word, he vanished into the living room.

Where are you, Jewel? Where?

I paced the length of the kitchen, my heart hammering so hard that my head was spinning. The schoolhouse wasn't far away. She'd never been this late before. Never this late.

Never. Once, last month, she'd stayed behind looking for her boot, but she hadn't been late enough for me to worry. She had always been so prompt.

Had—already I was thinking of her in the past.

This was no good.

I needed to stop, to think white-bread, ordinary thoughts again.

Oatmeal. Cake sprinkles. Cliff's face. Jewel's jacket. White bread. Thirty-five minutes.

The clock had an ugly smirk on its face, ticking a little louder and a little louder. Jacob was back in the kitchen saying something. I wasn't sure what. Reaching for the clock, I wrapped my hands around its smirking face.

"Take that!" I shouted. Pieces scattered. The clock stopped ticking. Jacob scurried, howling like an injured pup.

The door flew open.

Like magic, Jewel was standing on the other side. My legs went to rubber.

I should have smashed the clock before, long before, if that was all it took to bring her home. Ripping the lunchbox from Jewel's hands, I wanted to swing her around in the air and laugh for joy.

"Mumma, you broke the clock!"

"Forget the clock. It only makes fun. Where have you been?"

"Donalee's. I was at Donalee's to see the little brockle-face steer." My heart dropped into my stomach. Anger erupted in me with volcanic force, flashing red molten lava. "You took my ordinary, plain-as-white-bread day and changed it into a nightmare to go to Donalee's? I thought you'd been captured and no one would ever know. I carried my fear back and forth across the kitchen floor. You weren't here. You were supposed to be here. The clock was screaming. I sprinkled your porridge with bright candy for breakfast on a plain, ordinary, white-bread day. Your father disapproved. I wiped your face. And you were at Donalee's?"

"Mumma, don't. You're scaring me."

"Scaring you? The you who didn't think twice about worrying your own mother half to death because of some stupid steer standing in a pasture? I thought the dark prince had you."

"Mumma, please. I won't do it again." Big tears wetted her cheeks.

Cliff barged though the door just then, taking up more space than usual. "I could hear you all the way from the end of the pasture!" Jewel ran to him, sobbing. He latched onto her, stroking her head. "What have you done, Lizabeth?"

Jacob scurried toward him, too. Three giant steps put Cliff at the cupboard, the floorboards rattling beneath the weight of his thumping feet. He opened the door and took out the little box of pills Dr. Scott had given him. "Did you forget to take one again?"

I knocked the box out of his hands. Tiny pills skidded across the floor. Jewel and Jacob ran to his side again. They stood together, the three of them, hanging fast to one another.

Ninnies.

Their side.

My side.

An invisible line separated us.

"Lizabeth! You're acting crazy." He said it so quietly I could barely hear his words.

Something crept into my body and turned me to stone. The gap between us expanded and I knew then that I was not supposed to be there. It wasn't right. Everything was wrong—the look on their faces, the broken clock, the scattered pills—every bit of it was wrong. I had to get back my plain-white-bread day. I had to make the day feel right, calm, and ordinary again. I saw that the door was unguarded and raced toward it. Cliff grabbed for me, but I slipped from his grasp. The outdoors welcomed me with a song that stretched out across the horizon, filling me with an inner peace I'd never experienced before. Finally, I'd escaped from the enchanted castle, my burden gone. I could do as I pleased without Cliff's constant watch over me. I rolled the thought around the tip of my tongue, eager then to take an even bigger bite. I was free. There was no stopping me. Taking in a deep breath, I welcomed the taste of freedom on my lips.

Jewel

I had only planned to stop off at Donalee's pasture for a little bit. What difference would a few minutes make? Mumma had taken us there just last week to see the new calf because Jacob still missed Bright and Lion, and he wouldn't be quiet about it. We stood beside the fence and reached our arms out to the calf, but it kicked up its feet and ran away. If I went alone and was very quiet, I might get to touch it.

Along the path I saw some dandelions and stopped to pick them. I thought it might please Mumma if I brought some home to her. She always said they were her favourite. But when I stepped out of the ditch with a bouquet in my hands, someone was standing in the middle of the road. Even from a distance, I knew it was Jeff Peterson. A stampede of feet on the gravel road brought with it the rest of the Petersons, yelling for Jeff to wait up. He waved at me from where he was standing, but it wasn't a friendly gesture. All day long he'd been pestering me. When he started walking toward me on the playground first thing in the morning, I was sure he was coming to settle the score for the broken windows. But when I saw the look that spread across his face, I knew it had nothing to do with what had happened that night, that he hadn't guessed who was responsible.

"Do you know what I heard, Jewel MacKay?" he said, braced off in front of me. "I heard your mother's been crazy all her life ever since her mother jumped in the ocean and drowned herself." His words bruised me in a way I'd never experienced before. He was lying. How could he possibly know something about my family that even I didn't know? There was a picture of a woman in Poppy's living room, a pretty, small-framed woman with sad eyes, but Mumma never ever spoke about her even when I asked. "I was only five when she died," she'd say. Not even Poppy would say anything about her.

"Tell us, Jewel MacKay, do you suppose craziness runs in families? Who knows, you could be next," he said, jumping toward me. I flinched, thinking he was about to tackle me. His laugh was bitter, sharp around the edges. Running toward the schoolhouse, I felt a ball of fear pulse inside me. Mumma wasn't like the other mothers in the Forties Settlement, but I thought it was a secret, something no one else knew.

It was foolish of me to have stopped to pick flowers, and I made a wish that I'd gone straight home instead, a wish I knew couldn't possibly come true. In the distance, Jeff called out, "Loony Girl!" and I started to run. At recess, he'd locked me in the coat closet, but Mrs. Carver had caught him and given him a strapping. When he got out, he swore he'd get his revenge one way or another, so when he called at me from across the expanse, I knew he was coming to settle the score. A shortcut through Donalee's pasture would bring me right behind Poppy's barn. There was a path through the ditch and across a small wooded area a few feet from where I'd picked the dandelions. I hurried toward it. Still clutching fast to the flowers, I scrambled under the fence. They ended up ruined, their bright yellow heads squished into the ground. I dropped them but held fast to my lunchbox, pulling it beneath the fence with me. I didn't dare come home without it. Springing to my feet, I willed my legs to carry me to safety.

There were no signs of the new calf or any of the other cattle as I raced through the pasture. I found a well-worn trail the cattle used and ran, praying I'd make it to Poppy's in time. But the path was narrow and lined with rocks and bushes, difficult to manoeuvre around while running. My foot caught on a rock and I went down on my knees. The thumping of boots vibrated in my ears. Before I could scramble to my feet, Jeff knocked me down flat to the ground. My lunchbox went flying through the air. I wrapped my hands around my head, waiting for whatever was coming as Jeff pushed my face into the earth. I squirmed to get away, but he shoved his knee into my back. The pungent smell of green grass filled my mouth and lungs. I could barely breathe.

"Now, what were we talking about earlier, Loony Girl?" His breath was forced and filled with rage. The earth thumped with a stampede of running feet as the rest of the Peterson kids came to a halt, screaming at the top of their lungs. "Loony Girl, Loony Girl," they sang, parroting Jeff. Instead of the flurry of fists I expected to come down on me, I felt Jeff grab me by the scruff of the neck and set me on my feet.

"What are you going to do with her?" Alice Peterson asked in a soft voice. "I don't think you should hurt her."

"She's as loony as her mother," Jeff had said to Alice

the day he forbade her to ever talk to me again. "Don't go near her with a ten-foot pole." I'd catch Alice looking at me during the day. I thought she'd eventually come around, but she hadn't spoken to me since.

Jeff circled me, tapping his chin in contemplation, as he decided what he'd do. "Can't just let her off scot-free," he said. "She got me a strapping. It was all her fault. And when you cross a Peterson, you've got to pay…the…price." He poked me in the chest three times as he spoke. I stumbled backward, afraid he'd figured out who had broken the windows in his house. I was sure he'd kill me if he had. Legs trembling, I looked across the pasture. Poppy's barn beckoned to me in the distance, too far away from where I stood.

"Give her a black eye," said Greg. "A nice big shiner."

"No!" yelled Alice, yanking on Jeff's arm. He brushed her aside like a feather.

"Look, I ain't hitting no girl," said Jeff, pacing back and forth. I was relieved to hear him say this, although I was not completely convinced that he meant it.

"Make her eat a cow patty."

"Tie her to the fence."

"Take her shoes."

The boys threw out suggestions, and each time Alice would shout, "No!"

"I've got a better idea," Jeff finally said, ogling me for a few moments, his lopsided grin indicating it was something sinister. "Tell us your mother's a loony bin and maybe then I'll let you go."

"No!" I squawked, lunging at him, swinging my fists with a bravery I didn't know I possessed.

"Oh, I think you will," he said, pushing against my forehead to hold me back, as I furiously swatted air. I'd tear him to pieces if I made contact. Quickly playing myself out, I stopped swinging, straining to catch my breath. Jeff stepped backward, releasing me from his hold. He nodded to Greg, who then twisted my arm behind my back.

"Let me go!" I squawked, pain jabbing my shoulder as Greg pulled up on my arm.

"There's more where that came from, Loony Girl. Now say it. Say, 'My mother belongs in the loony bin.'" I held tough, preparing for what was to come. Jeff nodded at Greg again. This time he twisted harder. I yelled out, trying to get away, but Greg's hold was so strong. Alice yanked at Greg's arm, but she was no match.

"Let go!" she screamed as I cried out again.

"All she has to say is, 'My mother's a loony bin,'" shouted Jeff. "We don't go anywhere until she says that."

Another wrench on my arm and I could stand it no longer. I screamed out the offending words. "Say it again," Jeff shouted, and I did. Over and over. Jeff stood before me with a look of satisfaction. I kept screaming. I couldn't make myself stop. Tears ran down my face. Greg let go, pushing me away from him. I fell into a blubbering heap, my shoulder and arm throbbing. Alice ran to my side but was pulled away.

"Come on, Alice. You stay away from Loony Girl there," Jeff said. "She's crazy just like her mother and her grandmother." He booted me in the leg and walked away. As they hurried off, Alice stopped and turned back toward me. There was a haunting look in her eyes that burned a hole straight through me.

I didn't move for a time. The cattle came up over the hill, the little brockle-face steer by its mother's side. I wanted to stay on the ground and not move for a lifetime, but in the end I had to go home. Mumma would be wondering where I was. I gathered up my lunchbox and walked back toward the main road, my arms and legs weak. Climbing the pole fence, I jumped to the ground. The crumpled dandelions were waiting for me on the other side. I stepped on them and flattened them farther into the ground. Mumma wasn't crazy, she was just Mumma. The same way she'd always been.

"There's nothing you can do here," said Daddy. There were dark rings around his eyes. I could tell he'd been up most of the night. "You might just as well be in school. Now eat your breakfast."

I started to protest. School was the last place I wanted to be.

"She'll be back," he said, as I swallowed a spoonful of lumpy oatmeal. "It's not for you to worry."

Last night, lights had moved about the pasture and into the woods. From the window upstairs, me and Jacob had watched. Through the small crack of the opened window, I heard Daddy calling out to her.

"Where do you think she went?" Jacob said, his big brown eyes yearning for an answer I couldn't give. I turned away to keep him from seeing my tears. If I hadn't been late coming home from school yesterday, this never would have happened.

But then, Mumma was standing by the stove when I came through the door that afternoon, stirring a pot as if nothing had happened the day before, as if she hadn't disappeared into the woods and spent the entire night alone in the dark. She looked perfectly fine, or as close to perfectly fine as Mumma ever came.

"Mumma!" I gasped, nearly dropping my lunchbox on the floor. At school I'd pushed her away and made myself stop thinking about how she was gone. I'd concentrated on the numbers in my mathematics book and imagined running barefoot down the road to Poppy's house once summer came. I'd thought about Jacob and me burying more treasure down by the shore on our next trip to Uncle Dylan and Aunt Joan's, and riding on Dusty's back, nuzzling my face into her neck, taking her warmth just for me.

Mumma didn't speak that evening and neither did Daddy, and whenever Jacob made a noise I told him to shush. I went to my room; Jacob followed. I took out the book of bedtime stories Poppy had given us a few weeks ago and started to read. "Talk louder," Jacob said when we heard noises coming from downstairs. Later that evening, Mumma came into my room and crawled onto the bed beside me. Her body felt like a block of ice, and I lay there still as a stone, straining to hear if she was breathing.

Elizabeth

On a warm September evening I was out walking down by the foundry in Bridgewater when a stranger drove past me in his truck, then stopped and backed up. "Where are you headed?" he said, like he was showing up at just the right time to rescue me. There was something about it that made me laugh even though what he'd said wasn't the tiniest bit funny. I lied and told him I was working at the hospital as a nurse's aid. He didn't need to know I was just a laundry maid. He said it was warm for September even though the evenings cool down quickly, and before I knew it, I was sitting inside his truck, my hand gripped tight to the door handle. He could take me anywhere, I realized just then. He could be a rapist or a murderer for all I knew. Poppy had warned me to be careful the day he'd driven me into town to work. "Watch out for strangers," he'd said as I counted through the china teacups in my mind one more time. I looked across at the man whose truck I'd so eagerly climbed into. His brown eyes seemed trustworthy, but that could have been a trick. Too late to be remembering Poppy's warn-ing. But then I thought that if I befell some horrible fate, it would serve Poppy right for sending me away to work.

The man drove me up to the hospital entrance and asked if he could see me on the weekend. Never once did he make an inappropriate remark. "You don't even know my name. And I don't know yours," he said as I pulled up on the door handle. "Cliff. Cliff MacKay. In case you're wondering." I jumped out of the truck before telling him who I was.

"How about Friday night? We could go to a show...or something else if you'd rather. Will you be ready at seven?" Looking back at him, I smiled and nodded, then ran for the entrance. I was ready for bed by the time I realized that Poppy would be coming for me on Friday after work. Half the night I lay awake in bed until I finally got up and walked down the empty corridor. How would I manage to be in two places at once, and exactly which place did I want to be in the most?

On Friday morning I phoned Poppy to tell him he didn't have to come get me. He laughed and asked why I was being mysterious. All day I thought about the special sup-per Sandra would make for us on Saturday. She'd do it if I asked her to. She'd do anything I asked. I'd invite Cliff, and it would be perfect—just the three of us. I planned it all out, traced the entire evening in my mind. Poppy would be thoughtful, nodding and smiling, making polite conver-sation. Cliff would be gentlemanly. At the end of the eve-ning Poppy would look at me approvingly. "You did good, Elizabeth," he'd say. Maybe he'd tell me I didn't have to go back to work at the hospital now that I'd met someone.

When Friday evening came, Cliff picked me up at seven. It didn't take much to convince him to drive me home. We didn't even mention going to the show after that. He dropped me off at the house and promised to come back the next night for supper.

But that special supper never happened. Nothing happened—none of the good things I'd imagined, that is. Plenty did happen, and not one bit of it was good.

I saw what I wasn't supposed to see, a light kiss on the cheek when they thought no one was there, a knowing look one shares with someone they are far too familiar with—a look that told me there was more, so much more hidden in the shadows. A gentle embrace.

Words poured out of me, hate-filled and ugly. When I saw what I saw, and said what I didn't say, I ran, because I couldn't bear to think of what it all meant. The deeper I went into the woods the faster I ran, and the lies, betrayal, and broken trust all followed. Sandra had been coming to the house for five years, ever since Mrs. McGowan's left knee wouldn't allow her to do housework. I trusted Sandra's friendship, the way she scrubbed the floors, the bread she baked, the advice she gave so freely, her smile and friendly ways.

There was no place for me to turn. I wanted to disappear, run to Daniel and tell him what I'd seen, but I couldn't. Curling into a small, tight ball beneath the base of a large pine, I waited for Poppy to come find me. He never came. After dark, I slipped into the house. I couldn't face him—them. Neither one of them could I face, having seen what I had. In the morning I called Cliff. He took me back to the hospital that afternoon. He didn't ask why.

"You know what you need to do," I told Poppy before I left the house that day, and I wanted to beat my fists upon his chest and wail. And not until he'd banished her from our lives did I go back home.

Hurrying to escape from Cliff and the kids, I started down the trail toward Poppy's house but somehow ended up at the river. I made my way along the riverbank, feeling the gentle shuffling of my feet against the forest floor. A quietness descended over me the farther I went into the woods. Birds flittered among the tree branches, warbling sweet songs, and for the longest while I felt at peace.

Sometime later, I heard people talking, their voices came mingled with the trees and the breeze and the sound of the rushing river. I didn't know who could have found me. Not here. I didn't expect anyone to come looking for me this deep in the enchanted forest. No one had ever come looking for me before. Not even when I was a girl chasing after fairies. Perhaps it was the voice of the fairies, then, but they had given up on me long ago when I turned the corridor into adulthood. Then I saw Poppy's green checkered shirt through the trees—my knight in shining armour. I should have known he'd arrive. I stopped in my tracks. Something was wrong. I didn't need rescuing. I came to the woods to be alone, to get away from Cliff and the kids and their barrage of accusations. A knight in shining armour only shows up when someone needs rescuing. I hurried along the riverbank toward him, dodging mossy rocks and tree trunks, wondering what could have happened.

"I'm coming, I'm coming," I said as excitement built inside me. I had not felt this elated since I was a child waiting for Poppy to come rescue me and Mum from the dark tower. But as I neared the place where he was standing, my footsteps slowed and anger leapt into my throat, bitter as bile. He called out my name and I stopped.

"What's *she* doing here?" Fury pushed against my ribcage, making it difficult to inhale.

Poppy said, "We've been looking for you; me, Cliff,

everyone—you didn't come home last night." He was coming to meet me with outstretched arms.

"You made a worthless promise, Poppy. All those years ago. Look at you. It didn't mean a thing." Deceit spun in his eyes. I couldn't believe what I was seeing. How could Poppy be so blind? Even now, after all these years, she was trying to come between us, writing letters, making up lies about Poppy, expecting me to believe her stories.

"Listen to what your father is saying." I lunged at her with my arms flailing. She had no right speaking to me, not after all the lies she'd told. Poppy caught hold of me and held me back before I could tear her to shreds with my bare hands. My anger was so biting, I couldn't altogether make out what he was saying. He said something about home— taking me home. But I couldn't go home. Not now that I'd escaped. I'd tasted freedom, basked in its glory, and it was mine to have and to hold for as long as I wanted.

He told her to leave, and quite quickly she vanished without a trace and I was glad for that. "Everything's okay," he said, stepping closer. "No need for you to worry. It's all okay." His voice was gentle, like the soft patter of rain on the earth, the same tender words he'd spoken after Mum died. I clung to him, nestled in his warmth, his strong arms holding me, keeping me from harm. I didn't want to move. Even after the lies Sandra had written about him in her letter. I could have stood there for an eternity, safe and warmed, loved in a way that only a father could provide.

"It's time to go home, Elizabeth," he whispered. Lifting my face, he kissed me on the cheek. I tried to say something, but nothing would come out. "Now, you listen to what I'm saying, my girl. It's time for you to go home." And I went with him, not because I wanted to, but because at that moment, following was the only thing I felt capable of doing.

Cliff picked me up at the hospital one evening near the end of October and we went for a drive. "I've got a surprise," he said. I hadn't seen Poppy since September, not since I'd caught him and Sandra together. He had the power to bring me back home, he knew he did. He had to choose. His only defence was that I'd misunderstood, that it wasn't what it seemed. I asked him to explain. "You have to trust me on this, Elizabeth." But I couldn't trust, couldn't surrender to the notion that I'd misunderstood something innocent, not with that woman still coming to his house every week. "She has to go," I told Poppy, and she finally went. And for that I was grateful. But not until Cliff and I had been married six months.

"Keep talking," I said to Cliff as we drove along in his truck. I thought his voice might distract me, maybe stop my heart from flailing inside my chest at this talk about surprises. He launched into a speech about the plans he'd been making, plans he hoped would include me. The big surprise was a small grey shack down close to the water's edge. He'd put a deposit on it and was planning to keep fishing with his brother.

"We won't be rich, but it's an honest living."

"It's so cold by the shore," I said, feeling a chill creeping into my flesh.

The grey shingles on the house reminded me daily of how depressing life by the sea was; four small rooms to roam around in day and night and a view that consisted of rocks, gulls, water, and seaweed. The wind was forever blowing. Something dark and mournful lamented inside me. On nights when the moon was full and round I'd sit in the kitchen listening to the clock, counting the seconds until I'd be rid of that horrid house for good.

There's only so much cleaning you can do to four little

rooms. It took months for me to persuade Cliff to leave, and all that time Joan and Dylan were telling him stay, saying the *Maggie* was his boat too. Sandra was finally gone; it was safe for me to go back home. I dreamed of sneaking down to the wharf at night, lighting the boat on fire, watching it all go up in flames.

Jacob

They woke me. Feet stomping. Hinges squeaking. Talking. Laughing. Chewing tobacco and spitting it on the floor. I was sleeping in the manger, curled into a tiny ball, but I heard them come into the barn. When I straightened out my legs, my feet hit the side of the empty manger. The manger was hard, but I put hay in the bottom, two flakes that I broke off one of the bales we bought special for Dusty. Clover hay—it's the best, sweet and hardest to find. It doesn't grow in our field. Daddy bought it just for my pony. I begged and begged until he said yes.

Then Mumma got mad.

"Dusty's special," I said looking up at her.

"Nothing's special in *this* life," Mumma said, stomping away. Then she wouldn't say a word to us, not for two whole days, not until Daddy said a silly thing that made her laugh. Then she talked. She said he was full of shit. That made us all laugh. Everything was okay then.

Peeking above the manger, I saw two men standing next to the stable door. One man was skinny and had bright red suspenders. He pulled on them like they were horse reins and I thought he should be saying, "Giddy-up now," instead of talking about the weather. The other man had a stomach as big and round as a balloon. A tiny bit of his undershirt stuck out from between the buttons. His jacket wasn't zipped. It wouldn't fit around him anyway.

Looking at the man's big belly made me think about the poem Jewel read last evening. I could almost hear Jewel's voice in my head. Her bedtime voice, the one she uses only at night when we sit on the bed with the big book of bedtime stories in front of us. Sometimes Jewel reads stories about Mrs. Apricot and a parrot named Hustle Bustle. They all live on What-A-Jolly-Street and I think it sounds like the best place in the world to live. There's a story or poem for every day of the year and Jewel says we'll get through that whole big book some day. Sitting on the bed with the big book opened, there was only time for a poem last night. It was about a man who was selling magic balloons for a nickel, and I made myself believe while Jewel was reading. I pretended that I was flying far away, holding fast to a coloured balloon. I said the magical word, "Ho-abracadabra-hi-ho." I even saw the fairies and the rivers of pink lemonade, and I wanted to stay there in fairyland just like in the poem. Then Mumma yelled for us to go to sleep, and I couldn't make myself believe in the magic balloons anymore. I begged. I said, "Read it again." But Jewel said we'd better listen to Mumma. "She'll get mad," she whispered. We heard something bump downstairs. Heavy. Jewel snapped the book shut and I scrambled under the covers. I held on to my breath. Breathing made too much noise. I looked at Jewel. Her hands were over her ears as she tiptoed across the hallway. I pulled the book under the covers with me. Square, cold, hard. I stuck the corner of the book in my mouth and held it against my front teeth. Flipping through the pages, the papery wings blew the smell of the book back in my face. I thought about the balloons again and my trip to fairyland. I breathed in the magical word. I whispered, "Ho-abracadabra-hi-ho." Then I fell asleep.

I thought maybe there *was* a balloon under the man's shirt, and maybe he *would* float up, up into the air and away to fairyland. Maybe he would, but I knew better. "The Magic Balloons" is only a poem, and poems are make-believe. I wish they weren't. Looking at the man with the big stomach, I wished that words had the power to do what they say. I wanted to touch his stomach. If I could do anything I wanted, I'd reach out and give it a poke. Some things you need to know for yourself. If I let the air out of him would he sputter and swoosh and make funny noises, then fall to the floor flat as a pancake? Or maybe he was a balloon man who ran away from the circus. A man now dressed in farming clothes, pretending he was someone else because maybe being a balloon man isn't as much fun as it used to be. I wanted to scream out and make him tell the truth.

Are you the balloon man?

I heard Dusty moving about. Sometimes she'd paw the inside of her stall when she wanted to be heard and chew at the manger, gnawing like a wood grub. This time, she blew some air out of her nostrils and I wanted to go to her and touch the soft velvety skin on her nose and say, "Shush now, Dusty, you be good. You be so good."

Daisy struggled to her feet. Her muscles rippled, her tail swished. She made a jump and pushed herself up. The chain around her neck jingled. She bawled at the men standing in the barn with Daddy. Steam came out of her mouth, and she cried because she wanted them to leave. I wished it was Christmas Eve so that Daisy could talk. They'd be so scared to hear her they would die right there in the barn. I listened then to the sound of her mooing. She was crying because she didn't want to leave and she knew what they wanted. Daisy is such a smart cow. When her calf was born dead, she cried for hours in the cold barn last winter.

"Cows do that sometimes," Daddy said. "They aren't stupid. Not by a long shot."

"Don't be such a simpleton," Mumma had said. "What do animals know about loss?"

After Daddy took Daisy's calf away I stayed with her in the barn, and brushed her coat with Dusty's currycomb. I said, "That's a good girl, Daisy. That's a good girl." But she kept right on crying. Daddy came and carried me in the house. He sat me on the oven door. I shivered and shook. I thought about Daisy's baby. Daddy buried it in the manure pile, deep down at the bottom. That day Mumma said, "Life isn't always fair. Even for little boys who behave themselves." Then she rubbed the back of my neck.

The other night Mumma told Daddy that Daisy was worthless. "We can't even get a drop of cream." I heard her talking when I wasn't supposed to be listening. "We'll have to butcher her. That's all there is to it," she said.

Daddy told her to keep her voice down. "Jewel and Jacob will hear you."

"It's time they heard some things," said Mumma, and then she made a mooing sound. She mooed and mooed. After that she laughed.

I wanted to climb out of the manger, but I didn't know these men. Strange men came one day to look at the pair of steers Daddy had mated up. It took a long time for him to find a pair with the same white markings on their faces and across their shoulders. Cattle traders would come all the time. Daddy would show them the cattle and then send them on their way. He never planned to sell any. But they never knew that. He'd stand in the yard and watch them drive off. He always smiled when they left. But the last time some men came to look at the steers they took them away. Bright and Lion hurried out of the barn and onto the back of the truck like they could hardly wait to get away. Leaving behind their hoof marks in the dooryard, they lifted their tails and kicked up their heels when they got outside the barn. They looked out over the side of the truck box as they drove away. Big eyes rolled in their heads. They looked like they were smiling, and I wanted to cry, but I didn't. "Big boys don't cry, Jakey-boy," said Jewel, and I wanted to be big for Jewel. Daddy gave Mumma the money and she waved it in the air. She put it in the tin can that's in the cupboard and danced barefoot on the kitchen floor.

The skinny man with the braces walked over to Daisy. He put his hand on her leg and gave her a slap. "The price of cattle is way down," he said, walking to the front of the stall and pushing himself against Daisy to make her move to the side. "Would you be willing to dicker?"

"Might be," said Daddy, slow like he was considering it.

"Never knew a cattleman who wasn't willing to dicker," said the balloon man with a sloppy grin.

"It thorns me to let any of them go," said Daddy. "Had a fine pair of white-faced steers I sold a few weeks back. Broke them in last summer. Had plans of taking them around to the pulls. But plans get changed."

Last summer, when Daddy yoked up Bright and Lion, we hitched them to the drag. It was dry and hot, and we went round and round the dooryard a million times. The dirt stirred up high in the air. Daddy walked in front and

91

I followed. He called out "Gee, Bright" and "Haw, Lion" until they knew which way to turn. This summer I was the one supposed to be saying all the *Gee, Brights* and the *Haw, Lions*. Daddy promised. That's why I wanted to cry when they drove away that day, because of my *Gee, Brights* and *Haw, Lions*, only Jewel didn't know the real reason. Then I had to whisper it while they drove away in that big truck with the wooden box. "Gee, Bright. Haw, Lion," I said, but they didn't hear.

The balloon man pushed a ball of tobacco out of his mouth and it landed in the gutter, and at the same time Daisy lifted her tail. A steady, hot stream of pee hit the stable floor. Daddy threw a shovelful of sawdust on the wet spot, and then she lifted her tail again. Plop! Plop! Plop! The skinny man jumped back out of the way, but not before Daisy loaded his pant leg. He cursed. *Good*, I thought. *Now he won't want Daisy. He won't want a cow that splatters on him.* The skinny man looked down at his pant leg and laughed. He swatted at Daisy's rump and didn't look the least bit angry. Daisy flinched. She didn't like him. I could just tell. The balloon man talked about all the animals he had in his barn. He bragged that they were in such good shape. "They're fine," he said. Horses, cows, and oxen, he had them all.

Dusty jumped in her stall. She switched her tail and whinnied. Daddy said, "Whoa, girl. Steady, girl. Steady now," and it made her feel better. He patted her neck and rubbed her ears, all the things that she likes.

"I could take that little chestnut pony off your hands too," said the balloon man, pointing a fat finger at Dusty.

"Dasn't sell *her*," said Daddy. Dusty nuzzled against him. "I may as well move right out if I was to let *her* go."

The balloon man nodded and rolled his lip out toward

the floor. He might trip on it if he was to move. "If you change your mind," he said.

"I won't be doing that," Daddy told him, and I was never so happy.

I kept very still while they stood there talking. I'm used to being still when Mumma's running through the house, throwing shoes and dishes and anything she can get her hands on, until Daddy stops her. He holds her arms down tight so that she can't move. When Jewel whispers for me not to make a sound, I can be as still as a mouse. "Hush now, Jakey-boy," she says and holds my hand. Sometimes Mumma screams that Daddy is suffocating her, that she can't catch her breath. She tries to wiggle away, coiling and turning like a snake held up by the tail. "Please," she begs. "Please, let me go!" But he doesn't let go. Not until she stops screaming. Not until she breathes real quiet and lies limp in his arms.

Daddy walked to the front of Daisy's stall and patted her on the neck. Slowly, he unfastened her chain. It dangled against the side of the stall and made a tinkling sound.

Don't back up, Daisy. Don't leave your stall. Push your feet into the floor and be a stubborn old cow. She rolled her eyes up at Daddy and followed him out of the barn.

Jumping up out of the manger, I ran toward Daisy's stall. Dusty whinnied and pawed the floor. I spread my arms out wide, so wide, as wide as I could make them. But the stall felt empty without Daisy switching her tail and mooing at me. I grabbed Dusty's halter and pulled her head toward me. She pushed against my shoulder. I hugged fast to her neck and breathed in the scent from her chestnut mane.

A few weeks later, a truck pulled into the driveway. Daddy looked out the window and then went for his cap. I followed behind. "Stay in the house," he said. I didn't listen. I needed to see who was driving that truck. "Go back inside," said Daddy, turning toward me. I stopped right there in the dooryard. Tires crackled against the gravel stones as the truck came slowly to a stop. The door swung open. Feet hit the ground. I looked up, and when I saw who it was, I turned and ran toward the barn, screaming as loud and long as I could.

Jewel

The leaves on the maple trees shaded the ground where me and Jacob were digging. My bare arms were cold, but cold in a way that I didn't mind. The stone wall stretched across the length of the hayfield and it had quickly become our favourite spot to play. The rocks that made up the wall were covered with moss and we'd sometimes pick off large pieces and throw them away, leaving the stones naked and exposed to the air. Twigs that had fallen from the tree branches littered the ground and we were using the sticks to dig in the earth. It was a game we'd invented a while back, out of boredom and our need to stay clear of the house at any cost. Jacob was used to playing in the dooryard when I was at school, but now that summer was here we ventured farther from the house. We'd play for hours outdoors, coming in only when hunger forced us to, though even hunger seemed a better alternative than being near Mumma these days.

"Do you think there's anything good down here?" said Jacob.

"You mean like treasure?"

He nodded quickly, his eyes filled with expectation.

"Maybe," I said, injecting hope into my voice. "Like in the story I read you last night. Remember?" His eyes lit up and he began to dig more fiercely with his stick, dead leaves and bits of dirt shooting up into the air.

"And if we did, we could take the money and buy back all our animals and we wouldn't have to move away," he said, thrusting his stick into the ground with force. I joined him in his enthusiasm, digging and pawing into the soil, not sure if I should be laughing over our silliness at trying to unearth riches or continue with determination, holding fast to that small bit of hope that still lived inside me. I was glad Jacob could immerse himself in the games he made up when his whole world had disintegrated the day Dell Jameson came up the driveway. I was sure that day would go down in history as the worst day of our lives. From the kitchen window I'd held back my tears as Dell's cattle truck started down the driveway with Dusty tied on back.

A few weeks ago, we found some bottles near the stone wall; some were buried beneath the dead leaves, others deep in the dirt. The only hint of their existence was small bits of coloured glass sticking out of the ground. We carried them home in our arms and hid them in a hole we dug near the chicken coop. And now with summer vacation here, we played near the stone wall for hours when we weren't at Poppy's tending the white-faced steer calf whose mother wouldn't let it nurse after it was born. Poppy said some cows are like that: "No motherly instinct at all."

Summer vacation gave me a freedom I hadn't felt in a long time. No more worrying about what people might discover if they looked at me too closely; no more Petersons, even though Jeff had paid little attention to me since that day in Donalee's pasture. Some days we played in our empty barn. We didn't talk about Dusty or any of the other animals as being gone. It didn't seem right—a barn with empty stalls, without the sweet smell of hay this time of year— so we went about our day as though there was nothing wrong. We pretended to scrape down the stalls and throw the manure out the shutter door. Ignoring the empty short feed tub, we talked to Bright and Lion while dumping invisible cans of feed into the mangers for them to eat. Sitting on the milking stool, I'd make believe I was milking the cows while Jacob brushed Dusty's chestnut mane with the currycomb. And all the while we played in the barn we didn't once mention the fact that they were gone.

We spent little time in the house, not that Mumma noticed. Most mornings she stayed in her bedroom, not venturing out until late in the day. At night, she roamed the house and I'd sometimes wake, aware of her standing outside my open bedroom door. She was like a phantom, a thin, wispy cloud of vapour that haunted the house day and night. Poppy would stop by some evenings after supper, but she wouldn't come down the stairs, even when Daddy hollered up and told her Poppy wanted to see her. Poppy had always been Mumma's knight in shining armour, but now she didn't seem to care one way or the other. I only wished that whatever it was that had happened between them, it would go away. Mumma wasn't easy to be around at the best of times. Now it was next to impossible.

Since selling all the farm animals, Daddy had taken a job at the mill in Fraxville. "A stepping stone," he called it, "but don't tell Mumma. Not yet, anyway." We'd heard all about these stepping stones the last time we went to see

Uncle Dylan and Aunt Joan. They had it all planned out: Daddy was going to sell the farm in the Forties Settlement and we'd all move down to Chester so he could go fishing on the *Maggie* with Uncle Dylan. Convincing Mumma that it was a smart move would be the final step.

The day started out like any other. I got the cereal down from the cupboard, poured some into our bowls, and added sugar and milk like I'd done all the other mornings that Mumma refused to get out of bed. When we heard some stirring around from upstairs, we gobbled our breakfast and hurried off to the stone wall to play. The likelihood that she was up for the day was slim, but we weren't about to take any chances. Sometime in the middle of the day, I looked out from the stone wall and saw Daddy's truck come up the driveway. Dropping our sticks, we raced across the field to find out why he was home so early. When we reached the house, the sound of Mumma's wailing stopped us cold. It was a sound not unlike the wounded deer we found at the end of the pasture one day last fall. My blood turned to ice. I wasn't even sure I wanted to find out what had happened. I was almost certain that I didn't. But before I could stop Jacob, he barged into the kitchen. Mumma stopped moaning and looked up at us. She was sitting on the floor, knees drawn to her chest, resting against the cupboards. The skin on her face was red and blotchy.

"What's wrong?" I asked Daddy. My heart sank like a capsized boat when Mumma answered, "It's Poppy."

Daddy turned toward us. In his hands was the tiny box containing Mumma's pills.

Elizabeth

The letter haunted me, begging me not to open it, while some force deep within me told me I needed to know what was inside. I hid it from Cliff, from Poppy, but most of all from myself. When I could stand it no longer I ripped it open, ravenously devouring the words. I wanted it all to be lies. But I knew it wasn't. And then I took the letter to Poppy. I only wanted him to explain how he could do these things to me, to Mum, and how Sandra Peterson knew more about my life than I did.

I dreamed last night the house burned down, that awful grey house down by the shore, the one we were living in before Jewel was born. I stood watching the flames engulf the walls, thinking how that house was begging for a painting it was never going to get.

Good riddance! A wave of relief washed through me. I

closed my eyes, delighting in that feeling. Poppy was beside me with that gleam in his eye. It seemed quite natural that he be there and not Cliff, I mean. We held hands as the flames spread. That's when I saw them, Jewel and Jacob, standing in the attic window, waving frantically down at us.

"They'll die in there!" Poppy cried out.

"They need to die," I stated calmly. "If I want to survive, they'll have to die."

I awoke with those words sealed on my lips, a deep knowing rested in my heart, a secret even I hadn't known existed before that dream. It was as if I'd figured out some deep mystery, something that had been plaguing me for months; the mystery of me, who I was—Elizabeth Mackay.

I jumped out of bed, afraid that if I didn't, everything that was now so clear to me would end up murky, befouled like my very existence here in the Forties Settlement. The dream frightened me more than I wanted to admit. My words. *They need to die.* Spoken with such clarity, such conviction. I had to remove myself from Jewel and Jacob for fear of what those words really meant. When I came downstairs, Cliff was in the kitchen.

"Did you remember to take one?" he said, pointing to the small box of pills on the counter. "I think you might have forgotten yesterday. They won't work if you don't take them every day. That's what Dr. Scott said. Remember?"

When Cliff wasn't looking, I spat the pill out and watched it disappear down the sink drain. It was in good company with the small mound of little white pills already hiding down there in the dark. It was hardly something I could keep track of, but surely a healthy number had collected there these past months.

The dream taunted me throughout the day. When I could stand it no longer, I made up my mind to leave, to free myself from this house, from Cliff, from the secret I held deep inside me. In a brief moment, before hurrying out the door, Cliff reached out and grabbed my hand. A soft look settled over him, but it quickly disappeared. He knew about the dream, could see me for the monster I was, and him knowing all that left me naked and exposed.

"Lizabeth, stay," he whispered. I pulled back. I didn't need Cliff. What I needed was solitude. Peace. Quiet. To be responsible for no one, to straighten all this out in my mind, decipher the dream's true meaning.

I spent the night in the woods, sleeping on a bed of dry moss. Cliff wouldn't come looking. Cliff is not the kind of man to go searching for anything. He accepts what is, takes each day as it comes, never expecting or wanting more. This was not the first time I'd gone off in search of the solitude I find only in the woods, the smell of hemlock and pine, the swaying and creaking of tree branches, the whispering of thoughts that are trapped in my mind, things I can't say to Cliff, things only Poppy knows about. But then, I could always count on Poppy. Poppy never let me down. *You don't need to explain, Elizabeth*, he used to say. *No need to explain to me.*

Poppy appeared and settled beside me on the ring of moss. For a time I was content, cocooned within my own sweet memories, oblivious to the rest of the world—just Poppy and me. His words produced the same magic they had when I was small. And I listened while he weaved a vivid tale of a king and queen, and a beautiful princess named Elizabeth. I didn't interrupt. It had been so long since he'd told one of his stories. I absorbed every detail, saw it in my mind, felt it in my heart, relishing every bit. The tale ended shortly after the prince appeared. The prince brought darkness with him, so heavy and deep, the very mention of his name held me paralyzed with fear. His evil plot to capture the queen and the princess, and hold them prisoner, was eventually spoiled by a knight in shining armour who fought long and hard for their release from the cold dark tower they'd been imprisoned in.

I clung to Poppy's words, eager for more. His voice blended in with the night sounds. Sweet thoughts replaced all the fearful notions I'd been harbouring. I smiled. My knight in shining armour had come through for me again. With true fear comes salvation, and the brave knight always arrives in time. Maybe not in real life, but in the world of make-believe he does. I'd be willing to stay in a fantasy world if it meant I could stay here with Poppy forever.

Poppy cleared his throat. "Are you ready for sleep now?"

"Not yet," I whispered as disappointment ran a gentle hand across me. He hadn't yet told me his very best story. I wanted to remind him yet feared I'd sound ungrateful. Our time together was special, not to be frittered away with disappointment over an untold story. I would let go any wish, even the wish for Poppy's best story, for this precious time spent with him. I would. I would.

"You're looking to hear something more. I can see it in your eyes," he said, patting my head. I held my breath and crossed my fingers behind my back, waiting to hear what Poppy would say next. I settled down farther into the moss and waited for him to begin.

"You know about the fairies that live nearby, don't you?" Yes, yes, his best story; he remembered. I lay quite still, afraid that if I moved the moment would be lost, the story gone. Excitement churned inside me as he spun a tale about the fairies, the ones who lived deep in the woods not far from home. Nymphs, he called them, devilish creatures. How I longed to become one. To play tricks on unsuspecting folks.

Cruel tricks. Run barefoot through the Forties Settlement, open up barn doors and pasture gates as fairies have been known to do.

When the story was over I curled around Poppy the way I used to as a child. I could feel his warmth, his breath, upon my neck as he lay there softly snoring. I awoke much later, feeling about for him in the dark, sensing quite quickly that the place where he had been lying was empty. Moonlight, wind, treetops surrounded me. The moss crunched beneath my feet. I called out for him, but the answer came from the wind and an owl off in the distance.

"Where are you, Poppy?" I cried out. The owl quieted as I waited for a reply, and then the wind released a lonesome song. Darkness surrounded me, so thick and heavy I could scarcely draw a breath. "Where are you?" I whispered, falling to my knees.

And then I remembered.

He was laid out in the funeral home with his hands crossed at his chest. Cliff had taken me to see him. I'd looked down at him and shaken his shoulder. "Wake up," I'd said. "Wake up."

I cried myself to sleep, then; dry, hard tears that made my chest ache.

Sunlight pierced me in the early morning as it snaked a path through the treetops. I lay still and allowed the sun to spread inside me, to caress my very soul. And then I cried once again for my dear, sweet Poppy going in the ground that afternoon at two o'clock. Thin tears slid between the cracks of my eyes, but they brought no relief from my sorrow.

I hurried home to find Cliff in the living room with Jacob and Jewel, all three of them wearing their best clothes, Jewel with a blue ribbon up high on her head. It was obvious that Cliff had fixed it for her with his clumsy hands. They were waiting for me to come home, knowing I'd be back in time to say goodbye to Poppy. It was the one thing Cliff would count on.

Jewel raced toward me, but I held her back.

"I need to change," I said, running my hands through my hair.

"Wash your face," Cliff said. His words stopped me cold. He hadn't even asked where I'd been all this time. Could he tell I'd spent the night in the woods, Poppy there to protect me? Was there something about my appearance that gave my secret away?

As I hurried upstairs, I heard Jewel whining. Cliff was telling her something, but I couldn't make out what he was saying. A dress was laid out on the bed and I pulled it down over my head. I brushed my hair and washed my face and avoided looking directly into my eyes; the mirror wouldn't give a clear picture. How could it? I wasn't altogether sure who I was at that moment. I wanted to go and see Poppy. That was what I centred my mind on.

The smell of mothballs wafted about the cab of the truck with each bump we struck in the road. Jewel fussed about the hat Cliff had told her she had to wear right before we'd left the house. It was covering the blue ribbon in her hair, which was what she was objecting to—that and the smell of the mothballs.

"You can't go into a church without a hat. They have their rules," he'd said, opening a crumpled paper bag moments before we left for the church. When two mothballs fell from the bag and skidded across the floor, Jewel raced to pick them up, but he told her to leave them be, that they were poisonous.

"Where did you get these?" I said as he held out a hat with a small, stiff veil.

"Joan—I got them from Joan."

I pulled my hand back.

"I already told you. You can't step foot inside the church without a hat, Lizabeth. Do you want to miss out on your own father's funeral because of some stupid church hat?" I took a cleansing breath. I wasn't about to let my concentration fade, no more than I was about to forget the whole purpose of the day. I put the wretched thing on my head. I'd rather have worn a tattered dishrag than anything Joan Mackay had set her hands on, but I had little choice.

Staring at the road ahead, I waited for the church to come into view. A sea of vehicles was parked along both sides of the road as we pulled up to the wrought-iron gate. There was an empty spot beside the hearse, waiting, ordering us to come closer. Jacob squirmed beside me. Finding his way closer to the edge of the seat, he peered through the windshield.

"Look at all the people!" he cried.

> *Here's the church*
> *here's the steeple*
> *open the doors*
> *and see all the people.*

But we didn't need to open the doors to see the people; they had spilled out of the church in search of a place to sit. They were standing and sitting. Waiting. Chairs were lined up outside.

"I knew there'd be a big crowd," Cliff said.

We didn't get out of the truck for a time...seconds, minutes, I can't be sure. The only thing I was sure of was our sitting outside the church in Cliff's old truck, a horde of onlookers waiting like vultures, Jacob squirming to get out, and the smell of mothballs filling my lungs.

Cliff took my arm as the undertaker headed toward us. My feet moved toward the church while my body remained inside the truck. Cliff's grip on my arm tightened. "Come along, Lizabeth," he whispered.

There was a pause before we entered the church, as we stood upon the threshold of neither here nor there. A split second held us in limbo. A voice boomed out, "All rise." There was a shuffling of feet. My breath stopped. A sharp pain caught me in the chest. I wanted my fairy ring, the bed of moss Poppy and I had slept on.

I wanted.

I wanted.

I wanted.

My knees threatened to give way. I wasn't ready, not one bit ready.

I wanted my fairy ring.

I wanted the feel of Poppy's hand in mine, his breath on the back of my neck.

Whispers came from both sides of the church as we stopped in front of the casket. Poppy was lying so still, his hands clasped around a single red rose. His hands were pale, his fingernails bleached white as if he'd never done a hard day's work.

What a lie, what a miserable lie his hands were telling.

I freed the wretched flower from his grasp. A tiny prickle caught my finger.

Why a rose, Poppy, when you never liked the smell of roses? Why not a tomato stalk—green and healthy? You took such pleasure in growing tomatoes.

Cliff grabbed the rose and placed it beside the satiny fabric near Poppy's shoulder, but not before a drop of my blood hit the coffin lining. I didn't want to stop looking at the blood stain after that. He was taking me with him—at least a small part of me—to a faraway land where the dark prince would never find us.

"Lizabeth," Cliff whispered. "Sit down."

The first night after Cliff told me Poppy was dead, I heard him outside our bedroom window. I recognized the dull clank of his ox bells, heard Poppy give a quiet, "Whoa."

I raced to the window, but he'd already gone.

The organ began to play. Long, drawn-out notes echoed throughout the church. The music was Cliff's idea. He'd insisted on doing it all. He picked out the oak-grain coffin with light blue lining. (Poppy never looked good in blue.) He ordered the flowers. The night the minister came Cliff made me sit quiet while he thumbed through the hymn book looking for something he said would be fitting. I could have told Cliff that he wouldn't know "fitting" if it jumped up and bit him in the ass.

"What do you think of this one, Lizabeth?" he asked, poking his finger at the page.

And I then thought I saw Poppy move. I couldn't look away after that. I waited, watched, waited, and watched for one tiny little breath, the one thing that would tell me this was all make-believe. If only he'd gasp, draw some air into his lungs, I knew he'd come back to life. We could all go home. I could laugh at Cliff and say, "See, Cliff, he really was outside our bedroom window the other night!"

The choir began singing. Cliff grabbed my hand when I jumped up.

"*I come to the garden alone.*"

"Sit down, Lizabeth. The family stays seated."

"*While the dew is still on the roses.*"

"Lizabeth!"

Cliff's arm wrapped about me as we sat back down. Some woman hit a high note. Feet shuffled. Pages turned.

There was too much noise. It was drowning out my thoughts. I tried to think then whether Poppy liked hymns. For certain he didn't like roses, even if they were dripping in dew.

"And He walks with me, and He talks with me."

When the music ended, the minister spoke. He opened his book, his voice echoed. I searched his soul through the window he opened when he looked down into my eyes. He knew no more about Poppy than he had the other night when he came to the house asking questions.

"Everett was a good family man, a man of integrity who gave back to his community, a man who put his family first; a simple man, a farmer, municipal councillor for many years, and a friend to all, as is evident by the number of people here today."

Say it all, damn you—a man who loved life, who could weave a fairy tale and make it come true, a man who would always be my knight in shining armour—say every last bit!

There were things I still needed to tell Poppy, words I needed to take back. I'd forgive the past, make no mention of it ever again, if only he'd open his eyes. I looked quickly back at Poppy, but saw nothing. No breaths. No movement. I shouldn't have looked away, shouldn't have allowed my concentration to waver. He might have moved and I could have missed my only chance. It was the church's fault, and the tall skinny minister who wouldn't shut up. He talked about seasons and time and living and planting and war and love and Poppy's life—something he knew nothing about. Cliff had no business telling the minister anything about Poppy the night he came to the house.

And then we put him in the ground beside Mum.

Green carpet.

Deep hole.

Down...down...down.

"Earth to earth; ashes to ashes; dust to dust."

Tiny beads of dirt fell from the minister's hand, skidded across the oak casket, and formed the most unusual pattern, which slowly became one with the wood grain. It was beautiful. I wanted to stay and watch it forever, but Cliff pulled me along. I stumbled across the green turf, toward the crowd with their mournful faces. People were speaking—a whole line of them. Bodies and voices and faces and arms wrapping around me, suffocating and restrictive. Shuffling and speaking and touching. Their voices came all at once like a hundred whispers in my head.

"So sorry, Elizabeth. So sorry. A darn shame. He'll be missed. Sadly missed. Take care. Deepest sympathy. Sympathy to all. Sympathy. Sympathy. Sympathy. Sorry. So sorry...."

A cluster of clouds then drifted across the sun, covering me with shadow. I shivered. A whisper broke through the din; it slid out between the shadows and blew in my ear, carrying a sinister message, one that brought the past along with it, the past that had been neatly put away, the lid closed and locked up a long time ago. I drew back when I saw who was whispering in my ear as spikes of bitter rage cut into me like a knife. She had no business being here, no business at all.

Joan

We were all mortified. Elizabeth started carrying on like a wild woman, beating her fists upon some poor woman's chest right there for the whole Forties Settlement to see. I swear she tried to push her into that open grave, and would have had Cliff not stepped in to stop her. She whined and sobbed and lamented then stomped out across the cemetery, leaving Cliff to make excuses for her behaviour. What could he say after all that, other than Elizabeth had been very close to her father and was extremely distraught over his death? Well, *distraught* didn't even begin to describe what we'd just witnessed. I thought about that day in April when Elizabeth nearly went beside herself and all because Jacob and Jewel were down playing by the shore, something they'd done countless times before. That was the day I reached my limit. I told Cliff that he and the children were welcome to come anytime, but there was no way I was going to turn a blind eye to the hurtful things Elizabeth had said to me.

That's where I drew the line. Someone in the family had to stand up to her, and that someone was me.

People at the graveside started mumbling, telling Cliff not to worry about apologizing for what had just happened, that it was no worse than the time Sue Jordan tried to stop the undertaker from lowering the casket into the ground when old Duff died. But this really wasn't the same at all, since Sue hadn't been right from birth and everyone knew she didn't understand an ounce of what was happening that day. And it wasn't as if she knew it all meant she'd be sent away to live in a home somewhere, since Beth was in no real shape to look after herself, let alone a forty-nine-year-old with the mind of a child. Elizabeth, being mature in mind, had no excuse for her behaviour. She was just acting out like the spoiled brat she was.

There had been a bit of a fracas near the casket when they first walked into the church. I was at least satisfied to see that Elizabeth and Jewel were wearing the church hats I'd lent Cliff. And I'll say, they did look halfway presentable, which was all any of us could ask for at that point. It's not as if Elizabeth was going to gain any kind of fashion sense about her at this point in her life. I also took note that she had on the navy blue dress I'd mentioned to Cliff over the telephone. Really, it was the only decent thing I'd ever seen her wear, and I knew it would go quite well with the hat, and none of that had been a coincidence on my part.

The casket lid should have been closed before they ever came into the church. Anyone with a little common sense would tell you that. I'm not sure whose fault that was, but as I told Dylan later, it would be a cold day in hell before I'd ever let Westcott's look after one of my own when the time comes. With everyone standing in the church it was difficult to see what was taking place, although I knew something wasn't quite right by the mumbling I heard. I elbowed Dylan to get his attention. He was next to the aisle, and I was sure he could see what was going on. He leaned over and told me to never mind.

Time paused for the longest stretch. I kept straining to see, but there were too many heads in the way. When Cliff finally managed to steer Elizabeth into the pew, I breathed a sigh. Imagine if she had caused a hullabaloo right there in the church. Why, we would never have lived it down. Everyone from the Forties to Chester Basin and beyond would have heard about it, and I can't begin to wonder what I would say to the church guild then. I gave up making excuses for her years ago when they moved away from Chester shortly after they were married. I wasn't about to start trying to convince everyone that she was someone other than who she was. Yet, God help me, I didn't want Cliff and the kids to have to suffer any more than they already had.

Somehow Cliff managed to get Elizabeth through the service without making too much of a fuss, although I did see him pulling her back down into the pew a few times during the service, when she kept jumping up out of her seat. Each time I bit the side of my cheek, hoping she wouldn't act out. *Not now, dear God*, I prayed, *not in front of all these witnesses. Not in your house, of all places.*

It was a picture-perfect day for a funeral, scarcely a cloud in the afternoon sky, and when I stepped outside a sparrow flitted in front of me and perched on top of the church spire. I took it as a positive sign as I followed the mourners out to the cemetery, but that was just the hopeful part of me. Up until that point, Everett had been given a good send-off. That much everyone agreed upon, and if Elizabeth hadn't been so selfish, she would have agreed with that too. It was a lovely service—if one could actually call a funeral lovely. Reverend Collins's eulogy was uplifting, and it was the first time I'd come away from a funeral feeling slightly glad for the dearly departed, which was a testimony to Reverend Collins's ministerial abilities. At least Everett's torment was over—all the things Elizabeth had put him through over the years is what I'm referring to. Only that meant it would all fall on Cliff's shoulders, and I dreaded the thought of what that would mean for all of us. Everett could usually be counted on to keep her in line—to some degree, at least—when he wasn't spoiling her rotten.

If Cliff and Elizabeth had done what normal people do instead of running off to a Justice of the Peace, I might have been able to keep Cliff from making the biggest mistake of his life. But they couldn't wait. They burst into the kitchen late one evening, shoving Elizabeth's wedding band in our faces like we should fall all over ourselves about their good news.

"We're going to stay at the Kelley place for now," said Cliff. "But we're planning to buy a farm in the Forties one day." He looked over at Elizabeth and smiled like he'd been put under a spell. Buy a farm and move to the Forties? Neither one of us could believe our ears. It wasn't like Cliff to hurry into something without at least talking it over with his older brother. First off, Dylan would have told him not to jump into marriage, that he didn't know this girl well enough. He'd also have told him that it wasn't a good time to be buying a farm and that no one ever *did* get rich farming. It was all her doing; somehow she'd brainwashed him into doing this reckless thing. He'd be sorry in the end, I was certain. But believe me, this was one time I wished I'd been wrong.

"What about the *Maggie*?" said Dylan, and when I saw the disappointment in his eyes it crushed me. They'd been fishing together since Jake died. Cliff didn't know a thing about farming.

"I guess she'll be all yours," said Cliff, shrugging Dylan off as if the boat their father had left them when he died was some old jalopy rusting in the dooryard. "I'll keep fishing for now." The *Maggie* had been their livelihood, Dylan's pride and joy. Dylan went out fishing with his mother after Jake passed away, knowing things like that always fall to the oldest in the family. Barely sixteen he was when he quit school, and never once made a complaint about the opportunities he was giving up: the chance for a good education, to make something more of himself. He gave all that up with the hope that Cliff would have the chance to do what he couldn't, and now Cliff wouldn't stand a chance at anything, being married to Elizabeth.

"How did we ever get ourselves tangled up in this mess?" I said after they left that night.

"It's not our mess to get tangled into, Joan. Cliff'll have to deal with Elizabeth as he sees fit. They're married now. We've got to stay out of it," Dylan said, as if having Elizabeth in the family wasn't going to affect us all one day. Maybe he thought I couldn't see the disappointment in his eyes as his brother drove off that evening. Maybe he thought I believed him when he wished his brother well. He put on a good face, but he wasn't fooling me. And I thought to myself, *Just give it a little time, Dylan MacKay, and see if I'm not right about this being a mess. You just see if I'm not right.* This family would rue the day that woman came into our lives.

Everyone has their own sad story, I guarantee it, even the ones you see smiling and walking down the street like they've got their heads in the clouds. But those same sad stories are what shape a person into being who they are in the present. I dare say it couldn't have been easy, what with Elizabeth's poor start in life, but after a while you just have to keep those things from bothering you. You can't hold fast to a moment in time while the rest of the world goes on living. You've got to pick up those pieces and start making sense of them. And so I made myself a promise the same night Cliff made his whirlwind announcement: I wasn't about to let Elizabeth be this family's undoing. And I wasn't about to rest easy until she was out of our lives for good.

If I was smiling out at the graveside, I hope no one noticed. I meant no disrespect. *A few more minutes and this will all be over*, I kept thinking, *a few more minutes*. And just when it looked as if things were about to go off without a hitch, Elizabeth started in. The way she carried on was more shocking than anything she'd ever done in the past. We were on sacred ground, in case she didn't realize it, which I'm sure she did, and if you can't behave there, you might just as well be given up as a lost cause. Looking back, all those other things she'd put Cliff and the rest of us through seemed plenty mild compared to the fiasco that took place out in the graveyard during the committal service. When Elizabeth attacked Sandra right there by her father's open grave, I staggered backward into Dylan. Thank God we weren't standing there as part of the family is all I can say. Dylan grabbed me and steadied me, and I whispered, "Dear God above."

"Are you seeing stars again?" he said. I was far from being faint in that moment. It was the horror of it all—bearing witness to such a ghastly scene while the world looked on.

"That's Sandra Peterson," someone next to me whispered. "The two of them have known one another for years." Dylan gave me the strangest look just then, like the things I'd been saying about Elizabeth all along were finally making some sense. He always thought I'd been too hard on her. Elizabeth started screaming at Sandra to leave her alone, and Cliff was shaking her, trying to snap her out of it. Why, that poor woman was simply offering her condolences, comfort, and sympathy.

With the scene at Everett's funeral, you might ask me then if I was surprised about what happened a few weeks later, and I'd have to say not one bit. Not one little bit.

Elizabeth

Fly high above the earth or crawl deep beneath its surface like a lowly worm. Be high and low. All in one breath. It's possible. No one knows but me. But it's possible. Maybe Poppy knows, but he's beneath the ground now. He can't get out into the wind, the air. I'd free him if I could. Open the ground up and lift that coffin lid with my bare hands and let him out into the world.

The day after Poppy was buried I stayed for hours in the cellar beneath the house, rocking back and forth in the dark. Earthworms and cellar bugs crawled through the ground. I could hear them making their way toward me. The smell of damp earth choked off my air. I wanted to scream, to jump up and run away. But I needed to feel that same misery of being underground, knowing that Poppy was feeling it too.

"What the hell did you do all day long?" Cliff demanded when he came home to find no supper waiting for him.

"What do you think I did? I picked my nose. I picked my frigging nose!"

Cliff stomped off to the pantry and reached for a loaf of bread. I saw the knife he was using to cut the bread running across the pink flesh of his left hand as he held the loaf toward himself to cut off a slice. It stabbed him in the chest, carved patterns deep into his body. I sat by the table, dazed by what I'd seen, until I saw the knife in my own hand, stabbing again and again. I ran screaming from the house.

I went as far as I could, like a deer running free in the wild, not knowing which way to turn. Wanting to turn each way...every way...all ways. Perhaps explode into a million pieces. Nothing I did, nothing I thought of, would stop the thoughts racing through my mind.

"I can't stay here," I told Cliff days later, hoping I could make him understand. "It's not safe for me to be here. It's just not safe."

"You're not making any sense, Lizabeth. What are you talking about?" He snapped out the question like a teamster's whip.

"I just can't stay here anymore. I just can't stay."

"Then you'll be dead, Lizabeth. You'll be dead to me, to the children. And you can't ever come back from the dead, no matter what...I won't let you."

Better for me to die than Jacob and Jewel, I wanted to scream. It had already happened in my dreams. The house had been engulfed in flames. They called out to me and I did nothing. Worst of all, I watched it happen—calmly, as if it meant nothing at all. Who knew what dreams would one day come true? And you need to be sure. When it's your own children, you need to be sure. I tried explaining what Poppy's death had done to me.

Cliff said, "People die every day, and the rest of us have to go on. Do you think you're special?"

I had no answer, because there was no answer; no rhyme nor reason for any of it. Poppy should have had more time, the way that man enjoyed life. If anyone in this world was ever cheated out of life, it most surely was Poppy. He deserved more. Better. Cliff couldn't see that.

"Things happen the way they're meant to. Everett lived out his life. His time was up," Cliff went on to say. People say things like that all the time to pretend that everything in life has some purpose. I saw no purpose in my misery.

And I believe in nothing.

Life is a stew pot, boiled and stirred, each of us jiggling about like turnips and carrots. Pieces of meat and potatoes. Onions. Seasoned with salt, peppered with lies. I should have told Cliff all those things the day he declared my death.

"Pepper, Cliff," I should have said. "Our marriage is pepper."

I knew what Cliff meant when he said I'd be dead, but then Cliff should have known. I was already dead. Teetering on the edge, at least, and then Poppy dying like that. Something he had no right to do, not when we had more words to say, more time to spend, more secrets to unravel.

I wondered then how many deaths we are allowed in a single lifetime. Certainly more than one—two? Much more than that.

I thought of Jacob, his plump fingers reaching down into my dough dish. Those little fingers I must have slapped a thousand times over the years. And the day by the shore, when he nearly fell into the sea, slipped from the rocks like a greased eel. I thought for sure he would drown, but I reached the beach in time to save him.

Three or four seems a minute number.

That seemingly ordinary day that Jewel went off to school all on her own. Grown up. She had no use for me that day. Then the end of the day came and instead of coming straight home she stopped off at Donalee's pasture to look at the cattle through the pole fence. I knew in my heart that something had jumped out at her along the way and dragged her into the woods, her body never to be found. Chewed. Devoured. I knew that to be the truth.

And Poppy, you must have died at least a hundred times. I know. I've seen it every time. At night when the house is dark and silent, before the dawn brings daylight into the window, when I sweep the floor and hang the clothes out to dry, when I go to the outhouse out back. Those are some of the times I've seen you die.

Then there was the money Poppy told me about years ago. Our secret, Poppy's and mine, hidden upstairs in his bedroom, beneath the floorboards. Of course, Poppy would have had no idea, no inkling what the money would end up being used for.

Mad money, Poppy called it at the time. *Mad.*

"Spend it on something you don't need. We get so caught up on our neediness, Elizabeth, that we lose all the fun in life."

So that was where I walked off to that day, out across the field to get the money out of Poppy's house. It wasn't a fortune, but it would be enough. There were plenty of things I didn't need, but I could put the money to good use. I'd take myself away from the children, as far away as I could get. Keep them safe. That was the important part. It all made perfect sense.

I stayed at Poppy's house longer than I'd planned, an entire week perhaps—I can't remember—pawing through his things, sleeping in his bed, on the same sheets he died on. The smell of his pipe tobacco brought me comfort. At night I stood by the window looking out at the stars, trying to remember all the stories he once told, the sound of his voice, the twinkle in his eye, the soft thumping of his heart. And not once did I think about the mistakes of the past. Not once.

We all make mistakes, Poppy, but yours followed you to the grave. I made sure of that. I kept your secret safe.

I don't know why I left Poppy's house, but there must have been a reason. I only know the money that should have been in my pocket was not there. My mad money. Look at me. I've lost it and now I'm mad. But I don't think that was what Poppy meant about mad money. He meant: use it to do something crazy.

Someone found me in the woods, someone with strong arms who picked me clear off the ground despite my arms flailing, scratching and tearing the air.

"Lizabeth," he said. "It's me. Cliff."

I looked closely at his face, inches from mine. I heard myself laugh. Jagged and rough like a cat's claw on a doorframe. And then I couldn't stop laughing. He looked so ridiculous standing there with my mad money in his hand. He must have found it. But where?

Ssh. I won't ask if you don't tell. He'd only lie. Whoever *he* is. Even though he thinks he knows my name, I've never seen him before. I don't know anyone who'd steal my money from me—Poppy's mad money.

There was a car that day too, and I watched the trees from the back seat whirring past like hummingbirds. Bizz...bizz...bizz. We were trying to catch the trees, but we weren't fast enough. I sat with my face resting against the cool glass, watching the world from a linear place, one that I surmised would let me enter if I could only ease myself in. The car was going much too fast for that. Something else was taking me away. I felt so small inside my body, like a child standing on tiptoes to see out a window.

I touched the glass and looked at my bare hand. My wedding ring. I thought suddenly of my wedding ring. But no. I'd thrown it away the day I left. It wouldn't come back on its own.

"Who are you?" I yelled to the people in the front seat of the car.

One of them turned around. Not the one who was driving, but the other one who'd earlier asked me if I knew who he was. When he looked around, I suddenly recognized Cliff.

"I'm supposed to be dead. You said I'd be dead. Now where's my mad money?" I knew he had stolen it, and to steal from the dead was a crime in itself.

"You must have lost it," he said, staring at me with hollowed-out eyes that looked like two piss holes in the snow.

"I did no such thing!"

Who did he think he was fooling?

I ordered them to stop the car. I had to go back, back to the beginning where it all started. Back to that place before the dream ever happened. Before the house burned to the ground. This was all wrong.

"What's the matter, Lizabeth?" someone asked. Cliff. I could make out his voice even though much of that day was cloudy, even though the world was trying to collapse in on me. I had to keep the things in the outside world from finding a warm spot in my body to hide. The trees, the sky, the green, green grass were all vying for a place among my organs and blood vessels, and there was no room left. I had used up all the room myself. I had stacked the events of my life on top of themselves, pushed and squeezed them down so that they would all fit. I had no more room. Even Cliff should have been aware of that.

"I have to go back, back to the beginning. I have to go back for Poppy's sake—for Jewel and Jacob, too."

I might have pleaded, although I was never one to plead for anything in my life. *Never* and *always* are such superficial, lie-making words. One seldom always or rarely never does a thing in this life. What silly words.

"Aren't they silly?" I said to Cliff.

"I don't know what you mean," he answered.

Of course he knew what I meant. I don't know why he was pretending otherwise. But then I suddenly knew why. He was trying to distract me, trying to take my mind off wanting to go back. I knew the truth of what was happening that day, with the trees, and clouds, and the green, green grass all trying to wiggle their way inside me. I was going somewhere far, far away, and I would never come back. Never see those trees or grass or clouds again. And it was the *never* part of that thinking that kept me from crying out. Cold glass against my cheek, as fast as we were moving I knew we would not be able to catch up to those illusive trees. I would *never* go back. *Never* see that burning house again. *Never* walk across the hayfield. *Never* see my Jakey or Jewel.

How I loved that word, *never*. How it filled me with excitement.

I could hardly wait.

Part II

1975

Elizabeth

There was a time when I would lie in bed at night and listen to the muted sounds of soft-soled shoes in the corridors and repeat my children's names until I fell asleep. I feared being snatched from my bed, hooked up to wires and gadgets, having what little bits of my memory that were still intact taken away. Of course, no one ever came at night, but still I found it difficult to let go of that fear. I don't remember many of the treatments I received over the years, although I can recall on several occasions begging for them to be administered. They left me numb, but at least I was able to function on some menial level. All that started sometime in the sixties.

It's impossible for me to explain what takes place in the mind, how your fears can be so overwhelming that you're desperate for relief even when you become aware that each treatment pushes you further and further away from the person you once were. You try not to think about that, concentrating on the moment you are presently in and what feels right and manageable. You see your past slipping away and yet succumb to the notion that it was worth hanging on to in the first place.

Except for Jewel and Jacob, I surrendered more of myself than I might have wanted to. I was never going to relinquish their names, their tiny little faces, into some empty chasm and walk away wiping the dust from my hands. There came a point, I believe, where I clung to them out of my own stubbornness and nothing more. I often wanted to place them inside some larger memory, a trip into town on a hot summer day, a special Christmas we might have had, or birthday parties with games and prizes to be won, but it is useless for me to try. I wouldn't know where to begin; which reality to set them in. If those times ever did exist I've never been able to remember, and couldn't begin to make it up. Over time, I couldn't pull their faces out of the fog. I was left with nothing more than their names, and the distant memory of tiny arms wrapped tight around me; the soft beating of their hearts against my chest.

I was married to a man I'm sure I didn't love; for certain he didn't love me. The bare finger on my left hand tells a tale of its own, that and the fact that he never came for me. He left me, dangling in the past from a thread barely strong enough to hold me. His name was Cliff. Cliff MacKay, and I remember little else. His name came to me in the middle of the night, waking me from a dream that I strained to remember. Nothing I did could bring the dream back or any of the secrets that might have been locked up tight within it. But once his name came to the surface, it wouldn't go away. Not that it makes any difference now, after all this time.

Knowing things about your life is not the same as having memories of certain events. For instance, I know I once lived in the Forties Settlement, but couldn't begin to describe the landscape or a thing about my life there. I was married to Cliff MacKay and had two children, yet I haven't any specific memories that include them. I know that I became ill and that illness lasted for many years, and that same illness, or rather the treatments that went along with that illness, is what destroyed my memory over time. I know the names of the two hospitals I was a patient in, yet the rest is cloudy, as if the memories I have of those earlier years didn't happen to me but to someone I know, and they're something I was told, not something I experienced for myself. Perhaps I imagined all of it or suffered from hallucinations during my illness. *What can't be remembered can't be ruled out*, someone once said to me. The one thing I do know is if there were some way to control the things I remember, I'd hold fast to the happiest moments in my life and never let go.

I stop short of knocking on Mrs. Weaver's door. A closed door means she doesn't want to be disturbed, although not everyone here pays attention to that. The door is open, it's all right to walk in without knocking, but still I pause. She'll think I'm a nuisance for interrupting her again. Looking up from her desk, she sees me outside her office. "Dartmouth, then Divinity," she says, moving the papers on her desk. Her answer helps centre me. The worry that was twisting and turning in the pit of my stomach escapes like a wisp of smoke. I sigh, feeling suddenly empty. I think, then, as I turn to leave, that Annie is right: too much worry can kill you, but a little worry at least lets you know you're alive.

Today is not shaping up to be a very good day. I thought that the very moment I opened my eyes and saw the daddy long-legs crawling across the ceiling in my room.

My room. I'm not to be thinking that way. The room is ours, mine and Mrs. Zimmer's; Mrs. Weaver is adamant about that. I thought I had time to get rid of the spider before Mrs. Zimmer woke when I should have ignored it, let it sit there spinning a web for Belinda's dust mop to catch. Most mornings I lie facing the wall, waiting until it's time to get up and dressed, but this morning as I rolled over something beckoned me to glance upward.

Steadying myself on the bed with a rolled-up copy of the weekly paper in my hand, I made a swat at the spider and missed. It scurried off into a small crack in the corner just as Mrs. Zimmer sucked in a gulp of air. Her snoring came to an abrupt stop and ended in a snort. When I went to get down off the bed, the mattress wobbled. Arms out to each side, I tried to keep myself from falling.

"That's my paper you've got! *My* paper!" Mrs. Zimmer squealed as she threw back the comforter on her bed. Her bare legs swung outward. She grunted and pushed herself forward, trying to manoeuvre herself out of bed in a movement that neither her weight nor her age would allow. She was wild-eyed and ready for action. I saw that same look the day Belinda moved the teddy bears on her dresser. Mrs. Zimmer was in the family room watching her soap opera at the time. If Belinda had put everything back exactly where it had been she would never have known. Mrs. Zimmer was out for blood that day, huffing and panting with her fist raised high, until Belinda threatened to tell Mrs. Weaver if she so much as laid a baby finger on her.

I was ready to use that same threat if Mrs. Zimmer came after me.

As Mrs. Zimmer inched herself closer to the edge of the bed, the veins on the back of her calves bulged beneath the surface of her skin, looking overripe and ready to burst.

Her nightdress bunched up to reveal a series of purple lines splattered across the back of her thighs. They resembled tattoos—and what a strange thought it was to imagine someone drawing on Mrs. Zimmer's white, scaly legs. My feet kneaded into the mattress as I hurried to get down off the bed, my hand gripping tightly to the newspaper that I had no business being in possession of.

"That's *my* paper! Mine!" Mrs. Zimmer bellowed with a force that would reach all the way to the kitchen if she didn't soon quiet down. Jennie would come stomping down to our room, telling us in her raspy voice that we'd wake the dead if we didn't smarten the hell up.

"Shut up!" I whispered fiercely. She only pretends to read it anyway, her finger moving across the page while she mumbles words under her breath. No one can read that fast. Sometimes the paper sits on her rocker, from one week to the next, folded exactly the way it came. I flung the paper in her direction. When it landed on the floor near her feet, she stopped squealing and bent down to pick it up. Just then, I caught sight of white flesh from the opening in her nightdress, wrinkled and flabby. I had a bird's-eye view of it all. A quick flash of brown peeked out at me as her fingers sought after the crumpled paper, and I stared at it for a few moments, finally realizing that bit of dark flesh that had me momentarily wondering was Mrs. Zimmer's dried, shrivelled-up nipple. I looked away, quickly making my way off the bed.

Days that begin with a kerfuffle spiral quickly downward. The day was bound to be spoiled. The nipple had been a sign.

"Dartmouth, then Divinity," I repeat silently as I head back toward the family room. "Dartmouth then Divinity. Dartmouth then Divinity. Divinity then…No." I stop in my tracks. Something sounded wrong that last time. The rhythm of the words got lost. It comes back to me in an instant. "Dartmouth *then* Divinity."

I continue on my way to the family room.

I wish those words would settle down inside me, but they get jumbled up so I can't add them to my list of important words. And the order of things is so important. Just ask anyone who would argue about the chicken or the egg, and right away they'll tell you just how important order is.

"Perhaps you'll remember more words over time," Mrs. Weaver once said. In all these years I've found only a few important words from the past—five to be exact—that stay with me at all times. Five measly words hold the key to my truth, the one I've been searching for. There would be seven if I could add Dartmouth and Divinity. A reasonable person would have given up a long time ago, especially with the vague promise that came with Mrs. Weaver's "perhaps."

"This is your home, Nick. Your roots are here now," Mrs. Weaver said a few months back. Nick was talking about wanting to leave Harmony House for good, swinging his arms and puffing his chest out as he demanded to speak to someone higher up than Mrs. Weaver.

"This ain't the only place I've been, and I got rights," he said, smiling like Mrs. Weaver didn't know what she was talking about. "What about all the other places I lived in before I came here, or don't they count no more? Maybe I want my own roots, not the one you made up for me."

Someone huffed. Mrs. Weaver is the best thing that has ever happened to us here at Harmony House. Everyone knows that. Something had sent Nick into a tailspin that day. I can't remember what. Knowing Nick, it probably wasn't much. He's usually bickering with someone, accusing them of some wrong. Most of us don't pay attention to what he says anymore. But that day I was paying attention.

"Those other places don't matter, Nick. That was all in the past, and the past is gone. The past doesn't matter anymore. The important thing is where you are at the moment."

"I want my old apartment back, the last one I had, and I don't give a good goddamn about where I am at the moment." Nick's head was bobbing around in defiance. I couldn't believe he was speaking to Mrs. Weaver that way. Taking a cigarette from his tobacco pouch, he held it between his fingers. *Smoked herring*, I thought, seeing the yellow stain on his index finger. No wonder he smells so strong after tobacco smoke. When he began feeling around his pants' pockets, I thought he was going to light the cigarette right there in the family room.

"We all have a truth, Nick, and this is yours," stated Mrs. Weaver, strong and steady in her unshakable voice. "That apartment's not yours anymore. It's likely been rented out a dozen times since you came here to live."

"Well, look at me! I ain't got no truth but this here one you gave me." He slapped his thigh. By that time, people had gathered near the doorway, looking more anxious than when it's time to head to the dining room for supper. Nick spun around with a foolish look on his face and pulled a silver lighter out of his pocket. A small click sounded when he flicked the cover open. I held back the gasp that was building in me. Mrs. Weaver has strict rules. He made a horrible face—his skin so red it looked as though someone had slapped him, hard—then stomped out to the verandah. I saw him through the screen door cupping his shaky hands around the cigarette. Blue smoke made a quick circle about his head before disappearing into the air. He was pacing the floorboards like a caged bear, fingers running through his greying hair. I couldn't make out what he was mumbling. He stayed out there for the remainder of the day, refusing to come in for supper. Darkness closed in around him until all I could see of him was a small round light from a cigarette glowing in the dark. Finally, Clive told him to get his arse inside before he got locked out for the night.

"You want to get chewed up by a bear, you crazy old coot?" Clive shouted.

Nick won't be allowed back to the apartment he once had or any other apartment. Anyone who knows him can understand that much. He hasn't mentioned his apartment on Jones Street again. And I haven't forgotten what Mrs. Weaver had to say about our truth. Ever since that day I've been trying to get to mine. Mrs. Weaver said we all have one. That means me, too. I've seen my truth in bits and pieces for a long time now. It comes in flickers—a word, a name, a colour, a smell that feels vaguely familiar. I struggle to draw the flickers together, melding the parts I know for certain with the parts I remember. All those little pieces must mean something. I just don't know what. As hard as I try to hang fast to them, they leave me crumbling apart like aged cheddar. I might argue that these flickers are better than nothing, but they're fleeting, as satisfying as a dream you can never quite reach.

I haven't said anything to Mrs. Weaver, but I know how Nick felt that day. I don't want my roots to be here either—not that there's anything wrong with Harmony House. It's a nice enough place. I just don't want it to be all there is. I'm not interested in where I am at the moment, no matter how important Mrs. Weaver seems to think it is. Once upon a time I must have been someone, someone with more than a name. I lived in a house. I had a family. I was someone who had a truth, a real truth, not one assigned to me. Surely I can scrounge up enough pieces to find out who that someone was.

I can't ask for anyone's help. I tried that once when I was at Divinity and it didn't work out. I sent a letter and it came back and I was left to live with the disappointment, watching it fester with each passing day until finally I had to give up. You can only starve hope for so long; eventually it needs something for nourishment. I had nothing to offer, not even a small morsel from the past.

But all that has changed. I have changed. This time I won't give up so easily. The hard part will be doing it all on my own, something I'm not sure I'm brave enough to do. But truth is a powerful thing and must surely be something worth fighting for, and if it isn't then I have to wonder what purpose there is in living at all.

I remember suddenly that Rebecca is still waiting for me in the family room. A group of us are going on an outing to the used-clothing store in town. We were almost set to go when my truth started niggling away at me. I told Rebecca I wouldn't be long, that I just couldn't go into town before I spoke to Mrs. Weaver. That's why I went back to Mrs. Weaver's office for the second time. The smell of floor cleaner is strong as I walk down the hallway and round the bend. The *Caution: Wet Floor* sign is in place. Donna's red bucket is right up ahead. Her mop slips and slides; the floor is glistening and wet.

"Slow down, Elizabeth. You fall and break your neck, who do you think they'll come after? You want me to lose my job?" I glance back over my shoulder at Donna, her hands squeezing the mop strands. Mrs. Zimmer would have told her she's a sloppy old cow and deserves to lose her job. She might even have raised her fists and told her to go straight to hell and back. I could resent the implication that I'm too dim to look out for myself, but I won't. I can't. There's no time for that with everyone waiting for me.

"Dartmouth then Divinity."

I stayed at the hospital in Dartmouth first, and was later sent to Divinity. The order should be easy enough to keep straight, and would be, if they didn't both start with the same letter. It's that darn *D* constantly mixing me up. Another letter would make all the difference. I could put both places in order if they started with two different letters. Each time I get it firmly in my mind, something comes along to undermine my certainty and I'm confused all over again. It could be that Sophie won't settle down until I sit with her, or Nick causing another fuss because Marie's helping out in the kitchen and he doesn't want to eat anything that Marie "messed over." It could be Mrs. Zimmer and her constant annoyance with me over the piddliest little matter. As soon as something shakes up my day the order of the words slips out of my mind. I've tried so many times to put them in my secret word place, but they won't stay put. *If they are part of my truth,* I often find myself wondering, *why won't they stay where they belong?* Truth should come easily, a slip slide as smooth as Donna's mop on the glistening floor.

"Do you have your purse, Elizabeth?" Rebecca asks from the doorway when she sees me coming. *Of course. My purse!* Someone in the group sighs. I turn around and hurry back to our room. Donna looks up and shakes her head as I pass by again.

"Dartmouth then Divinity," I whisper, remembering then why I forgot my purse in the first place. Mrs. Zimmer is sitting in her rocker fully dressed by this time. Pages from the newspaper are now strewn over the foot of her bed, wrinkled and half torn. Ignoring her, I look through my wallet to see how much money I have. Two fives, a two, three ones, and a ten. I put the wallet back in my handbag and snap it shut. If it wasn't for the comfort money I get each month, I wouldn't have two cents to rub together. We can't all have rich nieces like Mrs. Zimmer.

"Going out on the town?" says Mrs. Zimmer before I have the chance to make my escape from the room.

"Frenchys," I answer, heading toward the door with my handbag hooked onto my arm. She twists her face up. I could kick myself for telling. Mrs. Zimmer hasn't been to Frenchys for a very long time. She's never invited to come anymore.

"You have yourself a good old time, Elizabeth MacKay. I'll just stay here by myself. Don't mind an old lady with bad knees." Squeezing my purse, I hurry through the doorway. If she stays in our room all day, it'll be her own fault.

Sophie runs to greet me as soon as she sees me coming, squealing my name, grabbing my arm and grappling fast. They haven't left without me. They're all still waiting by the front door.

Annie has her black sequined purse and Marie the bright pink contraption on her head she got the last time we went to Frenchys. Missy is leaning against the door, teased brown hair and high-heel shoes adding inches to her height. The blue jeans and purple shirt she's wearing do little to hide her bony frame, but at least she looks presentable today. The first day Missy showed up at Harmony House I couldn't shake the idea that she somehow looked familiar. Keeping my distance, I studied her movements, the way she nervously moved her hands when she spoke, and even the way she'd take a drag off a cigarette. But no matter how hard I struggled to make that connection, nothing concrete ever came to me. But then, I reasoned, if I had met Missy sometime in the past, wouldn't she recognize me? The answer seemed obvious.

"Well, if it isn't the queen herself, making the rest of us wait," Missy says, smacking her gum while rolling her eyes toward the ceiling.

"What's your hurry, Missy?" says Annie. "It's not like we've got anything else to do—or maybe you've got something else pencilled into your day." A noise from within the group indicates their amusement. Annie has a way of lightening a situation, and I'm grateful for that today. Clearing my throat, I turn toward Rebecca.

"Are we all set?" she says, smiling at our little group. Shuffling begins, people moving toward the closed door. "Now, let's try to stick together this time. Annie, I don't want you hurrying on ahead."

Rebecca's the one bright light in our day. Her smile has a way of warming the coldest room. She never has a cross word for any of us, and I've yet to see her lose her temper even when someone refuses to follow instructions. The last time we went out, Annie disappeared on us. We found her up the street, sitting on a bench across from the liquor store, waving at the men coming out with brown paper bags in their hands. You'd have thought she was drinking herself, the way she was carrying on. We could hear her calling out, "Nice day, honey!" every time someone walked past. No one coming out of the store that day spoke to her or even nodded. They walked past looking in the opposite direction, scurrying away like field mice. Seeing Annie from that distance, I felt suddenly embarrassed. Rebecca wouldn't have cared about her going off like that if Annie had just told her where she was going. Sometimes Annie takes the bus to Halifax to visit her sister. At Christmas she goes for a few weeks. It's not like we're prisoners here at Harmony House.

Rebecca doesn't say anything about the bright pink hat Marie is wearing as she opens the door for us. Rebecca believes in being yourself no matter what the rest of the world thinks. Mrs. Zimmer says that's like giving everyone here a licence to behave like a simpleton. "They already think we're a bunch of lunatics from the nuthouse," she says. *They*, meaning the people in town who either stand back and stare or else ignore us altogether. After seeing Annie that day outside the liquor store, a part of me agrees with Mrs. Zimmer. I step out on the verandah. The bright blue sky greets me. White fluffy clouds bunch together like marshmallows floating in a giant cup of cocoa.

"Dartmouth then Divinity," I whisper. Hard to believe a day so brilliant could have started with a daddy long-legs spider and quick flash of Mrs. Zimmer's puckered-up nipple.

Annie and Missy take off as soon as we get outside. They light cigarettes while waiting at the end of the driveway for the rest of us to catch up. When the faint smell of smoke reaches me, there comes a flash. A flicker. A burst of memory. Dartmouth or Divinity—the memory comes from one of those places. I'm certain of it. Most everyone at the hospitals smoked. Sometimes the air would be blue. I reach out to grab hold of the memory, can feel it beneath my fingertips, but then the flicker is gone. A strange feeling passes through me, and I'm left with nothing. There's not a thing I can do about it, no way to get that flicker back. They come and go, as inconsistent as the weather, always leaving me longing for more.

Sophie hangs off my elbow like a trained puppy as we head down the street. It's the only way to keep her on the sidewalk; otherwise she becomes distracted by little things along the way. A while back she nearly got hit by a car while chasing after a candy-bar wrapper that was blowing around in the wind. No one noticed she'd fallen behind. Rebecca yelled out for me to stop Sophie just as the car came to a screeching halt. Sophie remained ignorant to it all, finally grabbing hold of the wrapper as it settled next to the curb.

"I got it, Elizabeth! I got it!" she cried.

"Look at you," I said, smiling, as I pulled her back onto the sidewalk with a strength I didn't know I possessed. Finding the nearest garbage can, she threw it in. I didn't start shaking until I saw the dark green verandah when we got back to Harmony House that day. Later, I kept reliving that awful moment. Each time I saw it in a totally different way—Sophie being hit by the car, her body dragged down the street, arms and legs flapping. Screaming. Lots of screaming. And blood. Always there was blood. A frozen eye staring off into space. "You look like something the cat just drug in," Mrs. Zimmer said as I sat rocking on the edge of the bed, unable to say a word. Even the nerve pill they gave me that day didn't help.

We take our time walking. There's no point in trying to hurry Sophie with her short leg. Even that special shoe she wears doesn't help a lot. Sophie has one speed, and we can't get her to change. Rebecca looks over her shoulder at us. She gives a tiny wave that starts Sophie waving back, fast and furious. Some people on the opposite side of the street look at us. I take hold of Sophie's hand to make her stop.

"That's good, Sophie," I whisper, grabbing fast to her arm as I pull her along.

As if to cause a distraction, the feather on Marie's hat shifts back and forth in the breeze. I point it out to Sophie, who is suddenly taken up with its whimsical play. The hat was a find on our last trip to Frenchys and Marie modelled it for us right in the store. She smiled from ear to ear and said she'd always wanted a feather in her cap. Rebecca laughed and told her it was quite the find. I imagined it being part of her costume come Halloween, not something she was planning to wear into town when she went shopping. Cars whiz past. A horn honks. A young boy is looking out the rear window of a red car, sticking his middle finger up at us. His lips are moving and he's making a face. I have no desire to hear what is coming out of his mouth. Missy gives two fingers back, both arms extended.

"Little asshole," she says, her lips curled into a gritty snarl. I look quickly at Rebecca, but she isn't watching. She's talking to Annie, her hands busily moving as she speaks, and so she doesn't see a thing. As we near the Frenchys, Sophie starts squealing with excitement.

"We have to be quiet when we go in a store. Remember what I told you, Sophie," Rebecca reminds her. As if a switch has been turned off, Sophie quiets down. It's hard to ignore the look on her face as her smile disintegrates right before us. But it's important for her to mind. Bad things happen when Sophie doesn't listen. We line up, waiting to go inside, the same way we do in the evening when it's time for juice and cookies.

"Now, let's raise our heads high and conduct ourselves with civility," Rebecca says as she holds the door open. "The world might not be ready for us, but we're here all the same."

We waddle through like baby ducklings all in a row before heading off in different directions. The store has that rummage-sale smell about it, familiar in a way I can never quite place. Marie and Annie head toward the shoes and handbags, gibbering about what all they're going to buy. Missy hurries toward a bin below the *Ladies' Lingerie* sign.

Quickly pulling out a black lacy bra with tiny cups, she begins to inspect it.

There are five other customers in the store, ten if I count us too. One time the store was so full I sat on a bench and waited until it was time to go home. There seemed no point trying to find a place at one of the bins with so many people there. When a worker came out and dumped off some clothes, two women started a tug-of-war over a blue flowered bedsheet. They were both hanging on tight, refusing to let go. It reminded me of the time Mrs. Zimmer tried to take the afghan one of the volunteer ladies had knitted for me off the foot of my bed.

There's a radio playing in the background, just loud enough to be heard. I head toward the rack of dresses with nothing particular in mind to buy. A bright red dress is dangling on one of the hangers. I immediately go for it, excited by the possibilities. Red has been inside my head for a few weeks now. It's been showing up in the oddest places. It began the day Mrs. Zimmer's niece showed up wearing a scarf so bright I couldn't stop myself from staring. It was mesmerizing; a colour that until then I'd never considered wearing. That night I dreamed about hundreds of red scarves, all shades and colours, billowing and blowing like flags in the wind. Since that dream, I've continued to see red most everywhere I go. Each time I wonder what, if anything, it could mean.

I pull the dress out for a closer look. Leaving the hanger in place, I slowly spread the material outward, the way Rebecca often does. My hopes drain. Just as I suspected. It's not the right size. It would hang off me like an old burlap sack—not that anyone at Harmony House would care. I've been thinking I might be brave enough to wear that colour, but my heart dips. Red is a colour best worn by someone who wants to be noticed. It's really too bright a colour for me. So I put it back, a tiny bit of relief hidden deep inside me. My side of the closet is filled with greens and browns and navy blues. Mrs. Zimmer likes flowered patterns and polka dots, blouses with thick vertical stripes that I wouldn't be caught dead in. Nor could I dress like Missy, low-cut blouses and tight-fitting jeans, short, short dresses and bright colours that scream, *Look at me!* I've always preferred to blend into my surroundings like a chameleon, and so red following me about, even entering my dreams, is not like me at all. Yet I am powerless to make it stop.

I continue to look through the remainder of the dresses without interest. The hangers squeak across the clothes rack as I slide them along. I haven't time to linger or to take a second look. If I stay in one spot for too long, Sophie will become restless. Annie is holding out a pair of brown shoes, insisting Marie try them on for size as I walk toward the ladies' sweaters. Missy is still rooting through the lingerie bin like a dog digging for a buried sausage. From the corner of my eye, I see a young woman holding up a pair of black pants.

"What do you think of these, Jewel?" she says.

Stopping what I'm doing, I turn to see who is speaking. *Jewel* is one of my important words, secret in a way that makes my heart flutter whenever I think of it.

"Almost like new. They'll probably fit you, too."

The answer is coming from the checkout department, but from where I'm standing I can't see what the woman looks like. I hold my breath. I can't get my hopes up. Yet I have to know, at least see for myself. Yes. No. I'm suddenly frightened by both possibilities. But it'll run around the inside of my brain for days, weeks, months if I don't find out for sure. I will my legs to move, to get a better look. This chance can't slip away. If I don't go now, she might disappear into the back of the store to sort clothing, and then I'll never know for sure. This could be the only chance I have. As I move toward the checkout, Sophie keeps pace with me, hanging off my elbow again. I stop near one of the bins and pretend to be interested, hoping to distract her so I can see the woman behind the counter. Sophie begins rummaging through the tangled mess of clothing inside. There are bright colours hiding near the bottom, and as she reaches in deep, I slip away. I could have told her to stay put, not to move, and she would have listened, but it takes a harsh voice to make Sophie mind. I can't bring myself to talk to her the way Mrs. Weaver sometimes does.

As I draw near, my gaze rests on the nametag above the woman's left breast. The letters jump out at me: *J-e-w-e-l*. Could it be? My body trembles from head to toe. Clasping my hand over my mouth, I stifle the cry that wants to escape. My past, my truth, my secret word, is staring me in the face. Jewel. Is it even possible that she could be *my* Jewel, the daughter I left somewhere in the past? What age would she be now? I try to make a quick calculation but it is useless. My thoughts are all jumbled. I have no idea how old she'd be, the colour of her hair. No idea at all. Tiny beads of excitement run up and down my spine. But as I get up the nerve to step closer, a woman in a green jacket brushes past and drops an armload of clothing on the counter in front of me. Just then Sophie calls out, hurrying toward me in uneven steps, clip-clopping like an old mare.

"Look, Elizabeth! A scarf! A pretty scarf. It's orange and red and yellow."

Embarrassed by Sophie's outburst, I look quickly toward this Jewel. She holds up a sweater and rings in the price while smiling at the woman in green. I study this

Jewel's face, unable to take my eyes off her. Sophie pulls on my coat sleeve, harder and harder until I'm forced to look down at her. Holding the scarf out to me, she waves it about.

"It's lovely," I say, wishing she would quiet down. When I look back, this Jewel is leaning across the counter.

"They're from Harmony House; you know...that place in town. Did you see the pink hat?" She gives a nod in Marie's direction, smiling behind the pair of blue jeans that she's now holding up. The woman in the green jacket is laughing. I don't need to see her face to know that.

"That's seventeen ninety-five," this Jewel finally says. The woman in the green jacket digs into her handbag. The register rings and the drawer pops open. Quickly making change, she puts the items in a used grocery bag. Laughter is dancing in this Jewel's eyes when she hands the bag to the woman in green, and I wonder exactly what it is she finds so funny.

I wait. Stand still. Wait. Watch for this Jewel to look me in the eye, to suddenly recognize who I am. She cranes her neck around and says something to the young woman who spoke to her earlier about the pants. By this time I've lost all interest in shopping. It would be difficult to keep my hands from shaking, my mind from wondering, my lips from quivering. And Sophie will no longer care to look in the bins now that she has a bright scarf. We step up to the counter, Sophie gibbering non-stop about her special find.

"I'll wear it on Sunday, Elizabeth, when I go to church." She places it on the counter and opens her change purse, her face beaming like a brilliant star.

"You'll look beautiful," I say, gazing directly at this Jewel. She rings in the scarf and tells Sophie the price. My hand trembles slightly as I help Sophie count out the change. She slides it across the counter toward this Jewel, grabs the scarf, and wraps it around her neck two times. Gazing up at me, she smiles like a child just given a lollypop. I look once more at this Jewel. Our eyes meet this time, but there's no truth in what I see. My heart quickly plummets like a dusty stone kicked from a cliff. Surely her colouring is all wrong. She's far too old. There is no possible way she is *my* Jewel, my truth, one of my secret words, and yet this realization does not feel unpleasant.

Sophie and I go sit on the bench outside the store while the others continue to search for some hidden nugget in the bins. Rebecca never minds our leaving the store early to wait outside. She knows where we'll be when she comes out. She has told me how reassured she feels knowing that I'm always there to look out for Sophie. I have often wondered where this sense of responsibility comes from, what part of me feels the need to look out for Sophie even when there are times that it feels more like a burden than a responsibility.

Looking out at the street for a fleeting moment, I think about running off, racing down the sidewalk by myself and never looking back. My leg muscles tense as I scan the street with a deep longing in my heart. But what would I do with freedom when the life I want lies somewhere in the past? I can barely function on my own; I need the safety of Harmony House and all that is familiar to me just to get through most days. Mrs. Weaver and Rebecca need me to be responsible, and most of all Sophie needs me by her side when we go out on errands.

The main road is visible from where we sit. It is a slow day, an empty day, the traffic sparse, the walkers few. A warm breeze blows through the trees, the coloured leaves tremble but hold tight to the branches. Rebecca might take us down to the little store at the end of the street for a choco-late bar, but I don't mention this to Sophie in case we don't go. Listening to her bellyaching all the way home won't be good for my nerves today.

Sophie becomes excited by a small, hairy dog being walked down the sidewalk by its owner, pulling me suddenly back to the present. She makes sucking noises, encouraging the dog to come over to her. The owner pulls on the leash when the dog pauses in front of her. He smiles quickly and hurries them both away. I look up into the azure sky, at the thick white clouds moving out across the horizon. There is a touch of freedom on my face, a whisper in my ear, a gentle breeze that is warm and willing.

I didn't find my truth today, but that's okay. In fact, it's good. I wouldn't have known what to do with it. It's not as if the truth can be given back, exchanged for something more to our liking. If that Jewel *had* been my truth, a small part of me might have disappeared for good, dried and puckered up like Mrs. Zimmer's nipple. My truth still waits for me to claim it. Bits and pieces have been scattered along the way. I have five words to start with, maybe seven if I can keep them straight, and all things must have a beginning.

"Divinity then Dartmouth," I say to no one in particular.

Jewel

I lie in grassland the colour of sunflowers as hundreds of ponies trot out across a field, their beautiful chestnut manes flowing behind them in the wind. Hooves thump against the earth as I lie with my ear to the ground. I don't want to move, I want to remain where I am forever, but something calls to me. I know I can't stay.

Mumma. Her name still sticks in my throat in the middle of the night, a foreign object. It's been years since I whispered for her, years since I dreamed of Jacob's chestnut pony. Climbing out of bed, I pull back the curtains and peer down into the street below me. In the first light of morning, a lone runner races quietly down the sidewalk. I strain to hear the soft sound of her sneakers hitting the pavement. I've seen her before, hair pulled back in a ponytail, the same sleek form silhouetted against the sunrise. Often fancying myself a runner, I lack the ambition, the resolve, to force myself out the door every day. Not even the allure of being in those

151

first few moments of twilight seems capable of swaying me. Morning used to fill me with hope when I was a child—a new day about to begin, untouched by words or deeds, not yet stained by sin. The runner slips silently from my view. Headlights from an oncoming vehicle light up the street below me as the city slowly begins to awaken.

It's too early to call Jacob, and what would I say to him if I did? He'd immediately know something was wrong, something even I would have a problem explaining. Neither of us is good at small talk. I don't want to explain about David.

Opening the wooden box on my dresser, I trace the small gold band with my finger. The neatly folded page in the bottom of the box beckons to me. Jacob loved that storybook Poppy gave us. Setting the ring aside, I unfold the yellowed page, careful not to damage the tattered paper. I have no recollection of what became of the book after we moved away from the Forties Settlement; nor do I understand what strange power prevents me from destroying the page I ripped out. The date at the top is July 29, 1960. I blink back tears as it all comes back to me, the story I've kept inside me and the secret I've yet to tell, raw as if it were still yesterday.

It was late summer and the field behind our house was yellow. The hay should have been made, cut down to stubble, baled, and stored away in the barn, but the winter had been a harsh one. The cattle were loaded onto the back of a truck in late March. Three months later the chestnut pony was gone as well. Jacob cried when the truck took away his beloved Dusty, and I rocked him on my lap in the kitchen, saying, "Shush now, Jakey-boy," even though I could feel a lump growing in my own throat.

I ran upstairs the moment the screen door slammed. Jacob was close behind. Through the window at the top of the stairs I saw Mumma heading back across the field, her hair blowing in the wind behind her, flowing like the mane of Jacob's chestnut pony. Face pushed against the windowpane, I laid my hand on the glass, wishing I could reach out and touch her. She walked with a purpose, her arms swinging back and forth until she reached the large granite rock at the far side of the field. I thought she'd changed her mind and was coming back, but she stopped and touched the rock before continuing on her way.

"Where do you think she's going, Jewel?"

"Away," I said as if "away" were an actual place. Jacob would be satisfied so long as I told him something.

I had wanted to go with Mumma, but she said no. "You stay put, Jewel. Don't you dare follow—neither one of you. You follow me and something bad will happen. Do you hear me? Something really, really bad." She squeezed my face in her hand and looked directly into my eyes. For a moment I thought she was going to slap me. Instead, she fell to her knees, grabbed both Jacob and me, and held us close. Her heart sounded like the beating of a far-off drum. The hold she had on us was suffocating. I worried she wouldn't let go. Struggling to be released, Jacob reminded me of the baby chick that had wandered into the tall grass a few days before. I'd scooped it up in my hand, and it had squirmed and chirped until I returned it to its mother.

Mumma's arms fell limp at her side as she said, "I have to go now. I really have to go."

"No, don't!" cried Jacob, pulling on her dress. His bottom lip trembled. Reaching into her pocket, she pulled out a crumpled hanky and, lifting his chin, carefully wiped the wet from his face.

"Be good," she whispered, tucking the handkerchief into her bosom. "Both of you...promise me you'll always be good. If I have that promise, I'll be all right."

"We promise," Jacob and I chimed, but only because it seemed so desperately important to her.

"A promise made in desperation is a worthless promise," Mumma once told me. I didn't know what that meant at the time, and I still wasn't sure.

"You can't ever go back on a promise, because a true promise can never be broken," she said. A strange look swept across her face. I moved away from her, frightened for reasons I couldn't name. This hadn't been a useless promise at all, but the kind that was meant to last forever. She stood and looked down at us, her whole body trembling. A shaky hand followed the contours of her waist as she smoothed out the wrinkles in her clothes. She was wearing the same dress she'd worn to Poppy's funeral a few weeks back. I remembered how her teardrops dripped onto the navy fabric in the church that day, forming a large dark spot above her left breast.

"You were always jealous, Cliff. Jealous of what Poppy and I had," Mumma cried after the funeral.

"You're talking nonsense again, Lizabeth. We've got to move on with our lives," Daddy said. "You can't bury yourself, too."

"A lot you know. I've been buried for years," she laughed. Her laughter cracked the air.

Jacob and I ran and hid.

Mumma drew in a deep breath. "I have to go now. I really have to go.... Stay where you are. Daddy will soon be home." She turned her head upward. There was a strange look on her face. Her lips were pursed, her jaw tense, her eyes glazed.

"Where are you going, Mumma?" Jacob asked as she made her way toward the door. I grabbed hold of him to keep him from following, shushing him as best I could.

We waited by the window as Mumma disappear from sight, waiting to see if she'd change her mind and suddenly reappear. It wasn't long before the sound of truck tires rolling over the gravel stones in the driveway sent us scurrying back down the stairs.

"Mumma's gone!" cried Jacob when he reached the bottom step. Daddy picked him up and laid his hand on the top of my head.

"She told us to stay here...and to be good," I added, my lips trembling. I bit down hard to keep from crying. I thought he would run out the door to go look for her, but he didn't.

"Don't you worry," he said, firmly. "We'll be all right. Mumma will come home. She always does."

But not this time! I wanted to cry out. *This time Mumma's gone for good.*

She hadn't run from the house like any of the other times. She'd been quiet, not screaming or yelling, but quiet and calm.

"Sit up at the table now. I'll fix us something to eat. It won't be fancy, but we're used to roughing it." Last week Daddy had yelled at Mumma and told her he expected to have supper waiting for him after working all day.

Daddy whistled a tune I didn't recognize as he took the lid off the stove. Once the fire was going, the kitchen became unbearably hot on top of that already hot July day. We ignored it. Pot lids should have been tapping and steam rising, good smells filling the kitchen. That's if Mumma was having a good day. Lately, there hadn't been enough good days to bother counting. Lately, Daddy was the one frying potatoes in the pan, cutting up pork scraps and onions for the hash while Mumma sat in the living room looking out the window toward Poppy's place. When it came time to eat, she'd sit at the table and push the food around with her fork. Sometimes she'd wash the few dishes we dirtied, but most times I did that.

Beads of sweat formed on Daddy's forehead. Cutting three slices of bread, he spread them with molasses. "Not quite a gourmet meal, but it'll fill that hollow spot for now," he said, putting a small plate out for each of us. He gave a stiff grin. There was a sad look in his eyes and I glanced quickly at the place where Mumma should be sitting.

Promise me you'll always be good.

Always is a very long time.

When the kettle began to whistle, Daddy brewed a pot of tea. I waited for him to say something comforting, anything to make us feel better.

"Where did Mumma go?" Jacob asked scooping the bread up off the plate. I kicked at him from beneath the table.

"I'm not sure, but it's nothing for you to worry about. I'll figure something out. I always do. Now eat up."

The smell of molasses made my stomach lurch as I took a small bite of bread. Daddy said not to worry, he'd figure something out. When it came to Mumma, he usually did. Except things were different this time; Mumma had walked away, leaving Jacob and me alone. Something bad would happen if we went looking for her, something so bad even Mumma wouldn't say what it was. The bread formed a ball in my mouth that wouldn't go down no matter how hard I tried to swallow. Finally, I pushed the gooey mass into my hand. Hurrying away from the table, I let it slip onto the floor. Daddy called out for me to come back, but I couldn't.

Hurrying up the stairs, I ran to the window, watching the tall stalks of timothy rolling in the breeze, my heart so tight I could hardly let out a breath.

Looking out across the field, my eyes rested on the granite rock where Mumma had stopped. Later, I snuck down the stairs and out the front door. I ran across the field, treading along the trampled grass where Mumma had stepped. At first I saw nothing but specks of dark granite and fine fractures along the rock's uneven surface. I wasn't sure what I expected to find. But then I saw a small gold band sitting on a crooked ledge. I grabbed it up quickly. Back at the house, I hid the ring under my pillow and made a silent wish, a wish that came from a place so deep and dark I couldn't even think it into being.

And Mumma didn't come home.

We pulled two chairs across the kitchen floor and sat by the window. The sun sank behind the trees and the house grew dark, but still Mumma didn't return. When Daddy told us it was time for bed, Jacob didn't want to go. "I'm a big boy now. Poppy even said. I can stay up all night and wait for Mumma if I want to."

"It's bedtime," said Daddy. "Come along, Jewel." He carried Jacob upstairs to bed while Jacob kicked and cried to be released.

"Aren't you going to look for Mumma?" he cried out. A strange sensation burned in my chest. I should have stopped Mumma from leaving. I should have found the right words to say. If I had done something differently, Mumma would never have left. I crawled into my bed and squeezed my eyelids together. I whispered my bedtime prayer and waited to hear Mumma's footsteps downstairs. Sometime later, Jacob came over to my bed with the book of bedtime stories tucked beneath his arm.

"I don't want to read tonight, Jakey," I said, while he sat on the bed flipping anxiously through the pages. "Go back to bed."

"Look, Jewel," he said. "That says, 'What-a-Jolly-Street.'" He pointed to some words on the page and sniffled. I'd been reading to him every night since Poppy gave us the book.

"It doesn't say that. You don't even know how to read." I pulled the book away from him. I wanted to rip out all the pages and tear them to shreds. What good were books with happy stories and happy endings? Places like What-a-Jolly-Street don't even exist. How could they? No one could be happy and jolly all the time, let alone a whole street full of people.

"Please, Jewel, read like you always do," whispered Jacob.

I read him one story. I hurried through it, skipping some of the parts because I knew Jacob wouldn't know the difference. When he was asleep I tore a page from the back of the book. I folded it up small and slid it beneath my pillow. When we finally made it to that missing page in the book, Mumma would come home, but not until then—I was sure of it.

Reaching back under my pillow again, I pulled out Mumma's wedding ring and held it up close to see. It sparkled in the moonlight, and I felt a sudden urge to kiss it. I closed my eyes and for a moment I dared to believe everything would be all right. But how could it be? Everything hadn't been all right for a very long time.

The day after Poppy was buried, that was the day Mumma hid from us. I thought she'd run away. She was in the dooryard one minute, and when I looked up she was gone. I didn't tell Jacob. I didn't want him to know that

Mumma was gone. I tried my best to make it better. I held his hand and traced a circle. I sang: "Around and around the garden like a teddy bear; one step, two step, tickly under there." My fingernails scratched his neck when I tickled him and he howled even more. He cried so much that it made me cry too. But then Mumma came out from the cellar and we ran toward her, wiping our tears.

"Ninnies," she said, hurrying past. She looked so mad, I wished then she *had* run away.

The morning after Mumma left, Aunt Joan and Uncle Dylan were sitting at the kitchen table when I came downstairs. I knew something was very wrong for them to be visiting, especially at that hour. They seldom came to our house, and after what had happened in April I was sure they'd never visit again. Jacob asked where Mumma was, and the kitchen fell silent.

"She's dead," said Daddy, clearing his throat. "Mumma's dead." But I knew right away what that really meant—he'd killed her. I can't say how I knew, only that I did. A worm wiggled its way inside my head and it spoke to me.

"*Killed*," it said, "*killed.*"

Aunt Joan jumped to her feet and asked if anyone wanted more tea. She rattled the dishes on the counter and kept moving things about. Mumma wouldn't have wanted Aunt Joan in her kitchen.

"When's Mumma coming back?" Jacob asked.

"Dead people don't come back," I whispered. He turned toward me with a strange look on his face.

Dead people.

Dead Mumma.

It sounded so wrong. Jacob saw it too. There had to be some mistake.

"Where do dead people really go?"

Daddy said he wasn't sure. "Some people say heaven."

"Is Mumma with God?" asked Jacob.

"With God?" Daddy ran his fingers through his hair and looked toward Uncle Dylan.

"Mumma says that God calls people home. So when's she coming home?"

And it was true. I'd heard her myself, the day she told us Poppy had died.

"Not that home…heaven. She meant heaven. That's what calling someone home means. You go to be with God." Aunt Joan forced a smile, as if being with God was a good thing, but I knew that if Mumma was with God, we'd never see her again.

There was no funeral, no people coming by to offer condolences, no flowers, no wooden box for Mumma to lie in. No Mumma. She had simply disappeared into thin air, like tiny wisps of cloud in the wind.

Killed. Killed. Killed.

The word rustled like the leaves before a thunderstorm. I waited and waited for the rain that never came. I waited for a Mountie to come and cart Daddy away, leaving Jacob and me alone in that big old house in the Forties Settlement. There had been a funeral for Poppy a few weeks earlier. That's what started it all, Poppy up and dying like that on the day before Mumma's birthday, and then that look that never left Mumma's eyes. They'd had a fight a few weeks before he died, but we didn't know what it was about. The soft pattering of her feet though the house at night told me she'd been tormented by the things that were said.

And for all the times I'd wished things were different, I never imagined it would happen this way.

Waiting for a more reasonable hour, I call Jacob's apartment. He's already gone for the day. A part of me is relieved. What did I plan to say, anyway? Whatever it was would only raise alarms, and it's taken a long time to convince Jacob that he doesn't need to worry about me. We can't go back to that, to him expecting me to check in with him every day, sometimes calling late at night just to make sure. I spend the morning straightening up, trying to fill the gaps that David left wide open. In truth, they weren't that large.

Another day passes and I haven't yet told Jacob that David has moved out.

Elizabeth

The strangest thing happened while I was watching a program on the TV just now. Suddenly, instead of being in the family room, I was looking out a window into a large parking lot below me. I became aware of someone standing next to me, a small, brown-haired girl who looked vaguely familiar, yet I couldn't remember where I'd seen her before. I turned to her and asked, "Where am I?"

"You're in Dartmouth, in the loony bin. That's where they put people like you and me." Her hands were jittery, trembling like leaves in a hurricane. Her fingernails looked red and sore, chewed down to the quick. A cigarette dangled from between her shaky fingers. She was wearing a cotton duster with large blue flowers, a baggy outfit that gave no indication of her shape. She was thin, disturbingly so, and the dirty white sneakers with the laces untied looked so out of place on her feet.

"Was the cute guy with the curly black hair your husband?" she said, drawing in a breath of smoke.

"I don't know anyone with black curly hair, but I knew someone with brown eyes once," I told her.

"Your husband has brown eyes, silly. He was just here," she said, giggling. She blew smoke into the air above me, and I couldn't for the life of me figure out how she could possibly know any of that. Then just as suddenly, I was back in the family room at Harmony House, and I have no idea if I imagined all of this or if it's a memory that found its way to the surface. The only thing I am certain of is how very real it seemed.

The drawer on my nightstand makes a small squeak as I pull it open. I look quickly toward Mrs. Zimmer. Her head is slumped forward and she looks perfectly uncomfortable, although I swear she could sleep standing on her head if she had a mind to. Usually this time of the day she's down in the family room watching soap operas, talking to the characters on the TV screen with her hand gripping the arms of her chair, and she would be right now if it hadn't been for last night's cabbage supper. She put in a bad night, moaning about the stomach cramps she had until Leith brought her something to swallow, and then she quieted down.

A small songbird, neck stretched outward with black musical notes trilling out of its open beak, stares up at me from the cover of the notebook nestled safely inside the drawer. I close my eyes and reach in slowly, forcing the lump in my throat to go down. Mrs. Weaver gave me the notebook a few days ago, but until now I haven't been brave enough to take it out.

I thought about the notebook last evening when the guitar players came. There was a rugged-looking man in the group who cradled a guitar that seemed almost babyish in his big arms, but once his fingers began strumming across the strings it was obvious that he knew his way around a musical instrument. When he started to sing a song about going home down a country road, I looked at him more closely, studying his features, searching for something familiar about him. But wanting is never the same as having. Pure willpower stopped me from jumping to my feet and demanding he take me home immediately. But he obviously wasn't anyone who knew me from before. It was just that song, digging its melody and words inside me like hands clawing into a bowl of raw hamburger meat. I daubed at the water in the corner of my eyes when no one was looking.

As the evening continued, I became anxious to get to my truth and suddenly thought about the notebook. I couldn't up and leave in the middle of the singing, and by the time the juice and cookies were passed around and I made it back to my room, it had slipped my mind. Shortly after lunch today I remembered the notebook again, only Mrs. Zimmer was in our room and I wasn't about to have her asking me a string of nosy questions. *"What have you got there? Where did you get it? What are you writing down?"* She hoards questions inside her the way a stingy miser hoards money, allows them to build over time, waiting for the right moment to let loose. I finally got tired of waiting for her to leave and marched down to our room to see why she was still there. That's when I found her asleep in her rocker.

"If you write things down, you'll be sure to remember them later," Mrs. Weaver said when she first presented the notebook to me. For a few moments I considered the possibility of writing down the things I want to remember and thanked her profusely. The last gift I received was on my birthday back in July—some talcum powder that was supposed to smell like lilacs and a bottle of mauve bath salts that had no smell at all, even though it was also marked *Lilac*.

"In time, you might even use this little book as a diary," she said. "The possibilities are endless."

"A diary?" The words came out in a quiver, and my spinelessness made me want to give myself a swift kick. No one here at Harmony House keeps a diary, and the thought of endless possibilities put my brain into fast motion.

"Why, certainly, a diary! A diary's a great way to organize your thoughts. I've kept one for years." She touched my arm and smiled. "Don't look so troubled, Elizabeth. No one here is going to judge you. I just thought the notebook might be something that would come in handy. To help you remember certain things." My face must have showed my confusion, because she added, "You know—Dartmouth, then Divinity. It's sometimes easier than trying to keep all those things in our heads."

It would have been wrong of me to turn her gift down, to appear ungrateful, when I so seldom have anything given to me. I put the notebook in my nightstand for safe-keeping but was certain I'd never use it. The only things I write down are my doctor's appointments on the calendar pages above my bed and my Friday mornings helping out at the community centre down the street.

I search the drawer for a pen, moving aside the peppermint candy and the bingo daubers, the card of bobby pins that I won as a bingo prize a few years ago. I've never organized anything, let alone my thoughts. "An empty page holds so many possibilities," Mrs. Weaver had said, and I open the notebook with those words in my head.

There is something written on the first page.

To: Elizabeth MacKay, Harmony House, 1975.
May you find all the words you're searching for.
Mrs. Weaver.

The pages are so white, so perfect, filled with thin blue lines. Putting the pen to paper, my hand trembles. Where do I start? Mrs. Weaver makes everything sound so simple. I might write down something that I'll later come to regret, or else end up wondering what it all means. Or worse, much worse, I could write down some meaningless mumbo-jumbo that makes me look like a complete idiot if someone reads it. I flip through the pages. So many lines. So many blank spaces. So many words needed to fill it up. Going back to the first page, I press the pen to the paper again. I'm not someone who writes words. I only think them. What could Mrs. Weaver have been thinking?

"What are you doing?" croaks Mrs. Zimmer, her voice dry from sleep. I toss the notebook and pen back into the drawer and close it quickly. My heart is thumping so loudly I can feel it pulsing in my throat and ears.

"None of your business," I say, hurrying out past her.

That's it. I've made up my mind. I'll give the notebook back to Mrs. Weaver the first chance I get. It's impossible to decide what to write down, let alone try to do it in privacy. I can't write a thing with someone looking over my shoulder.

The remainder of the afternoon I spend waiting for Mrs. Zimmer to leave our room so I can get the notebook and give it back to Mrs. Weaver. I stay out near the solarium pretending to watch Nick and Howard help the workmen preparing the gardens for winter. I can see the door to our room from where I'm sitting. As soon as Mrs. Zimmer shuffles down the hallway and rounds the bend, I make a beeline for the notebook. Better to give it back than spend time worrying about what to write in it. If it's out of my drawer, the temptation will no longer exist.

"What's the matter, Elizabeth? Do you need some help getting started?"

I'm standing with my arm outstretched, waiting for Mrs. Weaver to take the notebook before someone comes along. I should have slipped it onto her desk when she was out, and would have had I not run into her just as she was leaving her office. If there's a question to be asked about something, you can be sure Mrs. Weaver will ask it. I always end up sounding like a bumbling idiot by the time I'm done answering. It would have been so much easier if I hadn't had to face her.

"It's hard to know what to put."

"Put anything, my dear. Who's going to know?" says Mrs. Weaver lightheartedly. "Come into my office. I'll get you started."

I don't tell her that I have no desire to start writing in a notebook that will take more than a lifetime to fill.

"Why not make a list of your important words, the ones you told me about a while back?" When I don't say anything, she continues. "Let's start by giving your list a title," she says, taking the chair next to me. She writes *My Words* at the top of the page and underlines it. "See? Nothing complicated to begin with." Sliding the book across the desk to me, she says, "Now it's your turn."

Nodding and smiling, she waits for me to start writing. Trying to position the pen properly in my fingers feels even more awkward with Mrs. Weaver sitting beside me.

"There's no right or wrong to this, Elizabeth. And you don't have to show anyone. I promise. You're the only one who will ever see it. Just write down your important words."

I look over at Mrs. Weaver. "It's no use," I say, laying the pen down. "It just doesn't feel right." My brain is scrambled, as if everything I know has suddenly become muddled, spinning in circles like an uncontrollable top. "This is too hard."

"You know what the first word is. Just write down the first word. The rest will follow." Mrs. Weaver gives me the pen again. With an unsteady hand, I make a *J* and jitter my way through the first word. The writing looks like something a child might produce, but I know Mrs. Weaver won't let me leave until I've done what she's asked. I start to form the next word. Eventually, I manage to write out all five of my important words.

> *Jewel*
> *Jacob*
> *Cliff*
> *Forties*
> *Poppy*

The words on the page hold me captive, as if writing them down has given them permanence and made them real.

"You should put down Dartmouth and Divinity," she says, her pink-polished nail pointing to the bottom of my list.

"Is it okay to? I can't keep them straight."

"Most certainly, it's okay. That way when you want to know, you can look it up for yourself. Eventually, you won't need to look."

I write out *Dartmouth* first and add *Divinity* below it, hoping that they will end up sealed in my memory for good. There should be no need for me to bother Mrs. Weaver about it now. Closing the book, Mrs. Weaver presses it into my hands.

"This is a fine start, Elizabeth," she says. Her smile is wide and approving. I have to wonder at her sincerity, although I have no reason to doubt it. Perhaps this is part of some plan to keep me from pestering her. The list is short. I haven't much to show for my life so far—a slim, almost nonexistent past, and a few tattered memories that refuse to mend. But at least now there are seven words instead of the five I began with. Surely that means I'm making progress.

"Now that you have a starting point, I'm sure you'll come up with more words. After all, the mind is a wonderful thing," she says, but her words come out funny toward the end of that sentence and then trail away as if she's said something wrong.

The little bird on the notebook draws my attention and I can't help noticing how the image on the cover has slightly changed. It's the words, I think, squeezing the book in my fingers, the power of those seven little words and a sealed promise that sooner or later the truth will emerge.

A cluster of leaves from outside catches my attention. Pressing my face to the glass, I watch them through the window in the common room; some bright green birch and maple leaves moving in the wind. They look to be carrying on a conversation with one another. I wonder what they are saying. The world outside is green and new, and a part of me longs to be out there listening to the leaves jabbering back and forth in the wind.

The brown-haired girl is sitting on the tiled floor with her legs drawn up and her dress pulled down over her knees, staring at the wall. No one is paying any attention to her. They walk past as if she isn't there. I go to her and look down at her, not sure what I should say or if I should say anything.

"What are you looking at?" she hisses, pulling her dress down over her knees farther, hiding her dirty white sneakers. She is the only one here who talks to me, even if it *is* just to ask for a cigarette. The others whisper about me in the corners until a nurse breaks them up, shooing them away like houseflies from a manure pile. The brown-haired girl is the only one who never whispers about me behind my back, and for that I am grateful. Two orderlies enter the room and pick her up by the arms like a life-size doll. At first she says nothing, does nothing, except to dangle in midair. But then she kicks and screams at them: "Take your goddamn hands off me!" She looks at me as they carry her away and stops screaming long enough to say, "Get yourself out of here, Elizabeth. No matter what you do. Don't let them keep you forever."

I turn toward the nurse, who is standing beside me.

"Where am I?"

If I'm going to get out of here, I have to know where *here* is.

"You're in Dartmouth."

"I promise," I whisper as the brown-haired girl disappears through the door. Her screams slowly fade away to nothing.

I spend the day thinking about the words in my notebook and go back to peek at them three times before bedtime.

"There's something not right with you. You're different," says Mrs. Zimmer as I climb into bed at the end of the day.

"The truth, Mrs. Zimmer—that's what's different." My words come out a bit giddy, but I don't care.

"Simpleton," she says, turning her back to me.

Once the lights are out, I go over the words in my mind, see them on the thin blue lines of the notebook, and wonder how someone's life can be hidden inside seven little words. I'm not sure what the answer to that is, or if there is an answer, or if that answer would even matter. I lie in bed and gasp, and suddenly think about that little brown-haired girl. I've yet to decide if she is real or if I conjured her out of want or necessity.

Slipping the notebook out of the drawer, I flip open the cover. Quietly, I jot down *The brown-haired girl* in my notebook. Is she a figment of my imagination or part of my past? If she is part of my past, that would make her memory, and if she is memory, why has she surfaced after all this time? I close the notebook, place it back in my dresser drawer, and settle down for sleep. One thing I'm certain of: finding my truth could end up being the most difficult thing I've ever done in my life.

Jewel

I stare down into the empty drawer that once held
David's clothes. We joked about what little space he took
up in the apartment after he moved in. "I don't know what
you're talking about. I've got plenty of stuff. Just ask some
homeless guy," he said. "You're just high maintenance, Jewel
MacKay."

"You mean because I own more than five changes of
clothing," I laughed.

Most of his clothes hung in the small side of the closet,
not that we'd agreed upon this beforehand, but it came
about as a natural progression. A toothbrush, some toi-
letries, extra shirts in case something became soiled, and
then, one snowy weekend in March, he showed up with two
friends and a pickup truck. He didn't have much; a stereo,
a beanbag chair, an acoustic guitar, and a goldfish named
Deja he'd inherited from his last relationship. The rest of his
things went to Goodwill.

"You're too perfect," I told him, placing the goldfish bowl on top of the TV.

"I'm travelling light through the world," he said.

That should have been my first clue.

Even though he hadn't technically been invited to move in, I agreed to give up one drawer of my four-drawer dresser and some closet space. It wasn't as if the apartment was meant for two.

He grew up with hippie parents—grounded, as he liked to say. They planted food and sold fresh bread and vegetables every Saturday outside a cafe where the owner was a friend of his father's first cousin. I told him I was a country girl and was prepared to get my hands dirty should he decide to ever go back to his roots. I knew he wouldn't. He didn't like the lifestyle he'd grown up with and made no apology about it. Maybe that's what attracted me to him in the beginning.

"There are a lot of ways to save the world," David used to say. "Being poor isn't necessarily one of them." He was studying to be a lawyer.

His parents separated the summer after he turned twelve. There was a teenage girl waiting tables at the cafe where they set up on Saturdays to sell their produce. His father took a liking to her and she, being young and inexperienced, thought he was cool. One day in late August they left town together. David consoled his mother through the transition, helped her sell bread and kale, him being the oldest of three. He hadn't seen his father since he was nineteen. They got drunk together one night at a local bar, his father promising he was back to stay while ordering another shot of whiskey. Marilyn was gone, he said, the relationship washed up, and David could hardly wait to tell his mother. When he woke up in the morning his father was gone.

Not that he ever criticized the life his parents had adopted, or even his father for leaving them, and from what I gathered his siblings were fairly well adjusted, but he wanted something different, he said. I could relate to that. I didn't speak of my own childhood; nor did I ask David any specifics about his, only what he'd volunteered. He got along great with Jacob, as if they'd known each other for years. Watching them together, the ease with which they conversed over matters big and small, sometimes left me a tiny bit envious. Why didn't our conversations have that same comfortable feeling?

Six months into our relationship I had a rushed coffee date with his mother—Journey, as she'd been calling herself for the past twenty years, although David could still remember when everyone called her Anne. It was summer and she was barefoot. We were in an outdoor cafe and a light breeze was blowing. There was an aura about her, a self-confidence, that I found intriguing, as if she knew where she fit into the world and was at peace with it. She was a woman who turned people's heads, in a good way.

"David tells me you grew up on a farm," she said, as if searching for common ground. She stirred her coffee thoughtfully, choosing her words with care. The bangles she wore tinkled like fairy bells. I sat mesmerized like a child. She had been living with a musician for the past eight years, still growing her kale and baking bread.

"Guilty as charged," I joked.

"Is that funny?" she asked, searching my face in earnest. I had worried she wouldn't like me.

"It was a wonderful life, actually. Hard work, but fun. I cried when we moved away," I added, quickly mending what might have become an awkward moment. It was true, I did cry, but not for the reason most would think.

Although I knew there was nothing about my and David's childhood that was vaguely similar, I gave the impression that I was a simple farm girl with an average upbringing. Neither David nor I had what anyone would call a conventional family life, but for totally opposite reasons. David liked to describe his childhood as abnormally wholesome, while I chose not to describe mine at all. Like me, David wasn't one for asking many questions.

I was accepted into Dalhousie right out of high school and settled into city living immediately. I was a girl walking down the street, sitting in class, studying at the library late at night. I became who I'd always wanted to be: Jewel MacKay—anonymous.

A noise breaks free from my throat, echoing against the vanilla walls in our bedroom. My bedroom. There's a stack of folded clothes on top of the dresser. I reach for it but stop myself. Closing the empty drawer, I curl up on the unmade bed, wondering if I should call Jacob. He would want to know about David.

Elizabeth

I look out the window in time to see the last of the coloured leaves trailing away in the wind. The trees are now naked, their branches stripped bare. They stand in silent protest against the harsh elements; their jabbering has subsided. The only sound they make comes from the creaking of their limbs back and forth in the wind. Paper snowflakes decorate the walls in the common room; big ones, little ones, medium-sized. Holly berry and green sprigs. Bright centrepieces on the tables with candles in the middle. Christmas—what happened to all those months? I look around me. The place feels different. Cigarette smoke hovers in the air. I close my eyes. Breathe in something fearful, frightening.

A girl used to be here, she had brown hair, but she never came back.

I look for her in the common room and any other place I can think of. No one will speak of her.

"Don't worry about it, dear," they say. "Concentrate on getting yourself better so you can go home."

"Where am I?"

"You're in Dartmouth, Elizabeth. You're feeling better now."

This morning, I woke with the words "little pony" on my lips and quickly added them to my list. I spent the next few hours whispering them in my mind. Trying to pull out a memory is like drawing a splinter out of your finger with a sewing needle. You pry and dig until you create a sore spot and still the splinter remains. In the end all you've accomplished is to produce a wound that wasn't there until you began picking at it in the first place. When I came back to our room to get ready for my morning at the community centre, I noticed the new calendar page Mrs. Zimmer had turned for November. There was a picture of a pony out grazing in a pasture surrounded by orange and red leaves. A crystal-blue lake was in the background. Opening the drawer on my nightstand, I quickly crossed *little pony* off my list.

At the bottom of the page, I wrote, *Be careful. Familiarity does not always mean memory.*

I underlined the sentence two times.

The wind scatters a cluster of leaves in front of me and into the street. They are sent flying back into the air by the first passing car. My fall jacket is buttoned all the way to the top, and I'm glad Rebecca suggested I put my cap and gloves on. Missy is a few steps behind me, getting in those last few puffs on a cigarette before we reach the community centre.

Hair being blown about, bare hands, rosy red cheeks—a white sequined dress and tiara would make her look just like an ice queen from a book of fairy tales. Walking along, I concentrate on the brown-haired girl and how she might or might not fit into my past. Each time I feel as though I might possibly have a breakthrough, the memory disintegrates out from under me. Perhaps I've only made her up. Who knows what all those treatments might have done to my brain cells, which parts they've erased forever or scrambled together, producing a conglomerate of happenings that never actually took place.

Every Friday there's a get-together at the community centre and a luncheon is prepared. Sometimes the luncheon is put on for the seniors or the bluegrass singers or some other local group. I've been coming here for several years now as part of a program Mrs. Weaver put together with the people at the community centre. Marie or Annie or sometimes even Jane comes with me.

"The program is only for those who are well enough to participate," Mrs. Weaver explained in the beginning, discreetly calling me into her office so as not to allow some of the other residents to overhear. When I told her I wasn't sure, she smiled and said, "Everyone should have a purpose in life, Elizabeth—even you."

Today there's to be a Halloween party for the pre-school in town, even though Halloween was two days ago. I was surprised to learn that Missy had agreed to help out this time. Missy doesn't know a thing about working in a kitchen, and I might have thought it would be unpleasant for her, being around young children and all. But when I met up with her at the front door this morning, she didn't seem the least bit troubled. She was leaning against the door looking into a little mirror, rubbing a powder puff over her chin and nose. The moment she saw me she snapped her compact shut, dropped it in her handbag, and said, "Let's get those little brats fed and on their way."

The centre is already decorated with jack-o'-lanterns and scarecrows when we arrive. Cardboard skeletons dangle from each of the windows. Orange and black streamers are twisted together near the ceiling, looped from one side of the room to the other. Balloons are fastened together in large bunches, black, white, and orange. Two long tables are set up with orange tablecloths, decorated with vases of coloured leaves and fall flowers made of plastic.

"It sounds hollow in here," says Missy as we walk toward the coat rack. Our boots echo with each step. She hooks her purse over a hanger and slips her fake-fur jacket over it. The slight breeze she causes smells of cigarette smoke. My cap and gloves shoved in my pockets and my jacket hung up, I head straight for the kitchen. Missy follows. Beverly is waiting to show us what needs to be done. There are so many rules when it comes to helping out in the kitchen. When I first started I was sure I'd never keep it all straight. There is something about Beverly that reminds me a bit of Mrs. Weaver, even though she's not nearly as stylish. The first time I came to the centre she met me at the door, welcoming me with her warm, friendly smile and dark, knowing eyes. Her cropped hair framed her face, making her look much younger than me, but the crow's feet around her eyes said middle-age.

"You must be Missy," Beverly says, looking toward the doorway where Missy stands twisting the ends of her hair. "Don't worry, we'll break you in. Won't we, Elizabeth?"

"Who's worried?" says Missy, and she laughs.

Clean apron, washed hands, hair tucked under a hairnet, I'm ready to go to work. Missy continues to lean against the doorway. It's not like her to be shy, although I find it difficult to picture her helping out in the kitchen. The one time she helped Jennie with dinner she ended up scalding her hand, nearly knocking a pot of boiling water to the floor and causing Jennie to ban her from ever entering the kitchen at Harmony House again. People murmured afterward, accusing Missy of purposely trying to get out of work. Not long after, Mrs. Weaver increased Missy's laundry duties, and that put an end to the rumours.

"The cupcakes and cookies need to be frosted, and there are snack trays to put together. The filling for the sandwiches is in the fridge. We're going with egg salad, ham and cheese, and tuna. Missy, wash your hands and grab an apron. Elizabeth, can get you a hairnet."

I reach for the drawer just as Missy says, "You've got to be kidding. I'm not putting one of those things on my head."

Beverly looks Missy up and down. Missy has on a white blouse and tight black pants that make her legs look like beanpoles. Someone should have told her to fasten one more button on her blouse before she left this morning. Usually Mrs. Weaver would do that, but she had an early morning appointment and won't be back until after lunch.

"We do have rules here," Beverly says taking a hair elastic from the drawer. She hands it to Missy. "You'll have to tie it back at the very least. I'm sorry, but there are regulations that need to be followed."

I hold my breath.

"And wash your hands properly. I suppose you're going to say an apron is out of the question, too."

I try to look busy while Beverly sets out the rules to Missy, and I whisper a silent thank you when I hear the water running in the kitchen sink behind me. I turn around just as Missy is tying an apron around her waist, feeling a sudden wave of relief.

A half hour later there is icing all over Missy's fingers. A daub of frosting waits to be licked from the corner of her mouth. Orange icing has trickled down over the edges of some of the cookies and hardened onto the parchment paper. A woman (I think her name is Ethel) is drawing the faces on the cookies. When Beverly asked if I wanted to ice the cookies with Missy or make sandwiches, I quickly chose the sandwiches.

Out in the main hall, the finishing touches are being added to the decorations, although I can't imagine what could possibly be added to what's already there. It all looks wonderful. Earlier, I heard people saying how perfect everything needs to be with the mayor's wife attending. Music is playing—snappy tunes that will appeal to young children. Grating on the nerves after the first few minutes, but I'm good at shutting things like that out when I need to. Sharing a room with Mrs. Zimmer has taught me that much.

Two older women go about putting together the fruit and vegetable trays. Tessa opens another loaf of bread and lays the slices out onto the counter. "I was surprised to hear the mayor's wife is coming," she says, casually making conversation. I open the egg salad container and start spreading one side of the bread while Tessa puts butter on the other.

"Why be surprised? It's not like she's any better than the rest of us," says Missy, picking up one of the cookies she's just frosted. "I heard she's got a thirst for the vodka. Those uppity-uppity types aren't nearly as perfect as they want everyone to think. She's probably got a little something going on the side...you know, with the gardener or someone, or maybe one of the town councillors." She digs at the icing and sucks it off her finger. A queer sound comes out of Ethel's mouth and the flab beneath her chin quivers. She might be about to say something, but stops. The kitchen becomes quiet. If only I could scratch out Missy's words the same way I do with the words in my notebook.

Ethel regains her voice. "You're one of the ones from that Harmony House, aren't you?" she says. Her voice reeks of accusation. I freeze, roll my eyes up at Missy. A gob of egg salad lands on the toe of my shoe and I quickly reach for paper towel. If only Annie or Marie or even Jane had come with me today. Missy brings the knife out of the frosting and shoots Ethel a hateful look. I can't help thinking that Ethel deserved that look, the way she said: *"You're one of the ones from that Harmony House, aren't you?"* like Missy is a leper, a carrier of some deadly disease, only I'm sure Missy won't leave it at that.

"What's it to you if I am? Do you have a problem with that, you old bag?" She points the table knife directly at Ethel. But she's not through talking. "Maybe you think I'm not good enough to be here. Is that it?" Ethel backs away from the table shaking her head, bumps into the table behind her, and hurries out of the kitchen like a frightened rabbit. Missy's laugh is harsh, breaking through the deathly quiet that has fallen over the entire centre. Even the music has paused, as if on command.

"Look at her running." Missy laughs, sticking the knife back into the frosting. "I wonder what crawled up her a—"

"The cookies look about done," interrupts Tessa before Missy has time to finish what she's saying. "Why don't you help Elizabeth with the sandwiches while I do the cup-cakes?" The music is back to playing again—a new tune. I breathe. Sigh deeply. Hoping all will be well.

"Not bad for a frosting virgin," says Missy, looking down at the cookies on the table. "It was kind of fun."

Tessa gives a tight smile. "They look lovely," she says quietly, reaching for one of the cupcakes.

I remind Missy to stop each time she gets to the edge of the bread and to scrape the extra salad dressing off before cutting the sandwiches into triangles.

"I'm so sick of triangles," she says before we're halfway through. We finish up the tuna and the ham and cheese and find a place for them in one of the refrigerators.

"Do you like the sprinkles?" says Tessa, holding out a tray of tiny cupcakes for our inspection. "Not very Halloweeny, but there weren't any black or orange ones," she adds.

"Hundreds and thousands," I say, staring down at the tiny balls of green, red, and white that are scattered on top of the white frosting, the words drifting up into my mind like a helium-filled balloon.

"Hundreds of what?"

"Thousands...they're called hundreds and thousands." A sudden flicker of remembrance strikes me and an odd feeling comes over me.

"Are you okay, Elizabeth? You look a little strange." It's not like Missy to show any concern. I blink back tears, blink again, and the feeling is gone.

"I'm fine," I assure her, pushing a thin smile at her. "Perfectly fine."

I open the refrigerator door for Tessa and she puts the cupcakes inside. Missy is watching me like she can read my thoughts, but that's impossible since I don't even know what those thoughts are.

I have a sudden urge to write something in my notebook.

A burst of sound and energy erupts into the community centre like the town fireworks on the first of July when the preschoolers finally arrive. The music becomes lost, soaked up by the sound of children's laughter and people talking. When it's time to eat we take the sandwiches and snack trays out and place them on a long table.

"They're like little animals," hisses Missy when one of the children nearly bumps into her and the tray she's carrying.

"Why did you say that about the mayor's wife?" I say to Missy when it is just the two of us in the kitchen. Missy bites into a tuna sandwich and makes a face.

"It could have been true," she says with a shrug, throwing the rest of the sandwich in the garbage and reaching for the egg salad. We finish our lunch and start cleaning the counters, and I'm not sure if Missy will want to come to the community centre to help out again.

When it's time for us to leave, the party is about over. The kitchen has been wiped down and the dishes put away. Everything is back in its original place. A few volunteers start taking down the decorations as the children head out the door. Removing my jacket from the coat rack, I feel a small tug on my dress. Big brown eyes stare up at me and I instantly freeze. He can't be any more than three or four. I look down at him standing there. Tear-filled eyes and a quivering lip prompt me to ask, "Are you lost?" When someone calls out, "Come on, Tyler," he spins around and races toward the door. My hands shake as I button my jacket. I can't stop thinking about the look on the little boy's face. I know that look, that feeling of being lost. The worst feeling in the world is to be left behind.

Noticing that Missy's things are gone from the coat rack, my mind quickly goes off in another direction. Trying not to panic, I search for her. She isn't in the kitchen or the main hall. I check the bathroom, but that's empty, too. My knees jiggle as I force myself to keep moving. I try to remember when I saw her last. We ate lunch in the kitchen and she helped wipe down the counters. After that, I'm not sure. I got busy sweeping floors and folding tablecloths and forgot to keep Missy in mind. My heart is making a strange beat. I ask Beverly and Ethel if they've seen Missy. I ask the volunteers who are taking down the decorations. Again, I check the bathroom, calling out her name to the empty stalls.

With nowhere inside the building left to look, I hurry down the steps. The breeze messes my hair. Pulling on my cap, I look up and down the street, frantically calling out her name. Missy isn't supposed to be out, not in town, not by herself. It's my fault—all my fault. If I go home without her I'll get the blame. "You're supposed to be the responsible one," Mrs. Weaver will say. My breath gets caught in my throat and I spin around, not knowing what I should do. Do I start searching the street? But which street? There are too many streets. I can't check them all.

One last time I yell for Missy. People are staring.

"Calm down, miss," says an old man. I scream at him to leave me be and his mouth swings open as if his jaw has become unhinged. Doesn't he understand that I've lost Missy? He starts to walk away and I realize he must think I'm crazy, shouting at him that way when he was trying to help.

"I'm sorry," I say, but he keeps walking down the sidewalk. The wind blows raw, slapping my face with an open hand. When Missy's coarse laughter finally reaches my ears, I stop in my tracks. I hurry back up the street and find her standing between the community centre and the fire hall, talking and laughing with two young men with long, shaggy hair. There's a lit cigarette in her left hand. One man has his arm around her waist. His fingers are sunk into the fake fur on her jacket. The moment she sees me, her face turns to stone.

"I've got to go," she says, throwing her cigarette butt onto the street. "I'll talk to you later." I clench my jaw and start for Harmony House, pretending I didn't hear what she just said. My legs push for more ground. Heat builds beneath my knitted cap. I could rip it off right now and not even mind the biting cold.

"You'd better keep your mouth shut about this," Missy says when she catches up to me. When I ignore her, she grabs my arm and yanks me around so that her face is inches from mine. There are faint red lines in her eyes and the quick burst of desperation I see hidden there surprises me.

"Did you hear me?" she says. The smell of stale cigarettes hits me in the face. I wrench free from her grip and tell her—no, shout at her—that I didn't see a thing. She smiles and nods her head, her face lighting up as she relaxes. "We were just talking. No harm done. There was nothing to see, right, Elizabeth?"

I'm unable to speak. Who knows what venom would pour out of me if I did? Missy knew darn well I'd be worried if she left the community centre without telling me. Mrs. Weaver doesn't let her go out by herself anymore—we both know that—so why wouldn't I be worried?

"You're mad, aren't you?" she says, slowing her pace. When she stops in her tracks, I turn to look at her. "No one ever gives me a chance," she says. "You make one mistake and they won't let you forget." She's pouting and might be about to cry. And Missy never cries, not even after what happened last Christmas.

"Why do you have to break the rules?" I say as my anger begins to subside. She doesn't say anything at first, just picks at a hangnail. She suddenly looks up.

"Perfect Elizabeth. Always making the rest of us look bad," she says, shaking her head. "You wouldn't say shit if you had a mouthful—would you? But you know what? At least the rest of us have a little fun from time to time. All you have are rules and a perfect little life where you always do what's expected. But what's life if you don't break the rules once in a while? Shit, you might just as well be dead." There's something frightening in the way she says this. A wild animal is hidden inside her, fighting to break out of its cage, and I have no desire to see it.

"You should have said you were going, is all." I'm immediately annoyed with myself for smoothing things over, for allowing her words to find their mark. The whole world walks on eggshells when Missy's around. The rest of the way home she dawdles along the street. I slow down to keep my pace with hers and hope that Mrs. Weaver doesn't ask what took us so long. Missy smokes another cigarette before we make it back to Harmony House. In the distance, I can see Nick sitting out on the verandah, feet up on the railing, relaxing. The closer we get to Harmony House, the more anxious I become. All I want is to get settled in, forget the incident at the community centre. Before we go inside, Missy grabs me by the arm again, stopping me in my tracks.

"Haven't you ever thought about not coming back here?" she says.

"Not coming back?" Her question leaves a gaping hole inside me. How could she? Why, I'd never....

"Yeah, you know, take off, go someplace else. Walk down these steps and never return. Maybe start a new life someplace new, where no one knows who you are." I stand in the driveway, frozen in time, unable to fathom the meaning behind her words, let alone come up with a coherent answer. "Forget it," she says, shaking her head. "You can't even let your mind dream." Spinning around, she starts running toward Harmony House. A strange sensation cradles me beneath the ribs.

Leave Harmony House? Impossible, I think as her shoes clack up the steps.

Impossible.

Elizabeth

"Welcome to Divinity Hospital, Elizabeth. Things are a bit more relaxed here. You'll have more freedom. Once you understand the way things work, you'll do just fine."

I don't venture out of my room for the first few days. I can't make my body stop trembling on the inside. The one thing they don't know—and it's the thing that frightens me the most—is that the darkness that filled me for all those years has followed me here. I sit on my bed holding the darkness in my hand like a rotten apple at the bottom of a barrel. It's heavy, but not as heavy as it once was. There's a tiny bit of light when I hold it up close and squint. And it's within that tiny bit of light that I see their faces looking back at me. For a time I didn't know who they were, but then it came to me one evening as I drifted into sleep. Jacob and Jewel—I had almost forgotten.

"You don't have to stay in here by yourself," the nurse says one day. "You should come out into the recreation room and get acquainted with everyone. Be sociable for once."

I want to hold that round bit of darkness up to the light all day, sit on the edge of my bed and marvel at that small bit of hope that is nestled inside, but I can't. I need to go out of my room and be sociable, allow them to fix what is wrong with me, listen to the ones who know more than I. Pretend to be normal or as close to normal as I can get so I can go home. The nurse takes me to a common room where people sit watching television and playing checkers. In the corner is a large pool table with coloured balls clacking and smacking into one another. I flinch each time one of the balls are hit, wishing I could go back to the solitude of my room.

"Who are you?" asks a young man with long, stringy hair. His pimply face is red and filled with whiteheads begging to be squeezed. He stares across the room at me for the longest while and I can't help wondering what he's thinking, what he sees when he looks at me.

"I'm Elizabeth," I tell him as if all the confidence in the world brought me here, even though there isn't an ounce of self-assurance left in me.

"Is that all you know?" He flips the question out like he's playing tiddlywinks, and without a crumb of sincerity. He chews at one of his nails and spits it onto the floor. Bright red appears around the rim of his nail. Examining the blood, he wipes it on his jeans, then looks up at me as if just noticing I'm still there.

"I don't like new people coming around," he says. "I told them not to let anyone new in here. No one listens to me. They all say, 'What do you want, Reggie?' and I tell them but then they don't listen. You're new here, aren't you?" he says, looking at me with suspicion until someone sitting in front of the television tells him to shut up.

"Up yours," he hisses and makes a rude gesture.

"Where are we?" asks an old woman sitting beside him on the couch.

"Divinity," he says, "and it's simply divine." Jumping to his feet, he throws his arms in the air, laughing like he's about to burst open at the seams. But then he looks over at me and suddenly stops, marches off as if he's been offended by the very sight of me. It bothers me for the longest time and I can't for the life of me imagine what I said or did to that young boy with the stringy blond hair to anger him so.

Back in the quiet of my room, I struggle to put things into place, to remember the small details of my life. The problem is I don't know what I've forgotten. I spend most of my days looking for something. Something got lost a while back and I haven't been able to find it.

At night someone whispers into the dark—over and over.

"Jewel and Jacob."

They are my children.

I am the one who is lost.

Curled up on my bed at night, I cry alone in the dark.

No one hears.

I am Elizabeth.

I have two children, Jacob and Jewel.

My husband's name is Cliff.

I live in the Forties Settlement.

That's not all I know.

I just can't remember the rest.

I don't like:

1. *farm animals*
2. *the ocean*

3. *the Bible*
4. *scalloped potatoes*
5. *church hats*

Right after I write these things in my notebook I think about scratching them out. It might be considered blasphemy to admit to not liking the Bible. And it seems childish to set down a list of things I don't like. I remember then what Mrs. Weaver said, that I won't be judged by the things in my notebook, so I decide to leave them be. I have no idea how these things figure into my truth, but they must. As for the Bible, there's a small copy of the New Testament at the back of my dresser drawer. I discovered it shortly after I arrived at Harmony House. Flipping through it one afternoon when I was bored, I stopped on one of the pages and started reading. When I came to the part about throwing yourself into the sea, a dark cloud swept over me, a feeling so heavy I could actually feel myself being pulled down... down...down. I pushed through the uncomfortable sensation and continued reading. When the passage went on to say that if there is no doubt in your heart your prayers will be answered, I snapped the book shut. It was too much for me to fathom. I've lost large portions of my life, and many memories might fail me, but not the whispered prayers that came up from my hospital bed when I had nothing left to cling to. I wanted no part of a Bible that contained lies.

I go back later and cross the Bible off the list.

As soon as the leaves were gathered this fall, there came another bunch to be rid of. Nick and Howard helped some workmen clean them up just last week, but you'd never know it to look at the ground now. Mrs. Weaver said anyone who helped clean up the yard would get a little extra when the comfort money comes this month. I hardly spend the money I get from one month to the next, but you just never know when that could change. I might come across something in town that will catch my eye. It's a good feeling to have money in my wallet.

Missy's question has been keeping me awake at night. Leave Harmony House—does she realize how impractical that would be for someone like me? I try to put it out of my head, but it's difficult to do when words get stuck there. Squeezing the rake handle, I try and put my mind in other places. Annie and Marie are supposed to be helping me put the leaves into garbage bags, but as soon as they got outside they lit up cigarettes and started talking about Missy.

"You can tell just by looking at her she's trouble with a capital T."

"I heard they're shipping her off someplace, maybe a different province if they can't find a place that'll take her around here."

"There's no controlling that one. She's a real pistol."

"She needs more tranquilizers if you ask me."

That's all everyone's been doing for the past two days. Even Sophie, who shares a room with Missy, has been making tutting noises when Missy's name is mentioned. I can't think Sophie even knows what she's tutting about.

"Who picks out her wardrobe? That's what I'd like to know," laughs Donna. I stop what I'm doing and glare in her direction, but she doesn't take notice. Someone should remind her that her break was over ten minutes ago and it's wrong for her to gossip about Missy to the rest of us. She works here and should be above all that—I'm sure that's what Mrs. Weaver would tell her if only she knew what Donna was saying. I can almost bet that no one here is going to inform her.

Missy has been in her room since Monday afternoon, right after I came out of Mrs. Weaver's office. Jennie sends meals down to her because she won't come into the dining room to eat. I've seen the plates going back to the kitchen with scarcely a nibble gone. She doesn't even come out of her room to smoke.

Someone at the community centre put in a report about Missy. I know this because I was called into Mrs. Weaver's office and she asked about the incident that happened on Friday. At first, I thought she was talking about Missy leaving the community centre like she did and the two men she was chatting with by the fire hall. It didn't make sense to me how she could possibly know this, since there was no one else around to see and I hadn't told a single soul. I wondered then if someone had been following me. I'd walked up and down the street that day calling out Missy's name. I should have known better, should have been careful. It was my fault Missy left the centre by herself. I've thought about it a lot since it happened, certain as I am that the whole thing could have been avoided. As I sat across from Mrs. Weaver I didn't say anything at first, since I wasn't sure what she wanted from me. She smiled and told me not to worry.

"I'm not trying to get anyone in trouble. I just want to get to the bottom of this." I went to answer, but the words in my head were jumbled. "Slow down, Elizabeth, and take your time," she said. I drew in a few jagged breaths. That's when she told me that someone had reported Missy for threatening one of the volunteers at the centre.

"Was there something about a table knife?" she asked when I told her I didn't know what she was talking about.

"Missy didn't threaten anyone," I answered, immediately shaking my head, but then I stopped. "At least, she didn't mean to. She was talking.... She just pointed the knife…like you would point a finger. She didn't mean any-thing by it." I shouldn't have raised my voice, but I couldn't have Mrs. Weaver thinking Missy had done this horrible thing. Missy is reckless and bold, but she wouldn't harm anyone, not purposely. At least, I don't think she would.

"When someone in the community puts in a complaint about anyone here at Harmony House it's my duty to check it out, Elizabeth. You understand that, don't you?" I stopped fiddling with my fingers and shoved my hands into my dress pockets.

"Missy didn't mean anything by it," I said again, my voice failing to carry any weight. "You can't hurt someone with a table knife. It's not even sharp…. Is Missy going to get in trouble?"

"That's not for you to worry about, Elizabeth. Some people just like to stir up trouble for those of us here at Harmony House. They don't think we should be here in the community. But that's where ignorance comes into play. There's a place for everyone in this town. I'll fight for each and every one of you here. Still, I have to check out any complaints, to see if they're valid. Perhaps someone misunderstood."

Missy was alone in the family room curled up on the couch when I came out of Mrs. Weaver's office. When she looked up and saw me, she pulled a knitted afghan around herself and sat up.

"That bitch at the community centre said I threatened her," she said, snarling. "What did you tell Mrs. Weaver?"

"I said you didn't mean to threaten anyone. I mean, I said you didn't mean anything by it. I told her you can't hurt someone with a table knife."

"That's what I said too, but I don't think the old battle-axe believed me."

"She's just trying to get to the bottom of it. Are you okay?" I asked, sitting beside her. It seemed as though I should say something else. I'm not very good at offering comfort. I patted Missy's hand, but she pulled it back like she'd been burned. Mrs. Zimmer was standing in the doorway when I looked up.

"So, you got yourself in a little trouble at the community centre, I hear," she snorted.

"Mind you own business," Missy hissed. "You weren't even there."

"Whose word do you think they're going take on this? Someone from the community centre or a little slut who can't keep her legs together...and her"—she pointed at me—"a cardboard dummy who can't remember when she ate last? So, tell me, who do you think they're going to believe?"

"Bitch!" yelled Missy so loudly that I jumped and gasped at the same time. Hauling the afghan around her, she ran out of the family room.

"I guess some people can't take the truth," said Mrs. Zimmer as she turned on the TV, her wide rear end settling down into one of the armchairs in front of the screen.

"You didn't have to say that," I snapped.

"Don't blame me. She brought it on herself. Now be quiet so I can hear my story," she said, waving her hand at me like she was swatting flies. Missy hasn't come out of her room since.

I'm not surprised that people are talking about Missy here at Harmony House. When she first came here she used to walk into town by herself. People said that men could get her to do things for cigarettes. They said she was like that from the time she was a teenager. Mrs. Weaver said that no one was a prisoner here at Harmony House and that Missy was free to go wherever she wanted just like everyone else.

No one had known Missy was pregnant, not even Sophie who shared a room with her. Not until last December when she found Missy under the Christmas tree one morning, howling into the floor. An ambulance came, bright lights and sirens. We crowded toward the windows to watch it drive in. Mrs. Weaver hurried to open the door, telling everyone to stand back out of the way. Missy moaned and groaned. "There, there, Missy," Mrs. Weaver cooed. And then Missy stopped making noises. One of the ambulance drivers covered her with a blanket, tucking it in all around her feet. Someone whispered that the afterbirth was still attached when they took the tiny bundle away.

"It must be dead," someone else said. "They covered its face. You can't see its face. There was no crying. Babies cry."

Missy was strapped to a gurney and wheeled out the door. Her eyes were lifeless, her head turned slightly to the side. She was smiling, wide and ready, but you could tell it looked fake. She came back to Harmony House about a month later, looking the way she always did. Someone asked her about the baby.

"What baby?" she said, like she hadn't a clue what they were talking about. If I didn't know better, even I would have believed her.

Pushing the leaves down farther into the garbage bag, I tie it tight and put it with the other bags. Annie and Marie take them down to the end of the drive. The wind pulls more leaves from the trees and they fall near my feet. I think then for a brief moment that Mrs. Zimmer is right; Missy did bring it all on herself. But for some reason that still makes me sad. A single orange leaf drifts down in front of me and I pick it up. I can't stop looking at it, how totally out of place it seems amidst all the reds, yellows, and browns. Missy's words echo somewhere inside me. I drop the leaf as a sudden impulse sends me hurrying up the steps.

"Hey, get back here! We're not done," cries Marie. "We're not done yet!"

"Bathroom," I call out before I reach the door. A warm burst of air meets me and I take off my cap and gloves. This won't take long, so I walk straight through. If I'm lucky, Donna won't catch me walking across the floors without taking off my footwear. Heading straight for Missy's room, I knock on the door. She doesn't answer, but I open it anyway. I stand with the door partly opened—half in, half out. Missy is lying on her side, clutching the balled-up afghan close to her chest. The blind is pulled and the room is dim. On the floor is her plate from lunch. The sandwiches have been pulled apart and some of the filling is gone. Looking up, she sees me in the doorway. When I say her name she doesn't move. Remaining steadfast, I wait for her to acknowledge my presence.

"What do you want?" she croaks, rising up on her elbow. It takes a moment for the word to form in my mouth, and I stand in the doorway staring at Missy.

"Yes," I finally manage to say. "My answer is yes." This confession leaves me weak, as if something has let go inside me. I'm entering into some unknown realm, and I sense that I am too far in to stop. I'll soon reach the point of no return. There is no going back from this "yes" of mine. I understand that and I am ready.

"What the hell are you talking about?" says Missy. "Are you crazy or something?"

"The other day, on our way home from the centre." My voice is quiet, not much more than a whisper. I'm not sure if I'll get the words out. I pause and close my eyes. When

I'm ready again I look directly at Missy. "You asked me if I ever thought of leaving here. That's what I'm talking about—leaving."

Missy sits up, bringing the knitted afghan with her.

"My answer's yes, Missy. I think about it all the time."

Each morning I go over my list of words when I get a spare moment to myself. Knowing my truth is out there, I've been trying extra hard to remember. It's useless to try and force memories into being. Whenever I do they end up distorted, mutilated by false expectations that wink at me from all sides, and I end up getting everything wrong, finally saddled with the new guilt those false memories bring. In all my imaginings I do everything wrong. I'm the one to blame. They'll never want me back.

I haven't added any new words to my list in a few weeks. I'd like to, but my mind draws a blank. No one's past can be made up of seven little words—no one. I've reasoned that out and it makes perfect sense. But regardless of how important the words might be, there's nothing I can do to bring them back. The key to the past rests in the few words that I can remember, if only I knew how they all fit together, how they form the missing pieces of me. But what if all the thousands of words I need to remember slid by when I wasn't looking? It might have happened in a dream or maybe they became mingled together with other words that held no meaning at the time, sporadic in nature and quick to materialize, but meaning nothing all on their own. Quick words bounce away like rubber balls. Once they're gone there's no way to get them back. It's a sobering thought. My truth might have come to me already, a single word at a time. Without continuity, they meant nothing.

"If the memories are in there, why can't they get to me?" I said one time.

"Life is filled with these little mysteries, Elizabeth. There's no possible way of knowing that," said Mrs. Weaver. I wasn't expecting an answer. The important part was being brave enough to speak the question out loud. So many of my questions go unasked for fear that I'll end up sounding like a simpleton. But I am well now, and I think perhaps that people who are well are supposed to question the life they have, at least from time to time. We can't just sit back and let life unravel. When we do, it becomes stagnant, a dormant cocoon waiting for the sun to hatch it.

They came to me in a dream the other night. Tiny faces and begging eyes. They cried out for me. I couldn't see their features clearly as hard as I tried. I woke immediately, wanting to cry, but having no tears in me, I lay there staring into the darkness. Truth held my heart in a firm grip and it squeezed hard. Feeling around in the dark, I opened the drawer to my nightstand and found my notebook. Mrs. Zimmer's snoring didn't falter as I wrote down *Mumma*. Hugging the notebook, with the glow of the full moon shining down on me, I rocked back and forth on the bed. They called me Mumma. I heard it in my dream, felt it in my heart, and knew it was the truth. That's why I went to Missy.

Elizabeth

A few flurries spit in my face; the wind that came up from nowhere is biting cold. Four people are waiting at the bus shed with us, moving about and trying to keep warm. A man with a thin brown coat is slapping his arms, moving up and down on his toes, his nose red. At least I had the good sense to put on my winter coat. Missy has on the pretty orange jacket she got the last time we went to Frenchys. It matches the orange in her oversized handbag, and she looks quite smart if I do say so myself. I wonder if any of these people waiting for the bus can tell what Missy and I have planned—but that would be impossible. No one can read the thoughts of another. It's stupid of me to entertain such a notion.

"You're sure you want to do this, right? Once we get on that bus there's no backing out," says Missy, eyeing me up and down. I tell Missy I'm sure as I've ever been, even though a part of me is dizzy with fright. I pull my handbag close to my chest. As I stare straight ahead, my resolve grows stronger. Some things you need to do regardless of how they make you feel.

As Missy roots through her bag, a pair of red lace panties makes its way to the surface. I quickly stuff it back into her bag before it falls out onto the street. I can't stop to wonder if anyone noticed. Unperturbed, she continues to rummage around in her bag. Pulling out a compact, she removes the shiny spot on her nose before the bus comes into view.

"Joey knows we're coming. I phoned him last night. He says he'll have lunch ready and everything. I hope it's something good." She pushes a broad smile across her face and looks one last time in the mirror, tossing the compact back into her bag as the bus pulls up. The brakes squeak as the bus comes to a stop. Eyes closed, I take a deep breath. Determination drives me forward. Sometimes people need to take matters into their own hands. I am now one of those people.

I haven't asked Missy how she knows this man in another town or how she came to have his phone number. I felt it was best for me not to go prying into her personal affairs. She's walking a fine line, and if I were her I'd be more careful. But I'm not her mother. It's not my place to hand out advice. I'm going along, not to keep watch over her, but with the promise that, once we're there, this Joey person will drive me to the Forties Settlement in his car. I've been thinking of little else since the dream put me back there. If I go and see the place for myself, it could trigger something important inside me. Writing down words in a notebook is fine, but I'm progressing at a snail's pace. There has to be something out there that will jar the memories loose. I can't go on waiting forever.

Missy hands over our tickets and boards the bus. The driver winks at me as I climb the steps. I quickly turn my head, shocked by his boldness. The people sitting near the front don't seem to have noticed his cheekiness. Head down, I hurry past him. He makes a small chuckle.

"Move your feet," Missy says to an elderly man who is sitting askew in his seat. His hands are clasped tightly to a walking cane. I smile awkwardly and nod as I walk down the aisle, hoping he'll accept it as an apology for Missy's rude behaviour. But there's not a hint of acceptance on his face as I pass by. I should apologize—someone should—but the words stay stuck inside me. It would sound stupid, me mumbling out an apology when I haven't done anything wrong. Even without the scowl he's wearing, his eyes give way his annoyance. There's nothing I can do about it now. I settle in close to the window while Missy pushes her bag in between us. As I squeeze closer to the glass, the bus changes gears and begins moving ahead. We pass by the shops, the cafe, the grocery store, through three sets of stoplights as we leave the town and Harmony House behind us.

There should be dozens of thoughts moving through my mind right now, but I can't seem to think of a thing as I look out the window. My heart should be rising up into my throat, my chest tight, my breathing shallow. I've never done anything like this in my life—at least, I don't think I have. It's strange to imagine myself ever being irresponsible, and yet I could have been as reckless as a schoolgirl in my younger years, ready to set out and follow my heart's desire.

The bus chugs along, filling the air with its rhythmic vibration. There are worse things in life than following your heart, I suddenly realize. Missy leans back in the seat and closes her eyes.

"Don't fall asleep," I say. If we miss our stop, I can't imagine what we'll do. We'll be stranded. I've never travelled on a bus before.

"I'm just resting my eyes a bit…. I didn't have to bring you." I don't remind her that it was my comfort money that bought her ticket. "I've got to have smokes," she'd said right after she took the ticket money from me. Reaching into my wallet, I pulled out another five-dollar bill and passed it over. I didn't mind giving her some money. Without Missy, none of this would be possible. I haven't a clue as to how I'd make it all the way to the Forties without Missy and her friend. It's not as if Mrs. Weaver would volunteer to take me. I've seen the pitying looks she gives me when I mention Jewel and Jacob. Besides, Mrs. Weaver doesn't believe in delving into the past and sees no importance in it. She made that perfectly clear to Nick the day he wanted to go back to his old apartment.

The rumbling of the bus continues to vibrate through my body as we drive along. I look out the window, see the grey November sky. There's a gentle tugging at my heartstrings as a cloak of doom settles over me. It feels so familiar, so natural, that I worry what it might all mean. I have struggled with these feelings of doom before, allowed them to swallow me up. It's a constant struggle to keep my head above water. Bare limbs on the trees do a poor job of hiding the clouds this time of year. I push these feelings of calamity aside. I have to. There are more important things for me to concentrate on. There's nothing more frightening than the unknown. A flock of cowbirds flies off in a singular movement, scared from the limbs they were gripping fast to moments before the bus passed. A cold finger walks the length of my spine. I shiver, and think other thoughts.

It's 10:13. Mrs. Weaver will soon be going to the kitchen for her first cup of coffee of the day. Mrs. Zimmer is back in our room, lying on top of her bed, staring at the wall as another day begins at Harmony House. I might be working on the jigsaw puzzle that was started the other day, the two thousand pieces Donna said would be impossible to put together—pastureland with lambkill and hackmatack, large granite rocks. Guernsey and Hereford cows, bull and heifer calves. Red barn. White farmhouse with a broad verandah. Mrs. Weaver did her share of coaxing until I finally sat down in front of the pieces.

"I wouldn't know one cow from the next. How do you know what they are?" she said after I listed off all the animals.

"I don't know," I told her, and it was true. I had no idea how I knew any of it. "I suppose we once had a farm," I added, but she made no further comment.

We drive past a large piece of newly ploughed earth not far out of town. A tractor is in the middle of the field with a wagon hitched to the back. A man bends down, reaching for something near his feet. When he straightens, he throws it into the wagon. He's picking rocks off the field—the realization curls around my insides, snaking a path that temporarily releases my mind from its dungeon. I know the feeling of ground beneath my feet, the smell of freshly turned soil. An odd sensation travels up to my head. It comes back to me all at once—a flood of words that forms a pool of sentences, thoughts, memories, as the bus drives on.

"All aboard the hippie bus."

"Oh, Walter, why do you call it that?"

"Look at it. Red and yellow flowers on it, the biggest

I've ever seen." Walter's eyes light up like fireflies as the bus pulls into the hospital parking lot. Sampson and Jeffrey, two orderlies from the hospital, are waiting with us to board. Sampson throws the cigarette he's smoking on the ground and steps on it, pushing it into the pavement.

"What do you think, Elizabeth? Does it meet your approval?" Sampson is forever asking me questions, forcing answers from me when I'd rather be left alone. It only reminds me how unimportant my answers are. It's not as if he really cares to know what I'm thinking. He's just making conversation, doing his job and being paid a pretty penny for it.

"I like the pea green paint," I say, knowing that he's expecting a positive answer. I wouldn't dare say it looks silly. The hospital doesn't like negativity. If we ignore the things we dislike, or the things that make us sad, they'll cease to exist—or at least that seems to be the belief here. A happy face means everything is going along smoothly.

"Pea green. Now, that's funny," laughs Reggie. He pauses for a moment and then breaks into song, "The residents of Divinity went to pick rocks in a beautiful pea green bus." Everyone laughs. I look down at the paved parking lot. It doesn't seem all that funny to me, twisting my words and making them something to joke about.

"They'll see us coming from a mile away," says Bernice, throwing her cigarette butt on the ground. The bus stops in front of us. I'm stricken by a change of heart the moment my foot touches the first step. My mind pokes a worried finger: *Do you really want to do this? Do you know what will happen if you do?* Before I have time to think of an answer I'm being ushered up the steps by those behind me. There's no place for me to turn, no going back in time. Like it or not, I have no choice in the matter. It's too late to refuse to go. It's just too late. Lowering myself onto the seat, I look out the window, waiting for the wheels to start turning. It's all I can do to pretend that everything's fine while my mind continues to silently scream in protest.

Do you really want to do this? Do you know what will happen if you do?

The answers come in quick, a flash that is nearly blinding.

No and no.

My face rests against the bus window and we turn off the highway and onto a dirt road. The bus shimmies over the potholes and I'm forced to remove my head from the window or else end up knocking it into the glass. Walter stands up when the bus makes another turn, this time off the dirt road. "Holy mother of God," he says and then whistles. Looking out the windshield of the bus, I understand Walter's reaction. Surely, I've never seen so many rocks before.

We're given instruction before we even attempt to get out of our seats. Throw the rocks into the wagon, don't bother with the small ones, and wear the sun hat you brought unless you want to get sick from the sun.

"It's not brain surgery. A five-year-old could do it," says Jeffrey as we step off the bus. "You'll all do fine, and you'll get a little money to spend." Hands clap at the sound of money. A few let out a cheer. Most of them wouldn't be here otherwise. I agreed to come only because of the strange dreams I've been having. I'm running across a hay field, desperately trying to take flight. But I'm unable to become airborne. I'm doing something wrong. I've forgotten some key part, something I should know. I thought being outdoors might help me remember, and then when the dream comes again I'll be prepared. I'll fly free as a bird, without a single care. Had it not been for the dream, I would have never got on that bus. I would have stayed inside the hospital walls, safe and sound, with no hope of ever making it off the ground.

The sun rests gently across my shoulders. Sweat gathers beneath my sunhat and the straw feels most uncomfortable sticking fast to my head. Reggie whoops and hollers as if relieved to be out in the wide-open spaces. The first rock clatters into the empty wagon, damaging the gentle sounds of the early morning air. Reggie's incessant noises continue to grate on my already frazzled nerves. I jump and gasp, gasp and jump whenever he shrieks. His voice is like a knife stabbing into tin. Blond stringy hair hangs down around his shoulders and he's forever pulling it out of his way. He refused to wear the hat they gave him. "I'm not a frigging cowboy," he said.

Without warning, Reggie starts singing at the top of his lungs. He oohs and aahs, saying "baby, baby," gyrating about like an agitated chimpanzee. He dances his way to the wagon with a rock in his hand, his long, gangly limbs making him even more of a spectacle. Jeffrey and Sampson take turns scolding him for acting out. Each time they do, Reggie makes rude gestures behind their backs. It's not long before he breaks out into song again. Eventually, someone from the group yells out for Reggie to shut up, but even that doesn't quiet him for long.

"It's a free country," he says. "If you can't sing out-doors, where the hell can you sing?" He has a point. If only he could carry a tune.

Cars speed past the field, dust flying from their wheels. A horn sounds and I look up to see arms flailing out the window of a black car streaked with dirt. Reggie stands up straight and shakes his fist. "Keep on trucking, assholes!" he screams. It's not long before the same black car comes from the opposite direction. Someone rolls down the passenger's window and a head pokes out, pointing in our direction.

"Cotton-picking rock pickers!" the passenger of the car yells as the car comes to a stop. Reggie makes a sound like a wounded animal. Everyone stops. He runs toward the car, taking giant strides. Screaming like a wild man, he starts throwing rocks. One. Two. Three. The car finally speeds away, tires spinning on the gravel road. Reggie stands perfectly still, his matted hair trailing behind him. Dropping to his knees with a rock clasped tightly in his fist, he sobs. Sampson goes to him and tells him he can wait in the bus if he wants.

"Just leave me alone," he says, pulling away from Sampson, and it looks for a moment as though he's about to start swinging his fists. He stays on his knees without a sound coming from him. This is not natural for Reggie. Finally jumping up, he marches across the tilled earth and continues where he left off as if nothing has happened. No one says anything for a time and Reggie has stopped singing. The chugging of the tractor and the loud bangs each time a rock hits the trailer are all the music we need.

On the way home, the bus stops at a corner store a few miles from the hospital. The store is tiny. The red paint around the large glass windows is peeling, and a big metal thermometer fastened to the side catches my attention. When we pull up to the store, Walter announces the temperature as if it's something to be broadcasted. Reggie is the first to shove his way off the bus. He buys two chocolate bars to eat on the ride back to the hospital. Taking the seat next to mine, he looks across the aisle at me.

"I'm going home soon, you know," he says with a mouth full of melted chocolate. Half-moons of dirt are pushed up under his fingernails and his palms are equally dirty. He should have worn gloves. There's a brown streak across his cheek. I tell him I didn't know that but it's nice to hear.

"Nice? Hell no, I hate those bastards in Antigonish."

"How could you hate your parents?" My hands tremble. If children can hate their parents, perhaps mine hate me. Perhaps that is why they never came.

"Of course I hate them. Don't look so shocked. Doctor Purcell says I need to own my feelings." It makes no sense to me that he'd be making plans to go home if he hated his parents the way he said. He crams the remainder of the chocolate bar into his mouth and licks the chocolate and dirt from his fingers.

Reggie talks about his weekend pass for weeks. In the dayroom he natters about the things he plans to do when he goes home and even his hatred for his parents, whom he claims are the reason he is at Divinity Hospital in the first place.

"They never wanted kids," he says, sounding pleased about it. "And look what they ended up with."

"Oh, Reggie," someone tells him. "I'm sure your parents would do anything to have you home." And I wanted to cry out, yes, yes, of course they would!

Some time later, from the window in my hospital room, I look down and see Reggie walking out toward the parking lot. This is the weekend he's been talking about for weeks now. What I wouldn't give to be in his shoes, to know I was going home, that such a place even existed for me. A woman is tugging at his long strands of hair and Reggie is shrugging her off. I can hear him shouting obscenities at her and I feel sorry for her. They get into a big blue car and drive away. I stand at the window until I can no longer see the tail lights.

The empty spot inside me grows a little bigger.

Snapping back to the present, I look toward Missy. "It's about time you came back to down to earth," she says with one eye open. "You were staring off into space like you were in a trance or something. Weird or what?"

As soon as she closes her eyes again, I take the notebook out of my handbag and write: *The Hippie Bus.* Below it I make a note.

What happened to Reggie?

Determination feels like grit between my teeth. I'll not let this memory lose me too.

Jewel

A chill comes over me as I fumble for the car keys.
I stop, unable to resist the urge to look up at the apartment
building across the road from where I'm parked. Most of the
windows have the curtains pulled, except for one. I take out
the pair of binoculars I sent for in the mail and hold them
to my eyes, fine-tune them until a clear picture comes into
focus. The walls inside the apartment are dull beige and
there's a framed picture—a family of five smiling for the
camera, wearing their best clothes, the children with wide
front teeth. Their smiles look too full, as if forced.

A woman moves toward the window and pulls the curtains shut. Her silhouette remains visible through the sheer
material. Someone approaches. They embrace. David—of
course it's David. I watched him walk into the apartment
building moments before. Putting the binoculars back in my
purse, I feel around for the rock I picked up a few days ago,
a chunk of loose asphalt, actually, and hold it in my hand,

feel the shape and size. Taking aim, I throw it with all my might, but it hits the side of the building and hurtles back down to earth. It was never going to reach its target anyway. I unlock the car, put the key in the ignition, and drive home.

My apartment feels bare. Snapping the TV on, I curl up on the couch and wait for darkness to descend. When nighttime comes, I curl up into a ball and lie in bed. This is where the pieces from the past come together, all the memories I've been fighting so hard to forget. I close my eyes and wait for the thumping, pounding, galloping. It's inevitable. Hundreds of ponies, they're coming for me, their beautiful chestnut manes blowing in the wind.

Again, I think of calling Jacob.

"Your mother went crazy," said Aunt Joan, squeezing her hand in between some rocks. Pulling out a shell, she removed some bits of seaweed from it and held it out for me to take. I reached for it, but the shell struck my fingertips and went flying into the air, hitting the rocks below.

"It's ruined," she said, looking down at it. "You've ruined it."

My throat hurt as if someone's thumb was pressed against my larynx, and I couldn't speak. I gazed at the broken shell and then at Aunt Joan. Neither one seemed to make any sense. Mumma ran away, took off one day and left Jacob and me all alone. No one knew where she went. In the beginning Daddy told us she'd died, but only because he didn't want to tell us the truth: she ran off and forgot all about us.

I had no idea why Aunt Joan was bringing Mumma up in the first place when I hadn't asked about her in weeks, and at a time when we were out searching the shore for shells;

not when we were in the kitchen together, her dough pan thumping against the table as she mixed a batch of bread. Her words sounded much different scattered on the ocean mist, the October leaves shimmering in the background, than they would have had they been contained inside her cramped little house filled with the smell of fresh-made bread and lobster.

I reached for the shell, but Aunt Joan told me to leave it be, the words shooting out of her mouth like sparks from a bonfire. I followed behind her, picking my way around the rocks and sand. There were lots of things I could have asked her about, questions that had been plaguing me since the day Mumma left, but I didn't know where to start. Several times in the past I'd mentioned Mumma, and each time she'd said, "Your mother left for greener pastures." Now suddenly she'd come up with this new story, but my heart said different. Aunt Joan was mistaken. I was the girl whose mother ran off one day, tired of being a mother and wife. I wasn't the girl whose mother went crazy. I just wasn't.

"How many do you need?" she asked, wrapping her fingers around a partly buried shell. She shook it gently and fine grains of sand trickled out the opening.

"Just a few," I whispered, although I no longer cared about having any.

"Here, hold it to your ear," she said. Obediently, I held it against the side of my head and waited.

"Can you hear the sea?"

I told her I could, but my hair was in the way and I couldn't hear a thing. Rubbing a small barnacle off the shell, I placed it in the wicker basket that was looped over my arm. A shell this size would make a good specimen for our school project. Ordinarily, I'd be happy about such a find.

A few more steps and she reached in between the rocks again, bringing out another shell, smaller than the first. Further inspection revealed a small hole on one side. She tossed it away.

"It was awful." At first, I thought she meant the shell. "Elizabeth frothing at the mouth and crawling in the dirt like an animal. She scratched your father. Dug her fingernails in deep...that was after your grandfather died."

The pink mark on Daddy's face had faded a few weeks ago. "A limb jumped up and bit me," he'd said when I asked what had happened.

Aunt Joan's face was long and drawn. There was something teetering on her trembling lips, unspoken words she seemed to be wrestling with. I'd spent enough days in her kitchen to know. There was always more she wanted to add.

I thought it must be the cold wind making her tremble, that it had nothing to do with what she was saying about Mumma, because *crazy* wasn't a word that would make someone tremble when spoken out loud, but an everyday word like *rock* or *sand* or *shell*. Except for the quivering in her lips, she'd made a quick recovery. Last week she'd spent in her bed with a rail-fence quilt pulled up around her neck, lamenting over Richard's sudden departure, until late Thursday afternoon when Uncle Dylan finally told her to stop it.

"Get yourself out of bed, Joan. The boy's not dead. He just wanted something else."

"That something else you're talking about," she croaked from the bedroom, "we could have given him that. If only he would have said something." She came out of her room then, her blue robe open at the waist, a too-thin cotton nightdress underneath. I could see her breasts beneath the fabric, two drooping shadows lying against her sunken chest. I wanted to laugh seeing her that way and suddenly thought of saying, "A pirate's delight...a sunken chest"—the same words Jeff Peterson said to Marjorie James one day, a girl in the tenth grade.

"Oh, Jewel, I didn't know you were here," she'd said, quickly pulling the robe shut, her eyes suddenly wide open at seeing me standing there. Her face was blotchy, her eyes and nose red and runny. The handkerchief she was clutching was twisted and wrinkled, both ends drooping out of her clenched fist. I looked quickly at the floor.

Her tears were nothing new to me. She was crying the day Mumma ran down to the shoreline after Jacob and me. Later, when I ran back into the house to get the drawing of Dusty, she was standing in the middle of the kitchen. I'd heard her wailing from outside seconds before I tripped the latch. She stopped when she saw me on the other side of the door.

"We're going home now," I mumbled, pulling the paper from the table. I could hardly wait to get away. The whole day had been ruined.

"It's best if you do," she sniffed. Her wailing picked up again as soon as I closed the door behind me.

The wind made a wild play, whipping up along the shoreline, and we stopped moving for a moment, waiting for it to subside. Branches of yellow leaves swayed playfully. And I wondered for a few moments what it must feel like to be a leaf ripped from a branch, fluttering against the breeze all alone without a thought or care in the world.

A small whirlwind picked up some bits of debris down on the beach, twirled it around, then relaxed. I wasn't sure if I was the only one who saw it. Normally, I would have said something to Aunt Joan, but not that day. Above us, a miniature gull shrieked out a chorus that dissolved into the clouds and fog. A cormorant stood on some rocks out in the water. Jacob and I would throw stones to make them fly, or else we'd chase them from the water, clapping our hands together and yelling. Aunt Joan would have thrown a fit if she ever saw us.

"Those poor, helpless creatures," she'd have said. We were always clever enough not to get caught.

A few weeks back, a seal washed ashore on the beach. It was close to death when Jacob and I found it. Jacob wanted to take it home and nurse it back to health. "We can keep it in the shed," he said.

"It's too far gone," I told him. "Besides, it would need water. Salt water. It belongs in the ocean." It had a glassy stare and a fly was sitting in the corner of one eye. It was barely breathing and was starting to smell. I hurried Jacob away. The next day gulls were swooping and landing on the sand.

"What are they doing?" he asked.

"I'm not sure," I told him. We didn't move closer and he didn't ask about the seal.

"Your father didn't want to send her away, but he had no choice in the matter. He couldn't have handled her, not in the state she was in. She was sick. Sometimes you've got to go forward in life without looking back. That's what your father did. We, Dylan and me, we told him he should."

"She'll get better," I said, patting Aunt Joan's hand. She shook her head and looked toward the water.

"I'm afraid not. There's no getting better. Not from that. Not for her. I saw her for myself, at the hospital. Your father and Dylan went too. I wouldn't have it said we didn't do all we could for her, because we did. I couldn't have lived with *that* on my conscience. Not that."

We continued to comb the beach, examining each item

we found before putting it in the basket—several more shells, a dead starfish, and a sea urchin. Two gulls landed on the beach not far from the water's edge, warning us not to come closer. I wanted to make my way onto the rocks and let the ocean rise around me, stranding me out in the middle of the water where no one could reach me. Let the water cover my head. Breathe. Once the water covered me, I'd take a deep breath.

Finally, Aunt Joan broke the silence. "Do we have enough? We can keep gathering if you want." I explained once more that we were only to bring in a few things. I'd been hoping to find something unique to take into school, something no one else would have.

"The sea urchin is different. The urchin will get you an A for sure." But there was to be no mark. It was for a display Miss Keddy was making called "The Bonnie, Bonnie Sea." We had driftwood and sand and small round rocks washed smooth by the sea; Miss Keddy said, in the beginning, to bring in only small rocks if we brought any rocks at all. There were three the size and shape of eggs in the display, ones Owen Burns brought in. The rocks seemed like a good thing for Owen to bring, simple and plentiful, requiring little work, and when Miss Keddy passed them around for us to hold I was sure I could feel some heat coming from them.

"See how the water has washed them smooth. Everything is made smooth by the motion of the sea," she said. It made me wonder if that was why Daddy had moved us down to the shore.

"I suppose I shouldn't be saying anything, since your mother and I didn't get along," said Aunt Joan, but it was too late for her to take back what she'd already said.

The wind pulled bits of her hair out from beneath her bandana and she yanked them from the corner of her mouth before speaking again. "But I want you to know, Jewel, that I tried. I tried as hard as I knew how to be your mother's friend, to treat her like family. And then the last time she was at the house—well, you remember that day, don't you?"

Of course I remembered. Mumma never went to their house after that. Whenever we went to visit, she'd stand by the kitchen window and watch us drive away. She'd say, "Have a good time," but she never came with.

"You're not supposed to know any of this," said Aunt Joan, walking up from the beach along the path that led straight to her kitchen door. "I wasn't to tell you…. And Jacob. Don't go telling Jacob any of this. He wouldn't know what it means, anyway. He's too young. Your father thinks you're too young, too. But he's a man. What does he know about girls? That's only for you and me to say."

Still nattering, she unlatched the door. "This is the last you'll hear of it from me," she said, shaking the sea mist out of her bandana and folding it up to fit in her pocket. I set the basket of shells on the kitchen table while Aunt Joan hung up her coat.

"It started back in April, you know that yourself. That's where it all started. Everything went downhill from there. But he's making some headway now, your father is. He seems happy for the first time in a long time. Have you noticed? I suppose she couldn't help herself," she added. "Your mother had her problems, that she did." She removed the shells from the basket, and then suddenly stopped. "Oh, I just wish she could have behaved herself, your mother. There are people who would have given anything to have what she had, anything. But some people are never satisfied. I guess your mother is just one of them."

"I don't think she could help it," I said, fighting the

urge to tell her to shut her mouth, that she had no right to be saying things about Mumma.

Taking a large shell from Aunt Joan's hands, I could see there was more she wanted to add. But she left all that was unsaid dangling like a pendulum back and forth, a slow tick-tock that droned on and on. The basket now empty, she put it back on the shelf in the hall closet and started rearranging the shells.

"We'll find a box for you to take them to school in. Just leave them here and I'll have them ready for you on Monday morning." She stopped me before I went out the door. I swung around. There was a pained look on her face. "Don't tell your father about any of this. If he asks, I'll lie. I'll say I never told you a thing."

Elizabeth

"See you later," the bus driver says. I don't turn my head or let on I've heard him. Stepping down off the bus, I look around for Missy's friend, the one who is supposed to pick us up. The sidewalk is empty. There's no one waiting at the bus stop. A part of me isn't surprised. Nothing seems to go as planned. My scalp tingles as if something is crawling through my hair, but it could just be the cold air. In my hurry to get going, I forgot to put my cap on this morning. I rarely go anywhere without it this late in the year. I wonder suddenly if Missy made it all up, that perhaps there's not a living soul waiting to pick us up and this was simply a ruse to get away from Harmony House, away from the rumours that were going around about her, with someone else paying her way. But that doesn't make any sense. Mrs. Weaver said the other day that what had happened at the community centre was a grave misunderstanding, even though it was agreed that Missy won't be going to help out at the centre anymore. The whisperings have all but stopped. Soon there will be something new to grab everyone's attention—some tragedy in the news or some new scheme the government has concocted that has everyone up in arms.

"Where's your friend?" I say, looking up and down the sidewalk. A young mother pushing a baby carriage is heading our way, behind them a group of seniors out for their daily stroll, but no signs of this Joey person. We could be stuck here in a strange town with nowhere to go, not that Missy would be overly concerned. She adapts to her environment like a chameleon, shifting and changing as need be, never worrying about a thing.

"There he is. Hey, Joey! Over here!" Missy gives a big wave as she calls out to him. "I told you he was coming," she hisses and I'm almost certain that it's relief I see sweep across her face. A man swaggers down the opposite side of the street. Head high in the air, he enters the intersection without even waiting for the walking sign to light up. I know it's this Joey that Missy knows. A car approaches, slows, blows its horn, but he keeps on walking. He looks like the cat that swallowed the canary, big smile that he has on his face. Lean muscle bulges beneath the T-shirt he's wearing, and I can't imagine how he can bear this cold November air without a jacket. There's a wave in his hair, the sides cut short, and I can't tell his age from this distance. When the gap between us lessens, I see the grey streaks near his temple—that, and a small tear at the shoulder of his white T-shirt. He's not at all what I was expecting, although I'm not sure what I *was* expecting. Pulling Missy toward him, he kisses her on the lips and I wonder if they're ever going to stop. He tells Missy he's missed her, and she hugs him like he's an overstuffed teddy bear.

"Still the hot little number I remember," he says, grabbing her rear end. Missy squeals and moves with tiny little steps, pretending she wants to escape his grasp. My face warms. I look away. I don't want Missy to catch me staring. I can imagine there are enough people on the street doing that already. Missy hooks her arm in his. I sometimes wish she'd give a damn what the rest of the world thinks.

"Come on, my place isn't far," he says. They turn and start down the sidewalk. They're walking away as if I'm not even there, as if I don't belong in this picture at all. I'm invisible. Nonexistent. Imaginary. The wind blows through me. It was a mistake to get on the bus. Mrs. Weaver will be so disappointed in me. I stifle a cry and shove down the fear. It pushes against me, rising. Again, I push it back down. If I had a nerve pill, I'd take it. Maybe even two. Yes, I'd definitely take two.

"What are you standing back there for? Aren't you coming?" Missy is turned toward me. My heart makes a leap. Hugging my handbag, I hurry to catch up. Missy's laughter spirals back at me like a whirlwind of dust. My knees tremble, but I force them to keep moving. *Step on a crack, break your mother's back.* The sidewalk is littered with cracks and I step over each one. Missy and Joey walk on through. I don't know why that silly little rhyme has me dodging the fractured concrete at my age.

Because your back is near broken already. The words come from out of nowhere like a birdsong on a ribbon of breeze. I flinch and step quickly along.

"I am well now," I whisper, taking a deep breath.

I hold my head up high.

Jewel

Yesterday, I ran into David coming out of the little coffee shop he and I used to go to all the time. His companion was a tall brunette, gorgeous in a way I will never be. They were laughing and being silly. The peculiar look that sometimes crosses David's face was there until he looked up and saw me coming through the doorway. I stopped momentarily. He nodded. His name caught in my throat. I wasn't sure what was expected of me. He mumbled my name and smiled, holding the door open for me to pass through. When I let out a small laugh, he seemed relieved.

I never expected he'd bring her to Julie's—the place we'd met.

The next morning, I awoke expecting to hear Mumma moving about downstairs, but the house was quiet, silent like when you're lying awake at night and you're sure you're the only one in the house. Once again, it took me a while to figure out where I was. It came to me like a slap of salt water against the shoreline rocks. I wasn't home in the Forties Settlement but in a little house down by the shore, across the hall from a room that now rumbled with the sound of Daddy snoring, in a room with white curtains and pink walls that made me sad the first time I saw it, even though Aunt Joan said it was a lovely little room for a girl my age. "It's like it was made just for you," she said when we moved my things in. I stood with a bag of clothes in my arms, wanting to scatter them all about, trample them into the floor to prove how wrong she was about the lovely little room down by the ocean.

I reached beneath my pillow for Mumma's wedding band.

"Here it is, Mumma, I've got your ring. I knew you'd come back for it. I knew you would." Mumma smiles and slips the ring on her finger, holds her hand out and admires it. "You found it," she says. "After all this time, you still have it."

I put the ring back under my pillow. Mumma was crazy, locked away where she couldn't get out. She'd never have the ring. I turned over in bed, the secret gnawing away at me. It nibbled on my fingers and chewed at my toes. I longed to tell someone that Mumma went crazy, hoping the monster wouldn't be so big if I spoke the words out loud, but Aunt Joan wouldn't let me.

The spoon slapped against the green ceramic bowl. The cake batter was runny and yellow, smelling of lemon. I counted the strokes, taking comfort as the number climbed higher and higher. When Aunt Joan stopped abruptly, the rhythm I'd found dissolved, and I was suddenly afraid of the thoughts that might take its place. I'd rather be counting. Counting covered things up. Counting stopped me from thinking. It put a large hole in the place where any thought should be and let me forget. *Your mother went crazy.*

"Your mother was a selfish one, always thinking of herself, especially near the end." There were small beads of perspiration beneath Aunt Joan's nose. I glanced down at Jacob. He was pushing his little cars across Aunt Joan's kitchen floor and making noises. "Brim brim...brim...brim."

Last night Daddy pulled three dinky cars out of a brown bag and a card with three sets of barrettes with tiny hair ribbons attached to it—pink, gold, and purple. Jacob grabbed the dinkies and tore off for the living room to play. Aunt Joan combed my hair and put the pink barrettes in place.

"You look like your mother," she said as if she'd made some startling discovery. "She looks like Elizabeth. Doesn't she, Cliff?" I ripped the barrettes out of my hair and flung them to the floor.

"Come back," Aunt Joan had called out. "Come back here at once. I didn't say nothing wrong. Nothing at all."

"You must have seen that yourself," continued Aunt Joan now, breathless as if she were forcing her arm to keep moving and could barely keep up, "some of her odd behaviour over the years, I mean."

I wouldn't have thought it was such hard work, beating cake batter.

"I don't think she could help herself. There are people like that, you know. They mean to be like the rest of us, but they can't stop themselves from being selfish. Like I already said, she was selfish, your mother was, always keeping our lives in an uproar. And secretive. She never told us the things she should have." She began beating the batter again, then stopped suddenly and looked at me. "I'm not saying any of this in a judgemental way. We all have our little ways about us. I used to try and talk some sense into her, but you can't make people see what they don't want to look at."

She added some flour and beat the batter a little more. "Your father's a good man, Jewel. Better than any I've known. To put up with your mother's shenanigans over the years and never once go complaining to the neighbours about her. Most men would have, you know. True blue, your father is...But that could be his undoing. It could, really. It could, and then where would you and Jacob be? Where then?" She clicked her tongue several times. "He's one of a kind, your father is. One of a kind."

More milk went into the bowl and she pulled her arm across her forehead, removing the strands of hair that had fallen down across her eyes.

"You're fortunate to have your father," she continued. "He's done a lot for you and Jacob—a lot. I dare say more than most men in his situation would have. Lord knows your mother never made his job easy. She fought him every step of the way. You must have seen things," she repeated.

"She burned one of my boots in the wood stove once... and she threw the clock and scared Jacob. Sometimes she'd just stare off into space." It all came bursting out of me like a flurry of snowflakes. Having held the words in for so long, once I opened my mouth I couldn't stop them from spitting out.

Aunt Joan shook her head and made more clicking sounds with her tongue.

"A mother should put her children first. That's what I did with Richard, even when common sense told me not to. He was a troublesome boy. But at least I can go to my grave knowing I did everything I could for him." She stared down into the cake batter, and when she looked up at me there were tears in her eyes. She wiped them away with the back of her hand and said, "I wonder if your mother could say the same. I wonder."

"Richard should have stayed...to help Uncle Dylan. And for you," I said in agreement. Some days she still cried over his leaving. A few weeks back she got a postcard in the mail from some place in Ontario.

"Here," she said with a faint smile. "Line the cake pan, if you don't mind. Take your time and do a good job."

I fumbled with the waxed paper, creasing it in a few places, but finally managed to get it inside the pan in a fashion that I hoped would satisfy her.

"Didn't your mother ever teach you to line a cake pan?" she said, looking down at what I'd done.

"Mumma said I was too clumsy."

"And a darn shame that was. A darn shame. I never would have. I never would have said such a thing. If you had been mine." She stopped abruptly, shaking her head. "I was asked to take you. After Jacob was born and your mother was sent to Roseland—both of you. Your father thought he couldn't manage. But then he had someone come in—through the day, he did. I had to say no. Richard was barely twelve. My hands were full with him. Besides, I told your father it wouldn't be right. You needed to be home. For when Elizabeth came back."

Adding some more flour into the batter, she began beating the cake again. I no longer felt like counting the strokes, so I watched the spoon move back and forth from one side of the bowl to the other.

"Mothers should teach those kinds of things to their children—the girls especially. Boys follow their fathers. But the girls need to be prepared for the day when they're keeping their own house. Soon enough you'll be grown and gone. But I'll show you. I'll do as much as I can." Her smile was weak and filled with pity.

"She threw rocks at Sandra Peterson's house one time," I said, feeling a sudden need to get back at Mumma for not doing all those things that mothers were supposed to do.

Aunt Joan stopped beating the batter and wiped her hands on her apron. "Sandra Peterson? Of all the things. She was that woman at Everett's funeral. Well, nothing would surprise me now.... Rocks, you say? When did she do this?"

"A long time ago. No one knew. Well, I knew, but no one else. No one else knew but me." I stumbled over the words. I had no idea why I was telling this to Aunt Joan when I'd helped Mumma throw the rocks at their house.

"Did she say why she did it?" said Aunt Joan. "I mean, Sandra Peterson is a neighbour. Didn't she keep house for Everett at one time?" She poured the batter into the pan and smoothed it with the back of her spoon.

"Her son, Jeff, took the pencil box Poppy made me and I think maybe Mumma got mad about that."

"You see? Right there is a prime example of the way she overreacted to things," said Aunt Joan, tapping her pointer finger on the table. "She led a tormented life, your mother did, a tormented life. And people who lead tormented lives drag down everyone around them.

"She's where she belongs now, your mother is, and that's all any of us can hope and pray for." She walked across the kitchen with the cake pan in her hands. "It's for her own good and everyone around her. It's one of those sacrifices people make through life. We let go of the ones we love when it's for their own good. That's what love is." She reached for the oven door. "One day, God willing, she'll see that we're all accountable for our actions. You can't go around throwing rocks at people's houses or burning your daughter's boots and expect there to be no price to pay. Your mother set the dye years ago and when you do that you've got to live with the consequences." She looked back at me and shook her head before putting the cake in the oven. "It's not your fault. None of it is your fault...or anyone's. She made your father's life miserable. I don't know why, but she did. Maybe she didn't mean to, but that doesn't change anything, now does it? But at least now he's getting some peace, your father is. At least now he is." She turned back toward me with a look of satisfaction.

Some weeks later Aunt Joan came to me. She made me sit at the table and told me she had something important to say. Her hands were folded in her lap and I watched the way she moved her thumbs, like a fly on the wall rubbing its back legs together. Her lip gave a sudden twitch and then she started in.

"We're going to see your mother again tomorrow," she said as she continued to rub her thumbs back and forth. "Your father wants to see one more time if he made the right decision—the right decision for everyone, that is. She was so sick the last time we went. They had to run electricity through her brain. I don't think they know how to make her well, to tell the truth." She was shaking her head as she spoke. "Your father would keep on waiting for her to get better if he thought there was any hope. I know your father. He's loyal to the core. He's given up so much...and he'll keep right on if we don't stop him. He'll run himself right into the ground and make himself sick doing it. Then you'll have no one. Just Dylan and me." She didn't say anything for a time. "But I've been thinking, Jewel." She leaned in close to me and spoke quietly. "If you were to tell him it was okay, that he didn't have to wait for her, I know he'd listen.

It's up to you, Jewel. Really, it's all up to you. Just say the word and I'll make it all right. I'll tell him you said it's all right to let her go."

Elizabeth

"Nothing ventured, nothing gained," says the nurse, gazing down at me with an eager look on her face. She might as well be showing me an alien instead of the writing tablet and pen. Her one eye goes off in the wrong direction when she looks at you. She's forever smiling, even when there's nothing to smile about. I can never tell if she's smiling at me or the person next to me. Some of the patients call her nasty names behind her back, saying things like she'd have to lie on her back to look down a well.

"Write them a letter. Why spend your time wondering where they are?" she says, and it makes perfect sense. Except that the pen is a foreign object in my hand, the writing tablet a terrifying bit of paper and lines the moment I try to gather my thoughts together. Still, I'm determined to get to the bottom of it, find out once and for all where they went. I have to make it official, a real letter, not a sloppy note jotted down in a hurry.

"What's the date?" I ask the nurse, and then I write down *September 16th, 1968,* right under the place where I've written *Divinity Hospital,* because with all the memories I've lost along the way, the most useless ones, like the proper way to write a letter, remain with me.

Dear Jewel and Jacob,

I stop, wondering what to write next. How best to make them want me back? If I write all the wrong things, they might rip up the letter without giving me a second chance. They left me to fend for myself, so it is not such a far-fetched idea. Fear stops the line of ink from flowing and I nearly rip the paper in two. What if I did something horrible to them in the past? And what do you say to the children whose faces you can't quite remember? And how do you tell them where you've been and what you've done when you don't know the answers to any of those questions yourself?

"I hope you are fine," the nurse says, smiling and nodding as she stands over me. I grab the pen and begin writing. The rest of the letter is a blur, a jumble of disconnected words that slip off the page the moment I write them. My hand shakes. I can't be sure they'll remember me, as fickle as children can be. But at least with the nurse helping, the letter will sound right, without a single word out of place. I insist she address the envelope. I'd only make a mess of it. With no lines to follow, it would look like a child wrote it.

"If there's anyone living in the Forties Settlement by that name, it'll reach them," the nurse says, licking the stamp. She puts it in the corner of the envelope, and my heart makes a slight hiccough. It's too late to take any of it back now. I'll find out the truth once and for all.

I wait weeks for the mail delivery, looking up each day when the parcels and letters are brought in, feigning disinterest, afraid to even hope something might come for me.

Not many letters arrive each day, but when they do there's a buzz of excitement as someone's name is called out and they're presented with an envelope or parcel.

When something finally comes for me, I tear it open and eagerly start reading.

Dear Jewel and Jacob, I hope you are fine.

There is something wrong. The writing looks oddly familiar. I flip over the envelope and my heart sinks. *Return to sender* is written on the envelope in bold letters. My one chance is gone. What little bit of hope I had of finding them has vanished. The nurse said I had nothing to lose by sending the letter. But she was wrong. I'm now left to wonder if I fabricated them in my mind, conjured them from out of the fog that feasts daily on my brain. If the returned letter proves anything at all, perhaps it is that. What if they're not even real?

In the days that follow, the darkness creeps up behind me, tiny steps so as not to be noticed by anyone but me.

It was always there.

It never left.

Now it's closer.

I thought perhaps there was something to be happy about, something to look forward to.

But there is nothing.

I'm nothing and no one, wrapped up in a tight little knot that's impossible to loosen.

But at least now I know.

I hope the two flights of rickety steps we're climbing, and the blistered paint, are no indication of what's waiting for us behind the door. Joey jingles a set of keys, takes them out of his pocket like a magician pulling off a magic trick.

I check my watch; 11:51. They're sitting down for lunch at Harmony House. They're about to discover that Missy and I aren't there. I try to picture the look on Mrs. Weaver's face, the disappointment in her eyes. She's always expected so much from me; too much, perhaps.

"I cleaned things up when you said you were coming," says Joey, pushing the key into the lock and twisting. The smell of stale cigarettes streams past us when the door opens. The kitchen and living room are joined together and visible at a glance. To the right, a door is opened and I can see a tangle of green and purple, a bedspread perhaps. Another door, which is closed, must be the bathroom. A coffee cup and dirty ashtray sit on a small table beside the orange flowered couch. A few magazines lie scattered on the floor. Other than that, the apartment is reasonably neat. Missy walks in like she's been here a hundred times before. Setting her purse on the table, she goes for the cupboards as if the apartment is hers.

"Where's your coffee? I'm dying for a cup." The cupboard doors thump softly as they are opened and closed. First one, then the other. She goes to the next set. This time her hand is wrapped around a jar. Joey plugs in the kettle and takes two mugs down from the cupboard. I stand in front of the living room window and look out at the street. Dried leaves blow along the edge of the road, finding a final resting spot along the curb. Brown stems stick out of the giant planters positioned along the street. I wonder if coming here was a wise decision. All these years the past has watched me from a distance, through a fog that I could never quite reach, but is it a past that I should go looking for or one that I should just leave be? There could be things there that I'm not prepared for, the reason I was left behind being one of them. Why *did* they leave me, the ones who were supposed to love me, the family who never once came? It could be that I was unlovable, a cold, vile person without a soft bone in my body. Or I might have been forgettable, as bland as mashed potatoes without a dash of salt or pepper.

"How about you? Do you want one, too?" Joey says, spooning coffee into the mugs. I should have waited until he poured the water before telling him I don't drink coffee. He laughs likes it's the funniest thing he's ever heard. Hot water splashes. I'd better not get the blame if he scalds himself.

"Who doesn't drink coffee?" Looking over at Missy, he says, "Your friend's a real hoot, Missy."

Missy gives me a look, shrugs, and takes a sip from her cup. "Don't mind her. She's just a little off," she says, twirling her finger next to the side of her head and rolling her eyes.

"I guess we're all a little crazy by times," says Joey, giving me a strange look. I wish I was like that woman I saw on TV one time who knew what people were thinking without them saying a word. But just as quickly, I'm glad I'm not her. Strange looks have a language all of their own. I really don't care to know what's going through Joey's mind at the moment.

"What have you got to eat in this joint?" Missy goes for the refrigerator and pulls on the door. She bends in to take a look, peering inside. "I'm starving."

"There's some bologna in there. Make yourself a sandwich. How about you? Are you hungry?" It takes me a second to realize he's talking to me. My first instinct is to say that I'm not hungry, but then I think better of that. I haven't had anything since seven this morning, and it's difficult to say how long it will take us to drive out to the Forties Settlement and back. And there's still the bus ride back to Harmony House later this evening. No one should wait that long to eat.

I end up making sandwiches for all of us while Joey and Missy watch some race-car show on television. So much for the lunch Joey promised. Missy doesn't seem to take notice. Her eyes are glued on Joey, who is cheering for his favourite driver and cursing the ones he doesn't like. Missy is calling out for number 23 to "get the lead out." I've never understood the appeal of watching cars racing around a track, crashing into one another, people risking their lives, going around and around. And the noise. I've never understood the noise.

We don't sit at the table to eat. Joey and Missy are on the couch, while I take the armchair. Sitting on the edge of my seat, I bite into the sandwich, careful not to lose any crumbs on the floor. I'm sometimes messy, especially when I'm nervous, like now. The race cars continue to make an ungodly sound as they tear around the track, almost drowning out the noise that is now coming from next door; shouting and cursing and screaming.

"Gerry probably forgot to come home last night. His old lady gets pretty sore sometimes," Joey says, smiling. "Just bang on the wall. That'll quiet them down."

The wall banging isn't necessary; the shouting stops as quickly as it began, followed by the loud slamming of a door. Joey looks up with a mouth full of bologna and asks what my name is. I only give him my first name. The less he knows, the better.

He laughs and says, "Elizabeth…. You mean like the queen?" I don't say anything. I'm not sure what he means. "You know, the Queen of England. Isn't her name Elizabeth?"

"I suppose it is," I finally say, although I fail to see the connection. Elizabeth is a fairly common name, and I'm nothing like the Queen of England, nothing.

Missy laughs and takes another sip of coffee.

"Don't mind her. She's got no sense of humour." Her comment momentarily dazzles me. My humour is as good as the next person's, but I don't speak up and say as much. I've too much to lose if I end up getting under her skin. Missy is like a cat, always waiting to pounce. She could kick me out and tell me to find my own way back to Harmony House. There's no way I could figure out the buses by myself. I wouldn't know where to start or what to do. I'd have to ask for help, but who would I ask?

I was hoping a bus might travel to the Forties Settlement, but it wasn't on any bus route when we looked. That's when Missy suggested her friend Joey. I couldn't see any other choice. If I want to go back to where my life fell apart, this is my best chance, and no doubt my very last chance. I take another bite of my sandwich. Best chances don't come along very often.

Joey says he wants to call me Liz. "I like that better than Elizabeth. Elizabeth sounds like a snooty name. You don't mind, do you?" And of course I mind, but I'm not going to say. No one calls me Liz. No one. I shift in the chair. It's difficult to sit still with the cars racing and Joey wolfing down his food, and calling me Liz with a ball of chewed-up bologna in his mouth. My mind is on the Forties Settlement, when we'll be leaving, and just what I'll remember once I get there. *Will I recognize the house I lived in? And will it still be standing?* It might have fallen down or burned to the ground for all I know. I've tried to imagine what colour it was, but you can't squeeze blood from a turnip, as Mrs. Zimmer likes to say. Then there's the nagging question that won't leave me be: *what if this life you've imagined isn't real—not one bit of it?*

I snatch up the plates and coffee cups as soon as they're empty. Putting them in the sink, I start running the water.

Joey and Missy are cuddling on the couch. They don't even know I'm there. I can't stop wondering when we're going to leave. It's not something I can bring up since I just met Joey a little over an hour ago. If I can get Missy alone, I'll tell her—no, ask her—to find out. The bus going back to Harmony House leaves at 6:30. Already it is past 1 in the afternoon.

From the kitchen window I can see into the neighbour's backyard. A small red tricycle is lying on its side and several bright yellow trucks are in a sandbox. An empty swing twists and turns in the wind, waiting for a child's weight to steady it. In the clouds, gigantic hands are reaching out to grab, then they slowly change into something I don't recognize. When I hear a door shut I turn back toward the living room. Missy's sitting on the couch by herself.

"Where'd he go?"

"Work. He's on the afternoon shift."

"Afternoon shift! But you said—"

"Yeah, well, do you expect him to miss work to drive some stranger around? You may as well watch something on TV. Joey doesn't get home until after ten."

"After ten? But it'll be too late then!"

She takes a small bottle out of her purse. "Here, take one of these." Pinching a pill between her fingers, she places it carefully in the palm of her hand.

I stare down at the pill, fighting the urge to snap it up. "It's just a nerve pill. Stop worrying. I save them up when the cart comes along. You know, '*Do you need one?*' Well, some days you don't, but I take them anyway. You never know. They won't give them to you when you really need them, only when they say so."

I take it because I know Missy's right and it's just a nerve pill, something I've taken countless times before.

"We'll figure things out in the morning. Now, loosen up."

"In the morning? But Mrs. Weaver.... We were supposed to take the evening bus back home. It's what we talked about, not spending the night away from Harmony House."

"Yeah, well, plans get changed so get used to it. At least I got you this far," she says, twisting a lock of hair around her finger the way she does. "That's more than you could have done on your own."

I hate it whenever Missy starts acting too big for her britches. I should tell her to go take a hike, that I'll find my own way to the bus stop. That would show her. But then I quickly wonder—how? I don't know this town at all, I can't even remember where the bus stop is. *Did we turn left or right when we came to Joey's apartment?* I was watching the cracks in the pavement, not the street signs. My heart starts telling me it's no use. *You can't go out roaming the streets on your own.* Locating the bus stop would be like finding a needle in a haystack. I have no sense of direction at all, even Rebecca jokes and tells me that. I'll have to stay where I am. I have no choice. My heart pushes against my eardrums. Wush...wush...wush...wush. I'm not sure the pill I took is going to help.

"Look, forget that old bag. What's she going to do, anyway? She doesn't even know where we are." The reality of what she's just said hits me. This was a mistake, a big, big mistake. I was a fool to listen to Missy, to think I could get away with something so irresponsible. My past is a lost cause. I've always known that. Regardless of any lame attempts I might make to get it back, it will always remain lost.

"We should have asked for permission." My words feel as though they will crumble on my lips. My chest is tight. I try to slow my breathing.

Breathe in, breathe out. Slow. Slow.

"Permission to do what? Come here to Joey's apartment? Are you nuts? Do you really think she would have agreed to that?" Missy takes out her cigarettes and opens the package. I know she's right. The last place Mrs. Weaver would let us go would be some man's apartment in another town. Annie visits her sister, but that's totally different. And she always has permission to go. She signs out. Mrs. Weaver knows where she is. I was such a fool to think this would work out, that I'd get a ride out to the Forties Settlement and something would jar my memory back in its place.

"Calm down, why don't you? Everything's going to be fine. You're too uptight, that's all." Missy taps the end of the cigarette against the package. Reaching into the pocket of her jeans, she takes out a lighter. Once again, I hope the nerve pill soon kicks in. I'm not sure how much more of this I can stand. And now there are my other pills back at Harmony House—two a day. It's always two a day. Has been for a very long time. I expected to be back long before morning came, and certainly before bedtime. My pills. How will I make it without them?

I walk out to the kitchen and go to the window, looking but not seeing, seeing but not looking. My feet want to move; back and forth, back and forth. The smell of cigarette smoke reaches me. Mrs. Weaver will be angry, disappointed that I got myself into this mess. Not to mention Mrs. Zimmer. Mrs. Zimmer will call me a simpleton again.

Of all the fool things, she'll say. Sophie will look at me and make tutting sounds. And the talk will be all over Harmony House. I'll be a laughingstock.

I sit in one of the kitchen chairs. My legs and arms are buzzing like something is crawling beneath my skin. It's 2:47. I'd be doing something at 2:47 back at Harmony

House, but I can't think what. I jump up and walk the floor. This is all wrong.

My notebook. I go for my purse.

"Just calm down," says Missy. A smoke ring hovers above her head like a ghost in the air. "No need to have a hissy fit." I fasten my purse. It's best if I don't take the notebook out. Missy might take it from me and snoop through it. I go back to the window, watch the clouds shifting, the swing moving in the wind. Biting my lip, I close my eyes. There is nothing to do but wait. For what, I'm not sure.

Missy's laughter is the only sound in the apartment aside from the kitchen clock hammering out a steady tick, tick, tick. When Joey got home from work, he pulled a grey army blanket out of the hall closet.

"Don't let the bedbugs bite," he said, handing it to me. He tossed a pillow onto the couch. "That should do you."

The couch is lumpy and I'm not sure if I should lie on my back or my side, and if my side, which side. The couch squeaks as I roll over. It's too narrow. My neck and face itch. The blanket Joey gave me reeks. I hope my clothes don't end up smelling like cigarette smoke as I pull the blanket around me. I don't think I've ever slept in my clothes, but I'm not about to take them off. Humming softly, I try to block out the muffled sounds coming from behind the bedroom door. It works for me when Mrs. Zimmer is snoring.

It's 10:36. Mrs. Zimmer has been asleep for the last two hours—yes, two hours, maybe more. The lights in the hallway at Harmony House have been dimmed. I'd be writing a few things in my notebook before bedtime if I were there, squinting in the dim light from the lamp on my nightstand. Mrs. Weaver is likely beside herself by now, concerned but

247

not wanting to raise any alarms just yet because it would only cause a kerfuffle all through Harmony House. And a kerfuffle that spreads will ooze into every crack and corner until it eventually takes over and everyone ends up affected—the residents and the staff. If Mrs. Weaver knew what Joey and Missy were doing right now, she'd be having a conniption fit. And there's not a thing I can do about that. I'm not her mother. I am *not* her mother.

"They're not hurting anyone," someone says.

"Who said that?" I whisper, looking around. But there's no one else in the living room. I'm the only one. I gasp and pull the blanket tighter, go back to what I was thinking before. My notebook with all my words. I'd be writing in it if I were back at Harmony House. I rub my face and turn over a few more times. Finally, throwing back the blanket, I get up off the couch. My legs and arms need movement. My scalp tingles. Goosebumps climb my arms. I shiver. Moonlight stretches out across the living room floor; a rectangle of silver shines on the wall. I sidle into the moonlight, careful of my movements. Movement is important and not something I can hurry into without shaking the delicate balance of darkness and light. Moonbeams cascade over me like a flowing fountain, lighting up my face, bathing me in their gentle glow. I can taste the full moon. For a time, I smile—face lifted toward the ceiling—and forget my present predicament.

When Missy's muffled laughter reaches my ears again, I hurry out of the moonlight and head toward the kitchen window. There's music in my head, a song I don't recognize yet wish I did. It might be coming from outside, the squeaking of the swing as it twirls in the wind. But the swing isn't moving. It's draped in moonlight and as still as a whisper in the middle of the night. I move away from the window.

Anyone on the outside could see me, and I'm not supposed to be here in this apartment that belongs to some strange man in a town I've never been to before. They might be looking for me—Mrs. Weaver, that is. I don't know who else would be looking. My arms are cold and I rub them. I need my pill. I'm never without it. Morning and night. Like clockwork. For years now. I can't be without it. I rub my arms.

I walk back to the couch. Flip through Joey's collection of magazines. Race cars, all of them, so I put them back. I scratch my head. The itching won't stop. Bedbugs or head lice. They could be living in the couch. I want sleep. Even a few hours. I'd settle for that. Something to make time pass before morning comes. But I don't even have a bedtime pill to help me sleep. If ever I needed one, it's now. The clock won't stop making a racket. Mrs. Weaver must be worried about us. We didn't sign out today. We slipped out and didn't look back.

The itching won't stop.

It must be the blanket.

Or the couch.

It could be both.

There would be too many questions asked if we sign out, Missy said.

"*They won't even know we're gone. We'll be back before you know it.*"

And I went along with it.

I scratch my head. The lice are crawling. The bedbugs calling, "*Elizabeth! Elizabeth!*"

"*The old bag will growl, but she's not going to send us packing. We got no other place to go. Besides, she deals with this stuff all the time. You're the only one who never makes any trouble. You never make waves. You're the good one.*"

"I am? I'm the good one?"

"A goody two-shoes. Perfect Elizabeth."

I'm talking out loud again, pulling Missy's words out of thin air, and I need to stop.

The moon lights up the apartment so the dark doesn't matter. With the living room curtains pulled open, it finds a way in. I could close the curtains completely, but I won't. There's nothing wrong with a little light in the middle of the darkness. I look through the cupboard, the drawers, the closet. Quiet, so as not to make any noise. There's nothing interesting in any of these places. I sweep the floor with the broom that's in the closet. I push the dirt under the couch when I can't find a dustpan. Organize things on the counter. Rearrange them. The toaster oven and the jar of coffee; the set of canisters with beige mushrooms and bright orange caps. Quiet. I need to keep quiet so that Missy and Joey don't hear. I wipe the counter down like I do at the community centre each Friday.

I go back and straighten the items in the drawers. The night will be long; a pause of infinite moments all stacked one on top of the other. It could go on forever if I just wait in the silence. The night might never stop. But I want daylight to come, so I keep moving. Joey promised to drive me to the Forties Settlement tomorrow. I stood beside Missy while she asked, my hands fidgeting.

"You can count on it, Liz," he said with a wink. And I *am* counting on it. I took his words, his promise, and laced it between my fingers, pulled it tight so it wouldn't slip away. It's the only thing I have to hold onto, the only thing that stopped the trembling in my hands.

I crawl back into the small rectangle of light shining onto the living room wall, crouch down close to the floor so that I'm totally engulfed by the moonlight.

"I am well," I whisper as I wait for the pink dawn to find me.

"I am well now."

Elizabeth

Sometimes I think it's Cliff's voice I hear; other times I think it's merely an echo, left over from the days when I lived in the Forties Settlement. There were forty lots, you see, of a hundred acres each, back when the land was being settled. It was a place filled with fairies and nymphs who wandered about the woods. They came out at night to play tricks on the people. I was told this in a story a long time ago, but so much of it comes filtered through darkness and shadow; whispered rememberings from a place so far away I can scarcely bring it in close enough to see. The memories are weak, fragile as the thoughts that enter my head, and don't often stay for very long. Perhaps I didn't pay close attention to the stories when they were being told. Maybe even then I knew I wouldn't be staying in the Forties Settlement forever.

Some people belong to a place and time along with every cloud and bit of the greenery in their world. They fit in as if they have always been there, as if they couldn't exist without that place and that place couldn't exist without them. They blend in like the sweet scent of apple blossoms on a spring afternoon with a breeze pushing them along; the sun forever shining on their face. I've never belonged to a place or a time, never set down any roots, never felt content. Never. Ever. Never. And for the life of me, I can't explain why I have these feelings or where they come from. Perhaps some deep, dark place in my mind that only allows in a little light at a time. Mrs. Weaver might have the answer to my questions, but there's no possible way I could bring the subject up. She's told me she's glad that I'm happy these days, so what else is there for me to say? She doesn't believe in digging up all the bones we've buried or questioning the past when the present is all that really matters. In some ways I believe she's right. There was a time when I wouldn't have, but all that has now changed. Still, I want to get all my facts straight. Iron out the bits and pieces of what my life once was. It will be important. When I meet Jacob and Jewel for the first time, they'll expect me to know certain things. I can tell them about Dartmouth and Divinity and my longing to be near them and the times no one would listen to what I had to say. Other than that, I have very little to offer.

The dawn is grey, heavy and dark. All night long I waited for the dawn to come, biting down hard to keep the mind-chatter from spilling out onto my lips. When darkness comes, my mind meanders without my bedtime pill. Last night I imagined all the things that Mrs. Weaver would be saying and doing. Each thought ended with Mrs. Weaver being furious with me. Certain rules at Harmony House have been in place ever since she was put in charge. She will have to go to the authorities if we don't soon come back.

We've left her little choice. Even Mrs. Weaver must answer to someone. I should have known better. Last night, my thoughts pitched fear deep into my chest, heaving it into a mound so high and dark I feared I'd never climb over it. That darkness was familiar. It knew me and I knew it, but I pretended otherwise in case I might be invited to stay. I knew I couldn't stay. I have places to go.

And then I wasn't sure which words were thoughts and which were spoken. I couldn't have Joey and Missy hear me, so I chewed at my lip until morning. Now it's sore and raw. I moved back to the couch sometime in the middle of the night and curled into a tight ball for warmth. Earlier Joey had complained that his landlord hadn't put the heat on yet. "It's cold enough for it," he'd said. "Not that *he'd* give a good goddamn, the cheapskate."

It doesn't feel as though I've slept a wink, although I might have drifted off toward morning. When the dawn brought a sky layered with thick grey streaks, hope slipped from my fingers. It sank like a stone in water. Eyes set on the window above the kitchen sink, I didn't want to admit what it might mean. I wondered if the sky could have a sudden change of heart, take pity on me in my weakness, give in and let me have my way as I waited for the pink dawn that never came.

The bedroom door opens and I jump to my feet. I don't know what to do with my arms, leave them by my side or cross them in front of me. I shouldn't have jumped up when I did. Now I'm forced to stand, awkwardly wondering which way to turn. Joey goes straight for the kitchen. He reaches for the instant coffee. It's not where he left it, but he doesn't seem to notice. It blends together, each piece on the counter exactly where I placed it. Perfect. Even though no one will notice. But *I* notice, and that should count for something.

"Did you sleep good?" says Joey, plugging in the kettle. "Fine," I say. "I slept fine." But he doesn't let on he hears.

It's 7:21. The breakfast sausage and toast Jenny cooked are gone by now. The hardboiled eggs, too. Cold cereal for those who can't eat the fat in a hot breakfast. Mrs. Zimmer is reporting to everyone that my bed hasn't been slept in. "*Simpleton,*" she's saying while shoving a whole sausage into her mouth and clamping her teeth down, "*she's nothing but a simpleton, taking off like that. Where does she expect to go, the one who can't get out of her own way most days?*" Whisperings will be circulating about the dining room as they realize that Missy didn't come home last night either. Some of them might think Missy forced me to go with her. And the speculations will go on during the day. Mrs. Weaver is not answering their questions. She's deciding what to do. Calculating her options. Harmony House is in the midst of a kerfuffle, one that I've created with my absence. A day ago, no one would ever have imagined this could happen, least of all me.

When Joey brings his coffee out to the living room and snaps on the TV, I head for the bathroom. I don't know what to say to him without Missy here. When someone is doing you a favour, you can't ignore them if they talk to you, but I'm not one for small talk. Who cares about the weather or what's happening on the afternoon stories or the strange brown mole on the side of Nick's face that may or may not be something for him to worry about? If Missy would only get up, we could get going, get this day over with, and be back at Harmony House safe and sound. No more gossiping. Harmony House would be kerfuffle-free.

I run the water in the bathroom sink for as long as I dare. My head itches again. It never really stopped, only my urge to scratch. A pill would settle me.

What about Missy's nerve pills?

It didn't help you yesterday.

Yesterday? Yes, yesterday, the day that never ended. I didn't go home last night.

I can't stay in the bathroom all day looking at the oval-shaped soap dish on the sink, so I take a big breath and shut the water off.

Breathe in. Breathe out.

"Make yourself something to eat," says Joey when I come out of the bathroom.

There's jam in the fridge, so I make some toast; apple juice, but no milk. I hate apple juice. Joey and Missy both drink their coffee black. A cup of tea would be welcomed, but I didn't see any in the cupboard last night. I usually eat an egg or two for breakfast. Oh, listen to me. One. I eat just one egg. I don't know why I thought two. I've never eaten two eggs. At least, I don't think I have.

The TV is louder than it needs to be, but at least it's not car racing again, so I concentrate on that instead. There are two people talking. Some author discussing the book he just wrote. He's got a bushy moustache and he looks like a giant walrus. His front teeth are much too long. I try to listen to what he's saying, but can't focus. All I can think about is leaving for the Forties Settlement. And soon. How soon?

It's 7:45. Carla is pushing the med cart out to the dining room. Everyone is lining up for their morning dose. Everyone but me. Missy—Missy isn't there, either.

With the crumbs wiped from the table, I go for my coat and purse so I can be ready the moment Joey says it's time to leave. Why doesn't Missy get up? We've a lot to do today.

"Look at you, all set to hit the road," says Joey, breaking my train of thought, and I flinch at the sound of his voice. He's across the table from me now, grinning from ear to ear. Dribbles of coffee have run down his white coffee mug. He wraps his fingers around them, unaware of the dribbles. He seems in a good mood, so I work up the courage to ask when we're going.

"My, my, but you're in a hurry, Liz. Don't you like my company?" He stretches his hand out toward mine. When I quickly pull back, he laughs. "I'm not going to bite."

I shake my head. "I just thought…I mean, we need to get back to Harmony House soon—Missy and me, I mean. People will be concerned. They'll come get us." Each word I speak buzzes inside my head. I don't believe it, the part about them coming for us, since no one has any idea where we've gone. My teeth vibrate, my jaw is tight. If I had something to straighten, rearrange, it would help.

Joey makes a loud noise as he drinks his coffee, and I think of Frank and the slurpy noises he makes when eating soup. Everyone at Harmony House laughs. Everyone except Mrs. Zimmer, who tells him he has the manners of an old sow pig. That's usually when he lets out a burp that echoes all through the dining room. "What's it to ya?" he says. "It's not hurting no one."

I want to move my hands, put them back on the table, but don't dare. Not with Joey's hands there, too. Why doesn't Missy wake up? If only there was some way to distract Joey and make him stop talking to me. I can't go to the bathroom again; I only just went a few moments ago.

"Look, Liz, the way I see it, we're all adults here. You'll get home when you get home. It's that simple. You shouldn't be answering to no one. They can't control your every move. People come and go as they please in this world. You should, too. You're not a kid."

But my pills, I want to shout. *My pills.* I can't expect him to understand. My mouth is dry as cotton. I go for a drink of water. Why doesn't Missy just wake up? She knew I wanted to get an early start. The bus leaves at 6:30 to go back home. If we are going to make it back to Harmony House tonight, we need to get going. Maybe I should wake her.

He's behind me, standing too close. I can tell without even seeing him.

I tilt the glass back, gulping the water. I feel him, the warmth of his body, the sound of his breathing. Far too close. Something grips me in the chest. I want to be someplace else. But I'm not. I'm here, wishing with all my heart that I was someplace else. When I turn he's facing me. I rear backward, knocking my hip into the counter. Quickly setting the glass in the sink, I move a little to the left.

"A little anxious to get going, aren't you, Liz?"

"It's important."

"Missy said your kids live out there in the Forties."

"Lived...they lived there once. It was years ago," I state quietly, even though fear is nuzzling against the back of my neck. When he touches my hair, I can tell he's not at all interested in what I'm saying. His eyes are partly closed and there's this annoying look on his face as if someone has painted it there. I cringe, pull back, scarcely able to breathe.

"Live. Lived. Does it really matter, Liz? They'd be grown up by now. Do you really think they still live there?"

Return to sender.

The letter that came back unopened all those years ago flickers across my mind. I should have written that in my notebook. Why didn't I write it down?

No, they don't live there now. Of course they don't. I don't expect to find them; only my past. My past and the ghost of memories still lingering in that place—trapped and unable to reach me. Not Jewel and Jacob. Jewel and Jacob wouldn't be there. No. Of course they wouldn't.

I don't know what to say. How best to answer his question. His fingers brush against my cheek, my chin.

"I...no...."

"See what I mean, Liz? You're all worked up about this, and for what? Look, I say the Forties can wait. Let's just get a little more acquainted here."

"Missy," I croak. "She should...wake up."

"Forget Missy," he says, lightly taking my hand.

"Don't!"

I shake my hand loose from his. He laughs.

"You're a feisty one, Liz," he says, reaching in past the opening of my coat and touching the collar of my dress. "I like that."

"Don't...call...me...Liz!"

I push against him with all my strength. The table legs squeak against the floor when he bumps into it. He pauses for a moment, a look sweeping across his face—first surprise, then anger. He grabs my arm and pulls me to him. His heart is beating loud and strong. Ker-thump...ker-thump... ker-thump. He breathes warm air on the back of my head. I won't be going to the Forties Settlement. Not today or any day. Not with Joey. Pushing my head down, I sink my teeth into his bare arm. He cries out as I wrench free from his grip.

"Crazy bitch!" He's baring his teeth, rubbing the spot on his arm. Cursing. He's cursing. "What the hell did you go and do that for? I was just being friendly."

My purse is on the little table by the couch. Racing toward it, I snatch it up without slowing down. My feet slap each one of the rickety steps as I hurry down them.

"Where are you going? Don't be stupid. You've got no place to go," he calls out behind me. My heart shoots hot blood up into my head. My breath comes in gulps—half tears, half air. There's an ache in my throat that won't let go. Why didn't Missy just get up out of bed like she was supposed to?

The concrete passes beneath my feet at a steady pace. My shoes are a good distraction. Right. Left. Right. Left. I'm glad that I thought to put on my sensible shoes, the ones I wear when we go to Frenchys. I walk through the cracks this time because I feel I must. Each thought I have keeps me stepping along.

A pill would help settle you.

If you had a pill to swallow, you'd be able to think all this out rationally.

I turn around and look, but Joey isn't following, so there's no need for me to hurry. I have to keep my wits about me. Pay attention to the street signs. The location of the shops. I need to stop my mind from racing. *Slow down. Slow down. Breathe in. Breathe out.*

It's 10: 27. Back at Harmony House, Donna has cleaned the washrooms and is taking an extra-long break before filling her red bucket with soap suds. There's a worried look on Mrs. Weaver's face. The staff are all looking at one another. "*I can't believe she took off like that,*" they're saying. "*Not Elizabeth. She was always so sensible.*" Mrs. Zimmer is smiling and snarling, snarling and smiling, and I'm sure she'd be both mad and glad if I didn't come back at all. "*What can you expect from a cardboard dummy?*" she's saying.

I don't know how to get to Harmony House. And Joey's apartment is out of the question. Especially now. Besides, I have no idea where his apartment is. I couldn't get myself there even if I wanted to. I look up and down the street, trying to get my bearings, ordering my mind to slow down and think, but nothing, absolutely nothing, looks familiar.

An *OPEN* sign flashes bright red—*on, off, on, off.* The cafe will be warm, a place for me to collect my thoughts and decide what to do next. A tiny tinkle announces my arrival and the woman behind the counter looks my way as soon as I step through the doorway. She's wearing a light blue uniform and her hair is done up into a tight bun. Loose strands have fallen out. There are dark rings under her eyes, and she reminds me suddenly of Missy. They could be sisters.

"Do you know Missy?" I say.

She gives me an odd look and says, "Missy who?"

"Missy Mullins."

"Sorry, I don't know who that is," she says with a shrug. Missy doesn't have any family. At least that's what she says. I know that, so why did I ask?

"What can I get you?"

"Tea...I'll have tea."

I open my wallet, but what little money I had in my purse yesterday is gone. Damn you, Missy. I should have known better. Hands trembling, I reach into my handbag and shake it around until some loose coins gather into the corner. Feeling them beneath my fingertips, I scoop them up.

"When does the bus come around?" I count out change for a cup of tea. Two times I have to stop and start over again.

"Six thirty or so. Sometimes it's a little late," she says, pouring my tea. Six thirty. Of course. I knew that. It hasn't changed. I didn't need to ask. All I need to do is to be at the bus stop before six thirty. I can finally get back to Harmony House. Missy will have to get back the best way she can. The rest of the change I put in the small zippered pocket in front of my purse. Grabbing the cup off the counter, I find a quiet place by the window. There aren't many people sitting at the tables. A man puts money in the jukebox and music starts playing. I recognize it immediately; an old

Hank Williams song. Squeezing my eyes tight, I manage to hold my tears in and clench my teeth at the parts of the song I remember. None of this makes any sense to me. There's nothing important about that song. It can hardly compare to the importance of remembering the past—my past.

I stay at the cafe for as long as I dare. People come, eat lunch, and then leave. You're supposed to order something when you go into an eating establishment; otherwise you're just taking the place of a paying customer. I've seen enough TV programs to know that much. You can't just sit there for hours on end and stare out the window into the street. Not only that, if I sit for too long without ordering something to eat, it'll arouse suspicion. Someone will wonder who I am and where exactly I came from. I'm not sure what I'd give for an answer if anyone asked.

The sight of a police car freezes me and I slowly close the door to the cafe until it has passed. By now I'm almost certain Mrs. Weaver will have notified the authorities and told them I—we are missing. Pulling my coat around me, I start walking down the sidewalk but remember then that Joey lives somewhere nearby. I need to find some other street to walk on, one that Joey wouldn't be walking on too. Making a quick turn to the right, I almost bump into a woman with a small dog in her arms.

"Sorry," I mumble as the woman and dog both start yipping at me. I hurry out of her way, but in my haste, I turn about and walk into a lamppost. My whole body vibrates. I look up, slightly dazed, the world spinning. Someone bumps into me then with enough force that I'm left staggering on my feet. I catch sight of him disappearing down a side street, his dirty white sneakers slapping the sidewalk. Heart in my hand, I yell out at him. Already it's too late. My hands scrunch up into two tight balls.

"Her purse!"

"Someone stop him!"

"Did you see that? He took her purse!"

Tears find a pathway to my eyes when it finally registers that my purse is no longer dangling on my arm. I can't hold back the dam. The pressure is too strong.

"Did you see that?"

"He stole her purse."

"Don't cry, ma'am."

"Did anyone get a good look at him?"

"Call the cops."

"No police…. Please, no."

My purse, without the money. The money was already gone. Change; there was a bit of change at the bottom. My hairbrush. My tissues. The compact I only use for the mirror. My empty wallet. Gone. All of it.

I could go to the police.

No, you can't. They'll put you in jail for leaving Harmony House without permission.

No, not jail. They'll put me in the hospital, not jail. Dartmouth or Divinity, and I'll never find Jacob or Jewel. Never.

Calm yourself.

And so I try, because there's nothing else I *can* do at the moment. My heart ignores its order to slow down. You can't expect body parts to do exactly as you say. Certainly not a heart that beats at its own pace. But my head, I can calm my head when I have to. Muscles trembling. I need a pill. I close my eyes and pull in a deep breath. A pair of dirty white sneakers flashes in my mind. I gasp. The brown-haired girl! Big tears splatter down my cheeks. Raindrops without the rain. I can't stop. Make it stop. I haven't cried in a good long while, not since the day I saw a pair of dirty white sneakers and the hem of a blue-flowered dress hanging in midair. I couldn't look up, couldn't look into her face. But it was there, somewhere. I know it was. Her name was Jill and she had brown hair. She used to talk to me when no one else would. It was so long ago.

I need to put the memory in its place. Calm my head. Do something, think something else.

Pulling myself away from the crowd, I tell them that I don't need help and not to worry. Injecting fake self-confidence into my words, they seem to believe me.

"There was no money in my purse," I say.

They are sympathetic.

"What's the world coming to?"

"And in broad daylight."

They don't know I'm from Harmony House.

Harmony House—so comfortable, so easily digestible. Mrs. Zimmer is most likely glad that I am gone. *"She was nothing but a pain in the A-S-S at the best of times,"* she's probably saying right about now to anyone who will listen. Mrs. Weaver might be out driving around town looking for me—for us. I know how these things work. They'll decide when last someone saw me—us. They'll ask people on the street. But no one on the street knows me—us. But that's not quite true. The ones who work at the community centre on Fridays know who I am. Perhaps they'll question Beverly or Tessa. But they know nothing. Nobody does. Missy knows people. Joey. And those two young men outside the community centre. My legs wobble, but I force them to keep moving.

I go in search of a payphone. I'll call Mrs. Weaver to come get me. There's one up the street. I dash toward it. And stop. I don't know the phone number at Harmony House. I've never called there before, and besides, there's no dime because my purse has been stolen. My purse. I gulp, then swallow my heart. A sick feeling comes over me.

The ticket. My bus ticket was in my purse!

How will you get home?

Back and forth, back and forth, I tread.

Stop yourself, Elizabeth.

My notebook! My notebook was in my purse, too.

Someone could be reading it this moment.

My list of important words.

My thoughts.

My private thoughts.

Gone.

Something inside begins to disintegrate. Fine silt filters into my veins, my limbs. I'm no longer able to hold myself up. Down. Down. Down. I trace out the items in my purse, the bus trip to Kentville, Joey's apartment, my notebook, my important words—*Jacob. Jewel. Cliff. Forties. Poppy. Dartmouth. Divinity.* But the words are so far away, pushed to the back where I can scarcely see them. They might disappear altogether and leave me standing in the middle of a strange street, in a strange town, with nothing.

The sidewalk is coming to meet me as farther down I crumble.

I whisper their names. It's all I can do.

There is no one to hear or to care.

The sidewalk is ice cold as I melt into it.

In the distance there is mumbling, but I can't make out what's being said.

"I am well now," I whisper, looking into the eye of the November sky.

But the pink dawn isn't there.

Perhaps it never was.

Jewel

Three days before Christmas. My last year of university.
In the middle of evergreen and decorations, wrapping paper
and shortbread cookies, cinnamon sticks and nutmeg. We
both came home for Christmas to be with Daddy. Aunt
Joan, her face on the other side of the door, knocking and
knocking. The wind pulled the latch from my fingers. The
door hit her in the chest, nearly knocking her off our front
stoop. Her hair was messy, her face pulled down into a
puckered frown.

"They haven't come in. They're overdue," she said.
"They should have come in by now." She was shivering,
the rain beating down on her. Her blue wool shortie coat
was flapping in the wind. "And I can't raise them on the
radio. They're gone, Jewel. I feel it in my bones. They're
gone." Before I had time to say anything, Jacob had invited
her inside. Taking the plastic rain bonnet from her head, she
shook the water off and folded it up before stepping inside.

He told her to sit by the stove and made her a cup of tea. Her lips trembled.

"We'll have but the one service," she said, twisting at the ties on her rain bonnet. "They were always together. I think that's best. What Dylan and Cliff would want." She emptied the pot of tea. The shortbread cookies burned black in the oven. She wouldn't shut up. I didn't have to open my mouth. All the talking in the house came from her. Her words lived on after she left, making it impossible for Jacob or me to say a thing.

Later, after the hymns and flowers, after the eulogy that she was adamant about doing herself, she invited everyone to come to her house. She clattered away about "the old times," opening her albums, showing pictures of Daddy and Uncle Dylan when they were growing up; pictures I'd never seen before.

"Maggie never realized what wonderful boys she was raising," she said, squeezing a white handkerchief in her hands. "And now, they're both gone." Looking out toward the water, she whinged like a lost pup in a snowbank.

Later, someone said they thought they'd seen Mumma at the service.

"I very much doubt that," said Aunt Joan, reaching for a cup of tea.

"Whoever it was, she was sitting at the very back, in the corner of the church, wearing some kind of orangish scarf on her head, wiping her eyes whenever one of the hymns played. She left before I could get a good look at her," said a woman I didn't know.

"But I'm sure it was Elizabeth," someone else said. "Where do you suppose she's been all this time?"

Speculations continued to circulate. "Elizabeth was always thin. I saw that same woman. No way was it

Elizabeth MacKay. Not on your life. Besides, she wouldn't dare show her face. Not after all this time. Not at a time like this, she wouldn't."

I knew that whoever it was, it couldn't have been Mumma. If she had been there I would have felt her presence. Somehow, I would have known.

When someone said, "Never say never," Aunt Joan turned deathly white. Her hands fumbled for the teacup and it scattered into bits on the floor. I bent down to help her pick up the pieces of broken china. We were inches apart, staring at one another, frozen until she put her hand on mine.

"It's okay, Jewel. It wasn't Elizabeth. It wasn't your mother. She didn't come back," she whispered. "She didn't come back. No one will know. It's okay. We're okay."

There's a place you can slip into with very little effort, a place so dark and heavy you can scarcely draw a breath without feeling pressure in your ribcage. It's there in the morning as soon as you open your eyes, a dull ache at your fingernails and in the roots of your hair, the enamel on your teeth. It pulses, reminding you of its presence the second you think it's gone. Sometimes you catch yourself smiling during the day, but then it pulls you back, asking what you've got to be happy about. You answer, "Nothing...there's nothing at all," and you know those words have become your truth. There are days when the darkness lifts a bit, but then another day comes and you realize it didn't go anywhere.

For months after Daddy drowned, I'd wake from a dream that I couldn't remember with the sounds of running ponies in the background. I'd sit up in bed, and the darkness would push me back down. In the morning, David would tell me to get up, reminding me it was time to get dressed and go to class. I didn't need reminding. I was fully aware of where I was and where I wasn't, and what I needed to do.

"You're not even trying," he'd say.

Jacob checked in on me, phoning in the evening, dropping by with pizza that had too many toppings. I used to wonder why Mumma stopped living after Poppy died. I'd watch her, curled up on the couch, and wonder why she just didn't make herself get up and do something. But then she was gone and I should have told Daddy to bring her home instead of telling him not to, because that's what families do. They stay together no matter what.

I asked Jacob one night, "Do you ever wonder what it would be like to disappear?" And then he wouldn't stop calling.

This time it isn't the dream that wakes me, the galloping of ponies in the distance. It's a loud banging at my door that won't stop. I wait, hoping whoever's there will get tired and go away. No one ever comes to my door. Pulling the ends of a cushion around my ears, I attempt to block out the noise. Still it continues. Groaning, I concentrate on willing it to stop and turn my back toward the door. My head is throbbing; the result of too much wine, even though I was convinced last night that another glass (or two) was in order. The wine was already chilled, and David's leaving was something that needed to be celebrated again.

"Jewel! Jewel!" I'm startled by the sound of desperation on the other side of the door. Jacob. He's supposed to be down at the shore visiting Aunt Joan this weekend. I gather up my raw edges and pull them around me like a cold cotton sheet in winter. The jingling of keys, the door opens, but before I can get up, Jacob's standing over me.

"How did you get in?" I say, looking up at him from the sofa. Soft dark curls frame his face. His brown eyes. The expression on his face. He reminds me so much of Daddy I can scarcely breathe.

Smiling, he says, "You gave me a key once, remember?"

BD—Before David. My first apartment and I was trying to be responsible. "In case of emergency," I'd said when I handed the key to Jacob.

I sit up and Jacob jumps on the sofa beside me. "What time is it?" I say, surveying the amount of light in the apartment. I look at the Pot of Gold box he's holding. "I don't want a chocolate, if that's what you're here for." I haven't been up this early on a Sunday since Aunt Joan used to hustle us off to a nine o'clock church service. Sitting at the kitchen table eating soggy cornflakes at eight in the morning, I'd complain to Daddy. "It's not the end of the world," he'd say. "Can't you just go along with it, Jewel? It makes Joan happy."

"Forget about the time. This is important," Jacob says, like he's about to burst wide open. "I found her, Jewel. I found Mum!"

I'm sure I didn't hear him properly. Found her? I didn't even know he was looking. The sound of galloping ponies echoes in my ears, but there are no ponies, there never were. It's only my heart racing.

"You found her? How? Why didn't you say?"

"She ran away. It was on the news. Didn't you see it?" His words come out in bursts as if a dam has suddenly let go. Jacob never speaks this quickly.

"Mumma was on the news?" None of what Jacob's saying makes sense. He went to see Aunt Joan; now suddenly he's telling me he's found Mumma. Fifteen years—it can't be this easy. It just can't be.

"Okay, look," he says, pulling me to my feet. "Her disappearance was on TV. They were looking for her. Where have you been the past few days? I saw this woman, the picture of her, I mean. And they said it was Elizabeth MacKay. But I was only five when she went away so I wasn't sure if it was her. I asked Aunt Joan and she said it was probably Mum."

"Probably? That sounds a little vague. A lot of people have the same name. There might be another Elizabeth MacKay. What if it's not her at all?" Jacob looks at me as if I've said a dirty word. I tilt my head, allowing a smile to camouflage my feelings. I walk over to the cupboard, place the dirty dishes in the sink, and wipe the crumbs from the counter.

"She could have come home. Her staying away, that was her own doing and had nothing to do with you and me. Now just let it go, Jewel. Whatever we did, it was the right thing."

"Aunt Joan didn't see the news, but she said it would probably make sense—that Mum would be living in a transition house, I mean."

"So now what?" The question comes out warped, bent like light refracted through murky water, pulling with it more meaning than I intend. I clear my throat.

"What's wrong, Jewel? I thought you'd be happy. We can find Mum. It's what we've always wanted."

"Nothing's wrong." Filling the sink with water, I watch the suds build. It's all so simple for him. He was five when Mumma left and cried more the day his pony was sold than when Mumma went away. He always thought she'd come back. As if he'd wait forever for her if he had to, that she was no farther away than the next room and could show up at any moment. A part of me had always envied that faith. He was always the good one, Mumma's favourite.

"Don't you *want* to find her?" His question is stark with accusations, pointing directly at me, as if he can see things I don't want him to see.

"I didn't even know we were looking, is all. Why didn't you tell me?"

"You're upset."

"I'm not upset. Would you just stop saying that?"

"She had a breakdown, Jewel. Aunt Joan said she went crazy after Poppy died, that's why she went away."

"So why didn't she come back? Have you ever thought of that? She could have come back. Fifteen years, Jakey. Where the hell has she been?" There is more emotion in me than I realized, fuelled by a series of unanswered questions that still haunt me—and then the part I played in it all.

"If she cared at all, she knew where to find you. Her staying away just proves she was happy to be gone. Mothers don't abandon their children, Jewel, not good mothers at least. Have you asked yourself how good a mother Elizabeth really was? Giving birth, that's one thing; raising a child is something else."

"We can ask all that after we find her," says Jacob. "Look what I've got, Jewel." He quickly removes the elastic from the chocolate box and, reaching inside, takes out a handful of envelopes. "Aunt Joan wrote these."

Figures. Aunt Joan saved everything in chocolate boxes.

"Here, read one. She wrote letters to Mum—for a lot of years she did. Not so much these past few years. But when we were small. She wanted Mum to know."

"*Mumma*, Jacob. We always called her Mumma!"

"Calm down, Jewel. It's just a name."

The hurt in Jacob's eyes causes me to quickly pull in my anger. This time I speak softly. "Don't you remember, Jacob? It was Mumma, always Mumma."

"I was only five, so I guess not. And then everyone stopped talking about her. You know what Daddy was like—all of them, really. It was a taboo subject."

I look into the box and see Aunt Joan's handwriting on one of the envelopes. *For: Elizabeth MacKay.*

Why the letters, Aunt Joan, when you said we were all better off without her?

"This doesn't even make sense, Jakey. Aunt Joan hated Mumma. Why would she write letters to her?" Jacob isn't going to let this drop. The conviction in his voice, the determined look in his eye. He saw Mumma. She was on the news. He'll get to the bottom of it—that's Jacob.

But there's so much he doesn't know.

Can't know.

Must never know—that's me.

He pulls a letter out from one of the envelopes, scanning it.

"Look, this one was about our first Christmas in Chester....She mostly wrote things about us. I read them all," he says, shoving the letter in front of me.

I push it away.

"I thought you'd be happy. I wanted you to know... before I call Harmony House. That's where she is. Harmony House." The letter dangles from his fingers. I look at him, wrestling the past in a single moment in time, juggling all the broken pieces, the ones that never quite fit.

Jacob wouldn't take the letters with him when he left. I couldn't change his mind. I didn't understand why they

274

seemed to please him so. "You need to read them, Jewel. When you're ready. They're really something."

"They're just letters, Jacob, written to a ghost; to some-one who wasn't here to know these things."

"Don't you get it, Jewel? All the things Mumma missed, they're in the letters, little details we wouldn't even remember."

I leave the letters on the coffee table, unread. Pulling in a deep breath, I settle myself back into the past, not knowing what I'll do with the flood of memories suddenly pushing their way to the top. Jacob is bound to find out the truth, that I'm the one responsible for our moving on without her.

Elizabeth

When I open my eyes, Mrs. Weaver is standing over the bed looking down at me. I gasp, pulling the sheet up close. I think suddenly of Missy, wondering if Mrs. Weaver has come to ask me where she is. And if she has, what will I tell her?

"I was beside myself with worry," she says, a slight pink colour touching her cheeks. "All of us at Harmony House were. We didn't know what to think, why you would leave like that. I thought you liked it here. I thought you were happy. This is so unlike you, Elizabeth, so unlike you." She is shaking her head and I'm not sure I've ever seen her this angry before. "I had to call the Mounties. Your picture was in the news. On TV. Asking the public for their help in locating your whereabouts like a runaway child. I always depended on you."

"My children," I croak, fighting the shame I feel at having my disappearance exposed for the entire world to see. "Jewel and Jacob...I wanted to find them." Mrs. Weaver sighs and turns her head. There's no way she'll understand. You can't understand what you don't feel for yourself. Mrs. Weaver doesn't have any children of her own. She has a fancy car and a husband who's a banker, a dog called Tillie that she leaves at the kennel when they go on vacation. She flies to warmer countries, for goodness' sake, and polishes her nails.

Outside the hospital room, people are talking and laughing. I wish the door were closed so no one could hear what Mrs. Weaver is saying. I know there is more to come, much more.

"How did I get here?" I suddenly wonder what day of the week it is, how much time I've lost. I might have dozed in and out, but for how long?

"Two days. You've been here two days. You collapsed on the street. You were exhausted and without your medication. What were you thinking? You can't just go off gallivanting around the countryside on your own. I thought you understood that." There's a wavering in Mrs. Weaver's voice that I have never heard before. She trusted me, but now that trust is gone.

"Missy...," I say.

"Missy came home—without you. She said she was trying to help you out and that you ran off on you own. Missy...of all people. Really? Elizabeth, really? What could you have been thinking?" Mrs. Weaver's face is pulled tight and she's doing that funny thing with her mouth that she does when she's highly annoyed.

"Jewel and Jacob," I bleat again, wishing she'd try to understand. "Missy said she'd help. We were supposed to be home. But her friend, he wouldn't keep his hands to himself. I couldn't stay and then someone stole my purse.... Missy said we'd be back in time. She promised."

Sighing, she shakes her head. She casts her eyes down at the foot of my bed, and I try to imagine what she's about to say. When she looks back at me, I want to dissolve into my pillow, disappear altogether and forget that I even exist.

"You're chasing an impossible dream, some ideal of the perfect family that only lives in your head, Elizabeth...*your* head. Harmony House is your life—like it or not. There's nothing you can do to change that. You might just as well accept it."

I don't tell her I'm not expecting perfection, that my only hope is of one day finding my children. After that I don't know what; after that my mind draws a blank. I just need to find my truth. She, above all others, should understand that. She continues, executing the final blow. "There is *no* next of kin, Elizabeth. Do you understand that? *No next of kin.* No one. All these years. Someone would have come forward."

I've heard tell of people being hypnotized, remembering all sorts of details from a past life. I saw it on a TV program one rainy afternoon a few months after I arrived at Harmony House: a woman who said she once lived in the court of some king a long time ago. She looked like a regular person, someone you would meet on the street or in the supermarket or even Frenchys.

"I was an ordinary housewife before any of this," she said to the person doing the interviewing, "until I started having these strange dreams."

"He took me back to the day I died," she said of the person who'd hypnotized her. She described the outfit she was wearing and headdress she had on, and said she was a lady-in-waiting. They called her Lady Sarah. She then described a battle scene that took place out in the courtyard one morning when she went to get water from the well. She said she remembered the weather that day and the people around her. The smells wafting in the breeze. It sounded so believable—yet unbelievable.

"The men came up on horses...a whole army of them. I dropped the urn I was carrying and ran, but then I felt the arrow pierce me. I counted the last few beats of my heart before my eyes finally closed."

Her voice was trembling. No one made fun of her. The whole audience listened intently to her story. There were ooohs and aaahs. People applauded. I couldn't help thinking that if someone from Harmony House had made that very same claim, no one would put them on the TV to tell their story. In fact, they'd either be ignored or else someone would up their medication to keep them from hallucinating any further, maybe land them in Dartmouth depending upon how convincing they sounded. Yet this woman spoke openly about this past life of hers as if she was completely sane and not the least bit embarrassed to have the entire country know her story. She'd written it all down and put it in a book.

The bangles on her wrist jingled when she moved her hands, which she did often enough. I wondered how many ordinary housewives had the time to dress up in bangles and makeup and red flowery dresses. And how many ordinary housewives sit down and write books?

But then her story began to trouble me at night—this idea about living past lives. I had another life, one I scarcely had memory of. But what if the memories of my children that I'd been clinging to all this time were not from this lifetime at all? What if the life I been hoping was mine had happened a lifetime ago, or maybe two or even three? I paced the halls at Harmony House, up and down the street, churning these thoughts over for days, wondering if this place called the Forties Settlement was actually my home, or did I just invent it? I died there the first time—for whatever reason, that thought kept haunting me. I had no idea where it came from. I'd close my eyes at night and pretend I had been put under a trance. I'd imagine a white house and a bright red barn in the distance. I'd place cows and a pony in the pasture. One night I thought I heard children's laughter. I sat up in bed and looked out the window into the moonlit street. There was no one there. And then the dreams began: flames and fire and voices crying, saying things I couldn't make out. There were people standing in the window of a burning house. I thought about the woman from the TV and wondered if these were indeed memories of some past life I'd lived, one that would be impossible to get back. I even decided it was the reason the letter I'd sent all those years ago came back. When I finally told all this to the doctor, he increased my medication and all that worry about those other lives, of death and being reborn, went away. I was happy for that. And so, for a long time, I stopped trying to delve into the past. Until the day Mrs. Weaver spoke to Nick about his truth.

On the drive back to Harmony House, Mrs. Weaver doesn't speak. I look out the car window at the people on the street. The world is drained of colour. It's depressing to watch. All those people, each one of them knows where they're going, moving with some purpose in mind. I had a purpose—for a short time, I did. I woke in the mornings filled with eagerness and a longing to add something new to my notebook. But the notebook is gone, stolen from me because of my own stupidity. My words, all my important words that I strained to remember, even my notes about the Hippie Bus and Reggie. My thoughts—some jumbled, some clear, but my thoughts—all of them. Gone. And this new memory of Jill, the little brown-haired girl I met in Dartmouth so long ago. Was it all for nothing?

When Mrs. Weaver pulls into her parking place, she turns to me and quietly says, "If they're real, Elizabeth, really real, where have they been all these years?" Her question shakes me to the core, erasing everything I've worked so hard for, the hope I held fast to when there was nothing else to keep me here.

Joan

The Lord only knows how Elizabeth's letter found its way to the shore that ordinary day in June. I've thought about it these past seven years. It was an omen, a sign of what was to come. Although I didn't recognize it at the time, it was surely a hint of what the future held. I was never one for believing in fate, that some invisible force was making things happen. Life is our own responsibility to make of what we will. We can sit back and let things happen, which amounts to little more than giving up, or else we can put things back on the proper track, the one we want.

Like receiving a letter from beyond the grave, all those years I pretended Elizabeth was dead to us, that she no longer existed. For all of us, I did this. Life was fine, as fine as I could ever hope it to be, until I looked down at the letter in my hand.

To: Cliff MacKay
The Forties Settlement

Lunenburg County, Nova Scotia

The address had been crossed out and it appeared that someone from the New Ross Post Office had written across the envelope: *Try Chester Basin, Nova Scotia. c/o Dylan MacKay*. Damn these small places that know more about everyone else's business than they do their own. When I took the mail out of the box that day I knew, before I even turned the letter over to see where it came from. Holding it to my bosom, I hurried to the house, hardly able to draw a decent breath into my lungs. Alone in the kitchen I opened it with a knife, my hands shaking so badly I had to stop twice to regain my composure before managing to get it open. Struggling to swallow with the lump that was festering in my throat, I set the letter aside, giving my heart time to slow. And when I reached for it again, when the trembling had all but subsided, I couldn't believe what she'd written. It wasn't a letter for Cliff at all, but one for the children.

Dear Jacob and Jewel. I am well now. Well enough to see you. I struggled to swallow—my throat hurt so—and continued. *I'm at Divinity Hospital. They will let you visit if you want to come. I really hope you will. I have missed you all this time and have never stopped thinking of you... Love Mumma.*

Half the morning, I walked the kitchen floor thinking on what I was to do with this information, how best to keep this family together. I couldn't tell Dylan about the letter, and certainly not Cliff. We'd made a decision years ago, and there was no way we were going to go back on it. I wouldn't allow it. Elizabeth was gone from our lives and she'd stay gone. Case closed. Cliff would buckle if he saw the letter; I knew he would. He'd take pity on her the way he did when they were still living together. He'd bring her back into our lives again, if I knew anything at all about him, and the mayhem would start all over again. All those years she'd been gone—how would we explain that to everyone? Besides, the children were making out fine without her; Cliff, too, for that matter. The spark was back in his eye. Jewel and Jacob were smiling and laughing. Life was calm. Life was good. We were all happy. Why now, I kept wondering as I paced back and forth the kitchen that morning, why now?

I had to decide how best to handle this. If I ripped up the letter, she'd likely write more, and if Cliff got the mail one day, or the children, it would be game over. Elizabeth would be back and all the craziness that went with her. Granted, she'd suffered that breakdown after her father died, but things weren't right way before then. Things were never right with Elizabeth. A few years in a mental hospital wouldn't have changed any of that. In her letter, she said she was well, but I knew that wasn't so. She wouldn't be in the hospital if she wasn't still sick.

And then it came to me—a stroke of brilliance if I say so myself. I slipped the letter into a brand new envelope of its own. I addressed it to *Cliff MacKay, The Forties Settlement*. I formed the letters so close to the writing on the original envelope that no one would know the difference. I even put her return address on the back, in the same place. I scratched out the address on the front and wrote: *Return to sender, unknown address* in large blue letters. And then I mailed it one day when we were in New Ross. Elizabeth would never bother us again.

You're never prepared for what life throws your way, no matter what you might have told yourself over the years, no matter how many times you've run things over in your mind, just what you'd do and how you'd get by if tragedy ever struck. I was certain I'd pull back my shoulders and keep carrying on, one way or another. I'd be the strong one, someone other women would admire. I'd imagine Dylan watching me from beyond the Pearly Gates, saying, "*That's my girl. You can do it, Joan, you can do it*," so full of pride in me it would make my heart about ready to burst at the seams. But the mind is a powerful thing. You can do all those things again and again, figuring you'd be as strong as the next person when life calls you to be, but when disaster *does* come knocking, all those things you imagined yourself doing, all that strength you figured you'd possess, gets thrown to the gulls.

I'd leave the shore, I used to tell myself, if something ever happened to Dylan. Sell this old house and buy another one as far inland as I could get, maybe get a job or do more volunteer work to fill my days. Start a brand new life, is what I thought. I wouldn't have to listen to the sea wind blowing or feel the rattling of the windows at night during another wicked storm, wondering if everyone was safe and who would survive come morning. I'd find a nice little spot big enough for me to grow some vegetables, maybe raise a few chickens just for the eggs. My life would become comfortable. And comfortable sure beats wishing things were something they're not.

Our lives changed once Cliff and the kids moved here. Not right away, but over time they did. In the beginning, things couldn't have been better. Dylan couldn't have been happier to have his brother out fishing with him, and it was heartwarming to see that old spark in his eye again. Cliff knew him like no one else. They were two peas in a pod. Most times, out on that boat, they didn't have to speak for each to know what the other was thinking. Dylan said it had been like that back when Jake was alive, too.

"Cliff could have been on the boat with me all along," Dylan said when I mentioned how content he seemed. And I had to agree. We both knew whose fault that was. I don't mind being the one to say that if it hadn't been for Elizabeth, our lives would have been much different. How one person has the power to change so many lives is beyond me, but Elizabeth had that power.

The day Richard took off to Ontario with Miles Tyrell, my very first thought was of Elizabeth. If I could have done something to stop those thoughts I would have, but my mind wouldn't keep me from seeing Elizabeth, alone in some hospital room, maybe wondering where her own children were. With Richard gone, I got to see first-hand what pain a mother goes through when she's separated from her child, what lengths she'd go to just to know they're doing okay. I knew I'd give my right arm to have Richard come on home regardless of how unruly he was. Elizabeth would be no different. And that thinking gnawed away at me day after day.

Kate Tyrell has six children scattered across the countryside and what all she knows about any one of them you could fit into a thimble. From the time they were old enough to toddle about, you'd see them gallivanting all over the neighbourhood like they didn't have a place to go home to. So long as they came back at bedtime and the cops didn't show up at her door, she never seemed to have a care in this world. I called Kate on the phone the day after Richard didn't come home. Someone told me they'd seen him with Miles the day before, and they looked pretty chummy, so I thought it was worth a try. I should have known hers wasn't a shoulder to be cried on, and I'd rather kiss a dead cod than ask Kate Tyrell anything, but I had to find out what she knew.

"Boys will be boys," she'd said, "and the less we know, the better." She gave a tittering little laugh. It's a good thing my hands were gripped fast to the phone receiver and not Kate's neck. I could have strangled the life out of her right then and there.

"Didn't you ask Miles where he was going?" I shouted. But no, she'd watched him pack a bag without asking a blessed thing. Maybe it's different with six sons. Perhaps with six sons there's room to allow one or two to slip away unnoticed into the fog, but what about those of us who have only one?

Even when Elizabeth wasn't in the picture, her presence was surely felt by the rest of us. It was why I went into Dartmouth with Cliff the second time. I had to see her for myself, let her know Jacob and Jewel were getting along just fine, and for her not to worry. If Richard's leaving taught me anything, it was that. But how was I to know what we were about to find that day? How could any of us have known? Tell her about Jewel and Jacob? Why, we couldn't tell her a thing. She was just sitting there with a blank look on her face. There wasn't anyone at home. Not a soul upstairs.

On the way home Cliff made up his mind.

"The children, they're doing fine without her," I said to Cliff as I looked out the window. "Jewel, she doesn't want her mother to come home. That's what she said, Cliff. I swear on old Jake's grave, that's what she said.... We're doing fine without her, all of us. It's the truth and you know it."

He drove for an hour or more, neither of us saying a word. I knew enough to keep my tongue still, let him simmer a little, see the way things really were, let him come to some conclusion on his own.

"You're right," he said, gripping the steering wheel when we were ten minutes from home. "She's better off where she is…and we're better off, too."

It wasn't an easy decision back then, but by God it was the right one.

We all find our own level of comfort, the one thing that makes an almost unbearable situation bearable. Maggie found it by heading out on the boat with Dylan after Jake died. She rolled up her sleeves and worked as hard as any man could. She never complained, just accepted what life had brought her way and found her own means of making it tolerable. The idea of the letters came to me when I got back home from Dartmouth that day. With the shape Elizabeth was in, it was hard to say if she'd even read them. In time, they might end up being thrown away, and all my time and effort would have been wasted, but I didn't let that line of thinking stop me. Elizabeth couldn't be there, that much we'd already decided, but it wasn't as if we were intentionally keeping her from knowing her own children.

Right after I wrote the first letter a strange feeling came over me. Something about it felt right, cleansing in a way that brought me peace. Sending it would be out of the question, but that didn't mean that someday she wouldn't get to read it. Life is filled with mysterious happenings. So I packed it away, a someday letter, knowing that someday Elizabeth might come into possession of it. There are those who might say it was a useless gesture. To me it made perfect sense. And it felt good. Each letter I wrote never seemed like enough. I'd wait a few more weeks or even months and I'd sit back down at the table again.

But then Jacob called the other night, asking questions—some woman he saw on the news—and I knew Elizabeth was back. Resurrected from the past, a past that was surely catching up to us all. How would I explain any of it without him thinking I was a monster? So I told him about the someday letters and suggested he might want to show them to his mother when the time was right. He came right to the house the very next day. When he read the first one, a smile spread across his face. It was like Christmas morning all over again, seeing that smile of his, knowing I was the one responsible for putting it there.

"It was a thoughtful thing to do," he said. "I'll show them to Mum when I find her." But a part of me trembled. Elizabeth was back. Everything was unravelling. It was all unravelling.

Elizabeth

The first white flakes of winter fly angrily in the wind like a handful of sand thrown from a child's clenched fist. I sit by the window in the family room, waiting for Mrs. Weaver to say she's sorry for doubting me, but she hasn't said anything, not since she barged in a few minutes ago and announced that Jacob is coming. A car pulls up into the driveway and I draw a breath of air into my lungs, my heart reaching for my throat. But then I recognize the driver. It's only Mrs. Burke's grandson, the one who always smiles and says hello as he parades down the hall with a big bouquet in his hands. Today, he's carrying a poinsettia that might end up chilled in these frigid temperatures. He really should have had it wrapped in paper, but men don't think of those things. The bright red leaves shift in the breeze as he strikes across the pavement with the pot tucked beneath his arm. I once heard that the leaves of the poinsettia plant are poisonous, and because of it I've never liked them for a houseplant. How could anything so pretty be a danger? Yet, every Christmas they're placed on the end tables in the family room like a deadly reminder to beware the beauty in this world.

A blast of winter air blows into the family room when Mrs. Burke's grandson enters. I hear him singing out his greeting, his feet making swift squeaks down the corridor, his voice disappearing with him as he reaches Mrs. Burke's room at the end of the hall. I wonder if Jacob will make such a flamboyant entrance, although a part of me hopes he doesn't.

Although it's nearly Christmas, this news Mrs. Weaver just delivered could have come at any time, even though she was smiling when she said, "Your son's coming, and just in time for Christmas." It is silly the way people place so much credence on things happening around the holidays, as if it somehow makes it that much more extraordinary. Jacob is coming. What does the month or day or year matter? He's coming. That's the important part.

"When?" I finally ask, feeling unprepared for this news. She places her hand gently on my shoulder, and I wonder if the gesture is meant as an apology, since just a few weeks ago she said they weren't real. It might be nice to have her acknowledge it in some way. Instead, she acts as though all is well. She smiles awkwardly and says, "At least some good came of that escapade of yours."

"When...when's he coming? What day?" I stammer.

"Soon. Sometime before Christmas. He apparently saw your picture on TV. That's all I know."

I add up the days in my head. Nine. But then quickly I wonder if I count Christmas Day. If I count Christmas, that would make ten. A flood of questions suddenly overtakes me and I can't shut up. "What did his voice sound like? Is it deep or soft? Did he sound pleased or just obliged to find me because my picture was on the TV? And what about Jewel? Did he say anything about Jewel?"

"My, my, you're filled with questions," says Mrs. Weaver, "but unfortunately, I have no answers. You'll have to wait until he comes and find out for yourself."

My heart is doing strange things in my chest. I turn and go back to my room and lie down. I fear that Mrs. Weaver is still annoyed at me for leaving Harmony House without permission. She's not behaving as if she is, with all the smiles she's putting out, but Missy told me so just the other day.

"She was wound up tighter than a clock, said she'd expect a stunt like that from me but not you. You're always responsible. She said I was a bad influence," Missy said, smacking her gum. "Why *did* you run off like that?"

That could be why Mrs. Weaver's not telling me much about Jacob, that and the fact that she was wrong about him being real. Perhaps she thinks his showing up now makes her look bad, since she refused to believe me all those times I spoke about my children. I think about the notebook she gave me to write down all my important words and how she'd encouraged me to make the list in the first place even though she didn't believe Jewel and Jacob were real. It was all to keep me from asking her about Dartmouth then Divinity.

Lying on my bed, I look at the ceiling and wonder if that daddy long-legs is still hiding somewhere in a crack above my head. I've seen him several times scurrying across the shiny white surface. I try to put my mind on anything other than the fact that Jacob is coming in time for Christmas. I'm not particularly fond of the holidays. The decorations, the music, the coloured packages all bring about feelings of indifference for me. I know it is not supposed to be that way. All over the world people sing and laugh, they buy each other gifts just for the sake of pleasing one another, yet that has not been my experience. The only Christmases I can recall are those spent here at Harmony House; dull and ordinary, the monotony broken up only by those family members who might drop by later in the day to wish us a Merry Christmas. And of course, our Saviour was born on Christmas—but for some reason that has always seemed secondary to me.

I attend the Christmas Eve service each year at the Episcopal church around the corner along with everyone else here at Harmony House, but I don't sing the carols or walk up the aisle for the bread and wine, and when everyone bows their head in prayer I secretly watch the minister to see if he knows the prayers by heart or if he must read them from his prayer book like the rest of us. It seems to me he should not have to look for the words, but he does. Now Jacob has found me and all this will change. In what way, I can't begin to imagine. Perhaps I won't even go to church this Christmas.

This is what you've wanted. All this time it's what you wanted.

"What's wrong with you now?" says Mrs. Zimmer from her rocking chair, her legs stretched wide beneath the hem of her dress as she pushes her feet into the floor, rocking. "Getting ready to take off again?" She's been making rude comments ever since I came back, but what else could I expect from her?

"My son is coming," I say, sitting up in bed and resting on my elbow. Mrs. Zimmer always said I was crazy to think I had children.

"What about your daughter? You said you had a boy *and* a girl. Why isn't she coming?" She picks something from her nose and flings it toward the ceiling. I don't look to see where it has landed. There's a smug look on her face as she sits there watching me like a gull waiting to dive into the ocean after bait. She can always find a way to take the wind from my sails.

"Mrs. Weaver didn't say. She just said Jacob." Doubt fills my throat.

I can't stop wondering why there was no mention of Jewel. If something happened to her—then what? All day I wonder, running so many *what ifs* through my mind that I make myself sick. I peck at my supper, pushing the peas and carrots around. When evening comes, there's a Christmas play on the TV that I pretend to be watching—some mushy reunion with family members who haven't spoken for eons but suddenly have a change of heart right before Christmas—but only because it's too early for me to go to bed. The storyline is old and tired and I can't help thinking that life is not all happy endings the way they are in the movies, and what will be my ending if, when Jacob comes, he's not at all happy with what he finds? What if he's filled with anger and bile from all the years I missed out on?

I shift my position and jump up from my chair. Pretending to stretch my legs, I walk around the room. Nick and Edward are playing cards in the corner of the room. The deck is worn and Nick complains that they can't even get a decent deck of cards in this joint. Mrs. Burke shushes them and turns the TV up a bit and I wish I could go to sleep for nine or maybe ten days and not wake up until Jacob arrives. When the movie is over, I go off to bed.

My mind needs to shut off before I can even begin to drift into sleep.

Sandra

News travels just like lightning in a small place like the Forties Settlement. I swear everyone must have been tuned in when Elizabeth's picture came across the TV screen that evening. The phone lines were surely buzzing afterward, everyone with a receiver up to their ear listening in. Even Daniel was taken up with the mystery, although that seems only natural, since I was the one everyone blamed for her disappearance in the first place. Not that anyone actually came right out and said it, but the insinuations were always there, and for months afterward people speculated on exactly what I'd said to her at Everett's funeral. I wouldn't have known that to be a fact if Marlene Lewis hadn't taken me aside one Sunday after church. She was the self-appointed spokesperson for the community and thought she could find out what the others couldn't. No one ever saw Elizabeth again after her stormy exit from the cemetery that day. It was as if she'd vanished into thin air. The next thing we knew, Cliff and the kids were moving back to Chester without her. And Everett leaving his house to me—no one understood that decision.

"Good Lord, come out and see this, Sandy—that's Elizabeth MacKay. Right there on TV," Daniel said, and I hurried out to the living room with a cup towel in my hand. I might have gasped, although I can't be sure. "Missing woman? Harmony House? Is that where she's been all these years?" Daniel was sitting in his armchair with his hands tucked in under his armpits as if warming them from a frost. It had been fifteen years, and her hair was pulled back into a ponytail instead of hanging down. There was a lost look in her eyes, some spark missing. It was Elizabeth, all right, but something about her had changed.

When the image on the screen disappeared, my mind started collecting all sorts of scenarios, running through the possibilities, wondering what this would mean for all of us.

It didn't take long for the incident at the funeral to find its way to the feed store where Daniel worked. I should have known it wouldn't. "Everyone's wondering what you said to set her off like that. Someone said she went wild." Daniel was talking as if he wasn't one of them. He enjoyed a good scandal as well as the next person. It was obvious in the way he was standing there half-smiling as he waited for an answer.

"I hardly remember," I lied. I knew better than to confide in Daniel. He would never be able to keep it to himself. The word *private* has never been part of his vocabulary. The first thing, everyone would know the real truth. Everett's good name would be tarnished and I didn't want that.

"Why didn't you tell me she attacked you? I had to hear it from Charlie Pence." The bemused look on his face said he was waiting to hear some juicy bit of gossip first-hand, something he could take to the feed store with him the next day. I knew more about the women in the Forties than most, thanks to their husbands and Daniel, who couldn't resist repeating the things he heard.

"Get away from me, bitch! I don't need you!" Fury had raged in her eyes as she pushed both hands against me. Cliff had spoken her name, scolding her.

"It's okay," I'd said, knowing I was the cause of her outburst. I should have known better. The letter I'd written a few months back was mailed back to me, ripped to shreds. Everett had asked me to wait. *"It's not the right time. Elizabeth hasn't been herself."* But I didn't expect there'd ever be a right time, and I was anxious for her to know the truth.

"She was upset, that's all," I said to Daniel as I scooped up a tobacco can of short feed from the tub and dumped it into the manger. Jennie stuck her head in and began chomping. I quickly grabbed the watering pail. I'd been hoping Daniel wouldn't bring the incident up, that he wouldn't want to know. But I knew better. Everyone at the graveside saw us. The funeral was well attended. Everett was an important man in the community. Tongues wag. They always do.

"So I heard. Enough for her to run away like that? Maybe she's got it in for you. Did you cross her in any way?" he continued, reaching for the barn shovel. I wondered what his friends had told him.

"Of course not."

"Maybe it was about the house, him leaving it to you like that? He told you, didn't he? Before he died, I mean. It must have made her spitting mad. She's a crazy one, she is."

"I was as surprised as everyone else when Everett left the place to me."

"Seems a strange thing, him giving it to you just because you kept house for him for a few years. What do you suppose got into him? Maybe the old-timer was going senile." I shrugged and wondered why he couldn't just accept the good fortune that had landed in his lap and be thankful.

"Elizabeth got his money—well, Cliff," I quickly spoke up, "and I suppose she already has a house of her own."

I should never have sent the letter. For days afterward I imagined her reading it, wondering what was going through her mind. The words I memorized, having read through the note countless times before sealing it into an envelope. I craved some acknowledgement from her as the days passed, waiting patiently for the mail delivery each day, but nothing came. I worried there had been a mix-up at the post office; perhaps it was placed in someone else's mailbox. But then she passed by me down at the Cross without turning her head, I knew the letter had found its way to her, and a part of me shrivelled inside.

"Back when you worked at the house, look how she carried on when Everett made her get out and get a job. She's crazy, that one is, always has been," Daniel said casually, scraping manure into the gutter.

He repeated that same sentiment last evening when the all-points bulletin came across the television screen, and like all those other times in the past, I chose not to speak up.

I would never have asked Everett to pick between me and Elizabeth, that wasn't why I wrote the letter. What I realize now is that discovering the truth can sometimes be more painful than living with the lies. A lie doesn't hurt as long as the truth is never revealed. That day, at Everett's funeral, the truth teetered and I faltered. I thought we might come together in our grief but I was wrong. Elizabeth wasn't about to accept me into her life, not then, not ever. Later, I made myself a promise to never tell. Besides, there was nothing to be gained by letting the truth out. People in the Forties Settlement thought Everett could do no wrong. Who was I to tarnish his good name?

I've asked myself a hundred times why Mom waited so long to tell me or why she thought I needed to know after all that time. But what I do know is that the longer you hold onto the truth the harder that truth is to speak. Even now, I wish that I had the courage to tell Daniel what I'd said to Elizabeth that day by Everett's grave.

"He was my father too, Elizabeth. He was my father too."

Elizabeth

"What will I say to him?" I ask Mrs. Weaver while straightening my dress collar.

"You'll do just fine, Elizabeth," she says, patting my hand. She looks toward the Christmas tree that is decorated and standing in the corner of the family room. The smile she's wearing is vague, and it makes me wonder if she's half as glad about Jacob coming as she pretends to be. She didn't want to believe he was real. "I know you'll do fine," she repeats, patting the words into place to make sure they stay.

Fine—but what if fine isn't good enough? What if fine doesn't make up for what was lost in the past? Fine is no better than mediocre and most times not worth the bother. Who would bother to come for mediocrity? Who would come back again for fine? What if he comes this one time but never returns? And what is the real reason no mention of Jewel was made? Butterflies continue to flit about inside me. I almost wish that Mrs. Weaver hadn't told me about

Jacob's most recent phone call. I ask her for an extra nerve pill, something that will cut down the jitters. My hands are trembling and there is no other way to make them stop.

"Don't be so silly," she says. "You don't need a nerve pill. This is all part of living. You'll do all right."

"But I wasn't expecting this."

"That's the wonderful thing about life, Elizabeth. We never know what's waiting around the corner. One day you're minding your own business and the next your long-lost son is coming to visit. What could be more splendid?"

I am sure I can think of other things that would appear more splendid than this sudden uprooting of my life. Not that I don't want to see Jacob; of course I do. I've dreamt of this moment for as long as I can recall, only in my dreams our reunion is unexpected, a chance encounter with both him and Jewel, recognition striking us at the same moment in time as we rush into each other's arms and hold on tight.

I suddenly work up the courage to ask about Jewel again.

"He didn't say, dear, but you can ask all that this evening."

"This evening? He's coming this evening?"

"Of course he's coming. I just told you he called again." Mrs. Weaver's quick flicker of a smile causes me to wonder if she knows more than she's telling. Seven days. There are seven days left before Christmas.

"Did he sound happy on the phone or just so-so?" Surely there is more to tell, not just that he's coming.

"Happy? I don't know if I'd use the word happy exactly."

"Then what? What would you say? Did he sound like he didn't care? I knew it," I huff, spinning abruptly toward the hallway. Mrs. Weaver takes me by the shoulders and turns me back around, nudging me toward the family room. "Go watch some TV, for goodness' sake. You'll drive yourself crazy asking all these questions."

The Christmas tree has been in place for some time, pushed back into the corner of the family room opposite the television. Every year they put the tree up too early in my opinion, and I suppose the stir that it causes when the tree is assembled somehow seems to make it worth the effort. It is all anyone talks about for a time here at Harmony House. *"Have you seen the tree?" "Isn't the tree lovely this year?" "Come look at our tree."* And on and on. I sense it won't make a good topic of conversation with Jacob, since I can't recall a single Christmas tree we would have decorated together when he was small. He was young, so young, and they took my past from me with the very treatments that made me well.

The tree is the first thing you see when you walk through the front door, and I'm certain Jacob will approve. Perfect round balls hang on every bough, the garland looped around both the front and back upon Mrs. Weaver's insistence. A small group of us stood back to watch the procedure. Lacking any sort of artistic abilities, I'm more than happy to have these things unfold before me. I wouldn't do it right anyway, and I'd spend each moment second-guessing where I placed everything. If it didn't look perfect, someone would complain.

"Garland in the back! No one's going to see the back," yelped Nick, and then Mrs. Weaver went on to tell him how everything must be done properly, speaking in a quiet voice; one that lacked conviction. But then, Nick likes to be spoken to that way even when he himself is screaming at the top of his lungs.

There was some discussion over the use of tinsel. "It'll look naked if we don't use the tinsel," Nick said.

"I like the icicles," said Sophie.

"*Tinsel*," Nick said, tilting his head to one side. "It happens to be called *tinsel*."

"It sticks to everything," complained Missy. "You get it on your clothes and in your hair. Down your underwear and in the crack of your ass. It's everywhere."

Everyone looked at Missy in surprise. Missy hadn't spoken to any of them since she came back to Harmony House claiming that it was all my idea for us to run away together.

"I couldn't let Elizabeth go off on her own," she'd told Mrs. Weaver. "Who knows where she'd have ended up, the way *she* is?" Mrs. Weaver had plenty to say to her and I thought she might have threatened to send her off, but she didn't. I wouldn't have known any of this had Mrs. Zimmer not told me.

"Missy was in Mrs. Weaver's office singing like a canary. Making herself out to be the good guy—as if." Mrs. Zimmer let out a loud grunt.

In the end, the tinsel was not put on the tree.

Mrs. Zimmer's side of the room is filled with teddy bears with pink and yellow ribbons tied around their necks. Each one of them has a silly name like Fuzzy, Beanie, or Skippy. She recently began a collection of porcelain dolls after her niece brought her one the day she came to visit. One day, while I lay on my bed with my back to them and pretended to sleep, I heard Mrs. Zimmer say to her niece, "Her mind's not worth a fiddler's fart."

"What happened?" the niece whispered.

"Shock treatments. You know what Swiss cheese looks like? Nothing more than a cardboard dummy. A frigging shame if you ask me." I got up then and walked out of the room and Mrs. Zimmer has not once apologized or made mention of the incident. I hope she won't listen in when Jacob comes to visit. I can hardly tell her to leave, for it is her room as well. Mrs. Zimmer has a habit of telling people more than they want to hear and I fear Jacob will be appalled to hear about Mrs. Zimmer's second husband who had an insatiable appetite for sex, as I once overheard her tell her niece.

I nearly jump out of my skin to see Mrs. Weaver outside our room looking in at me. I hurry to get off the bed in case she thinks I'm being a lazybones. I should be down in the kitchen helping Jenny or else watching TV in the family room like Mrs. Zimmer, not lying on my bed. But I haven't been sure what to do with myself since she told me that Jacob is coming after supper.

"This must be your lucky day," she says as she stretches out her arm. She's holding a brown handbag out to me and I realize it's mine, the one I lost in Kentville a few weeks back. She's smiling as if it belongs to her and not me, as if she couldn't be happier.

"But how?" I say, pulling it close. I never imagined I'd see it again.

"Someone found it—some honest person. And your notebook, Elizabeth, your notebook is what told them whose purse it was and where to find you."

The moment she's gone I flop onto the bed and unzip my bag. I'm surprised to find my empty wallet is still inside. Pulling out my notebook, I quickly flip it open to see the inscription Mrs. Weaver placed there. I turn to the first page, to my list of words. I quickly go through the other pages. It's all there, every last word, everything I wrote. I would never have dreamt that this notebook would bring me such joy. I'll show it to Jacob when he comes. I'll say, "See, I was trying to find you, all this time I've been trying." But as quickly as I think this, I know I won't have the courage.

After supper I begin pacing the hallway, looking out the window in the family room to see if he is coming up the drive, expecting I will recognize him immediately in the dim lighting outside Harmony House. Still, plans get changed and people show up early or late all the time. I start to worry that he won't come at all. I go to my notebook and write:

December 18th, 1975
Jacob is coming.

The carollers begin to arrive, hurrying in through the doorway with a rupture of cold air. Sheet music rustles while they remove their winter coats and migrate quickly toward the piano in the family room. Shortly afterward, musical notes are echoing all through Harmony House. They invite us to join in, smiling and laughing as they pass around a booklet that contains the words to the Christmas carols, even to those who cannot read. The booklet makes me uneasy. What will I do with it when Jacob arrives? I wish I hadn't taken one. I'd forgotten the carollers were coming this evening, when all day long I thought of nothing but Jacob and why no one mentioned Jewel.

At first, I mistake him for one of the carollers arriving a bit late until I see him speaking to Mrs. Weaver, who then leads him across the room to where I'm standing. My heart reaches for my throat, pushing with all its might. I didn't expect him to choose the very same evening as the carollers, but I smile when he reaches out to me, wondering if the worry I'm feeling is spread across my face. He has perfect teeth and looks much older than I'd imagined, handsome in his black leather jacket. His brown eyes and curly hair startle me somewhat and I gasp slightly as he comes closer. In my mind he was much fairer, more like me. But I was wrong. He looks like Cliff, and the fact that I recognize this so blatantly, in this moment, should be cause for me to be happy, but instead it threatens to bring me to my knees.

The piano music is vibrating so loudly that I can barely make out what he's saying. We exchange awkward hugs. I don't know which shoulder feels right. His cheek brushes against mine and I tremble, my knees beginning to fail, and I can't for the life of me think of a single intelligent thing to say. I cling to him much longer than I should, hoping to gain courage and find a way to untangle my tongue.

"Take your company back to your room, Elizabeth," Mrs. Weaver says, smiling. "It'll be more private there and a little less noisy." Mrs. Zimmer is sitting next to the piano player, her flabby neck stretched out in song. Relief floats through me like a downy white feather from the clouds; at least I won't have to worry about her saying something totally inappropriate.

To be truthful, I was hoping to stay in the family room, melding in with the singing and music, pressing our expectations somewhere to the back, perhaps ignoring altogether the complexity of our situation. It's enough for me to see Jacob, to be in the same room. If we're alone he'll expect more from me than I'm able to give. Some things a mother just knows, even a mother who cannot remember.

"So noisy," he says, unzipping his coat as we settle into the room I share with Mrs. Zimmer. I can't take my eyes off him. "Here. I brought you something." He places a small package in my hands and tells me to open it. There are tiny pink and white soaps and powder with a bright pink puff wrapped up neatly in a clear plastic package that is impossible to open. The scent comes through the packaging and I take a sniff.

"I wasn't sure what to get...what you might need."

"It smells wonderful," I say, flipping over the package. "Magnolia. My favourite." He seems pleased. I fumble with it for a bit longer until Jacob says I can get someone to help me later.

"This is so nice," I say, grappling for something more to say, something that will make it worth his while to have come. He looks about the room I share with Mrs. Zimmer, at her array of plush teddy bears, and I feel suddenly inadequate. What does he think now that he sees the meagre surroundings that make up my life, that his mother is a simpleton, a damaged part of society, as Mrs. Zimmer is always so quick to point out?

"You came a long way," I say, hoping to stop him from looking too closely.

"Longer than you think."

"I didn't know. Couldn't remember," I stumble, sounding immature, knowing what little I have to offer.

"It's okay," he says, touching my hand. "Mrs. Weaver mentioned that on the phone."

"Jewel," I say hesitantly.

He clears his throat. "She couldn't come," he says.

"You mean she's okay, then?" I close my eyes and breathe, my body weak with relief, but then I immediately need to know. "Where is she? Why didn't she come?"

"I'm not altogether sure. Maybe some other time," he adds, seeing the disappointment on my face. But the way he says it makes me wonder if there's something more, something he's not ready to tell, but I can't ask. That privilege is not even mine. I can't imagine giving up on Jacob or Jewel.

Real mothers don't do those kinds of things, but then real mothers, good mothers, don't go crazy.

"I don't think I wanted to leave," I try to explain. "I think maybe I had no choice."

"Then we won't talk about it. Not now, at least." I'm happy to be let off the hook. I've imagined there would be questions along with a whole list of *Do you remember*s that I know would reduce me to little more than the cardboard dummy Mrs. Zimmer once described me as.

"We can go out and listen to the music if you'd rather." Only we sit on the bed, not moving, until Jacob finally says, "Why don't you tell me a story?"

So I tell him how I picked rocks in the farmer's field one summer in the late sixties. I tell him about the Hippie Bus with bright red flowers that we drove in on each day and about Jeffery and Sampson, the hospital workers who went with us to the field, and the time Bernice grabbed the cigarette from Sampson's mouth and twisted it into the ground with her foot, and about the cars that would speed by daily, sometimes blowing their horns or waving their arms out the windows at us, and I even tell him about the little store where we'd stop on the way back to the hospital to buy candy bars. Most of all I talk about Reggie, the young fellow in the group who kept things quite lively, whooping and hollering at various intervals during the morning. When the day was over, when there was no time for Reggie to act the fool, he would often talk about his parents in Antigonish. Most of us envied Reggie, for he was one of the very few who got to go home on a weekend pass.

And all the while I'm speaking, I can see that Jacob is interested in what I have to say.

"I wonder what happened to him—Reggie, I mean," he says when I come to the end of the story.

"I'm so sorry," I say, feeling suddenly foolish at the way I've rambled on. I'm no better than Mrs. Zimmer when her niece comes to visit.

"Sorry about what?" His face gives away his confusion.

"About Reggie. Telling you all about him. You didn't even know him. I shouldn't have gone on so. It was silly. It's just that I remember that time in my life. It's one of the few things I remember quite clearly. It wasn't unpleasant, you see. Most of the treatments were over. I was beginning to piece some things back together."

It's impossible for me to explain this to Jacob, this young man sitting on my bed. How peculiar it seems trying to imagine him as the little boy I left somewhere in the past.

"Did I tell you many stories when you were small?' I ask, trying to shake off my embarrassment.

"I don't remember you telling stories at all." I look to see if there is disappointment in his eyes when he says this. Good mothers tell their children stories, at least bedtime stories. Why couldn't I have told him a story he'd remember, something he could have carried with him all these years? "I don't remember a lot from back then," he says. "I was only five. Jewel used to read to me, though. We had this book of stories Poppy gave us."

"Poppy! That's one of my words!"

Eagerly pulling open the drawer to my nightstand, I take out the notebook and go to the first page. *Poppy*. I point to it. The word is right there, on my list of words.

"See, I knew it meant something important!"

"Poppy was your father."

"My father?... Really? I always thought it was a flower." I should have known better. Why would a flower hold any significance? And why did I have to admit my stupidity to Jacob just now? I quickly look at him, feeling embarrassed by my blunder. His smile is soft, his eyes brimming with understanding. "Can I see?" he says, reaching out for the notebook. I give it to him only because I don't know how to say no. What if he laughs at my childish scribblings? Mrs. Weaver said no one would ever see it. Hugging fast to myself, I wait as he turns the pages and reads what I've written. When he is through, he puts it back and closes the drawer. A part of me is glad not to know what he's thinking.

"You'll have more to write about now," he says.

Tears blur my eyes then and I wipe them away. How ridiculous of me to sit crying on the bed with my son beside me, this son I haven't seen for years, this son I hadn't been absolutely sure existed until now. I'm not at all sure why I'm crying—if it's from having Jacob beside me after all these years or because I just now remember what happened to Reggie. We sit on the bed, Jacob with his arm draped across my shoulder. I look up into his eyes, through this veil of forgetfulness that plagues my past, only to see some deep understanding embedded there.

"He died." Jacob looks at me, surprised. "Reggie, I mean. We were told he hanged himself in the basement of his parents' home while out on his weekend pass."

It's all so clear to me now, the look on the nurse's face when she told us. Nobody knew what to say. He was too young to leave this world. Far too young.

We rock back and forth then on the edge of the bed, not in time to the music that is rumbling in the family room, the plink-plinking of the piano keys, but to a rhythm pulled out from the past, a steady, slow rising and falling of our chests as we breathe.

Jewel

On the wall to the left of the doorway are two laminated signs with roses on either side. One says *Helena* and the other *Elizabeth*, just where Mrs. Weaver said they'd be. Something gnaws in the pit of my stomach as I grip the Pot of Gold chocolate box. What if Jacob has already gone? The piano begins to play "Silent Night," and voices echo from down the hall, some slightly off key, others trying to keep the tempo, straining to be heard over the piano. The hallway is dimly lit for the evening and my steps slow as I draw near the open door. There's still time for me to turn back, take the past with me and keep it hidden.

Finally working up the courage, I spent last evening reading through the letters. Jacob is right. The letters hold all the things Mumma missed from our childhood, a time capsule of sorts, even though Aunt Joan's motives were less than admirable. Some of the letters brought back memories, things I hadn't thought of in a very long time, and when I got to the end, once the very last letter had been read, my heart opened wide and a flood of tears washed over me. I cried for all the secrets I'd kept and all the times I'd wished things had been different; all the things that had been lost during Mumma's absence, the fact that she had to face her illness all alone. And then I cried for Daddy and Uncle Dylan and David and even Jacob's chestnut pony.

Inside the small room Jacob is sitting on the bed, eyes closed, swaying to the music. The sight of him with Mumma catches me off guard. I'm unable to move closer, to spoil this precious moment, crumple it with my presence. Mumma looks up then, sees me standing in the doorway, and time comes to a screeching halt. The betrayal I've lived with all these years falls slowly away when I see the look in her eyes. My name rests on her lips, quivering between the past and present. She reaches out her arms to me. She reaches out her arms...to me.

"Mumma," I whisper softly. The box of letters slips from my hands and the envelopes scatter across the floor. Jacob opens his eyes. I see the same boy who looked up at me from the empty manger the day his chestnut pony went away and I know then, after all these years, Mumma has finally come home.

Part III

1976

Elizabeth

The wind blows in through the car window, tossing my hair in a carefree dance. I smile, making myself comfortable in the back seat of Jacob's car. It's not a big vehicle, but I like the colour of the interior, a plush grey that almost makes me feel like royalty when I settle myself in. The car is far from being new, and lately there's this noise that comes from beneath when he hits a rough patch in the road. I keep telling him he should get it looked at, but he's been putting it off, saying it's probably nothing. Jacob's not one to be overly concerned about what he calls the "little things." I like that about him, the way he can calm the worry that niggles inside of me. This is our first day trip together, the three of us. Day trip—just thinking about it makes me smile. For years I used to watch with envy when some of the residents at Harmony House got to leave for the entire day. They'd come back different, as if being away had altered them, at least until the reality of their lives set back in again, which usually came a few hours later. I used to think that I'd be happy just to experience that feeling of being different, even for a short time. I've been trying to stay optimistic, not expecting too much to change, but allowing the contentment I feel to spread however slowly it wants. I now have a reason to smile every day.

The sun beams down on me through the window of the car, settling deep in my core, as we pull away from Harmony House. A sense of euphoria comes over me, and I feel lighter than usual. This day seems perfect; something I once feared would never be possible. Mrs. Weaver gave me her blessing earlier this morning. She came into my room while I was going through my closet. I'd been planning to wear a dark navy outfit but found myself reaching for a breezy cotton dress I'd found at Frenchys last week. Sophie gasped when I went into the changing room that day with it draped over my arm. From inside the tiny stall I overheard her say, "Elizabeth doesn't wear red." Looking at myself from all angles, I had to admit that I liked the bright colour and the tiny yellow flowers. When I came back out and announced that I'd take it, Rebecca said she was very proud of me for trying something new. "I'm sure it will look beautiful on you," she said. I told her I wasn't sure about that but that the colour was certainly eye-catching. The scrunched-up face Sophie gave made us both laugh. At the time I wasn't sure I'd ever wear the dress, but as the days went by, knowing it was inside my closet reassured me in a way that an article of clothing had never done before. It's only a red dress, for goodness' sake.

Music is playing over the car radio, tunes that only young people listen to these days, certainly no one at Harmony House. Mrs. Zimmer would be sputtering and chewing that young people have no respect, but I sit here tapping my foot and feeling the rhythm of the song bouncing in my soul. Jewel is singing along to the music and every so often Jacob joins in. They look at one another and smile. From the back seat, I see the countryside pass by. As we approach a field filled with dandelions, I make a quick gasp, calling out for Jacob to stop. He pulls off the road and the three of us get out of the car.

"We used to pick dandelion flowers," says Jacob, smiling. "Our field would be covered in the spring."

"You'd put them in a glass on the table," adds Jewel.

Bending down to pick one, I decide against it. It will only stain my hands. As we get back into the car, I ask Jacob to wait for a moment before resuming our drive. Taking in the view, I absorb the scenery like a sponge. "I like dandelions," I say, gazing out at the field of yellow.

"Do you suppose it's something you remember from before? You always said they were your favourite." Jewel's eyes sparkle. I can see her reflection in the side-view mirror, her beautiful complexion, bits of blonde hair being swept up in the breeze. Jacob favours his father. I can see it even though I can't produce a clear image of Cliff in my mind. But Jewel, so much of me is in her; the way she turns her head and smiles, the look that crosses her face when she's contemplating something. Jacob laughs and says how uncanny it is, that we could pass as sisters. While I smile at the thought, I hope for her sake that it isn't true. I want Jewel to be strong and confident; all the things I can't be.

Jacob has promised that one day we will look at old photos together—when we're all ready, that is. One part of me is terrified at the thought, the other part filled with curiosity. I'd like to know what my life once looked like. I really would. I've been keeping my questions to a minimum, afraid that I might push them for answers they don't want to be truthful about for fear of hurting me. My illness got in the way of us living our lives. It robbed me, stopped me from being the person I was meant to be. Then there's Jewel, still grieving for her father, even though it's been nearly three years since he was lost at sea. I know what it's like to carry a heart full of grief. And so, we are not yet ready for photos.

Last night, I took out my notebook and wrote on a brand new page: *Tomorrow we are going home.* My hand trembled slightly as the words materialized on the page and I scolded myself for being weak. There's a picnic lunch on the seat beside me: potato salad, coleslaw and pieces of cold chicken, some early strawberries Jewel picked up at the store this morning that smell totally scrumptious. Both Jacob and Jewel insisted upon bringing all this food, even though I told them they shouldn't fuss and that sandwiches would be just fine.

"Who said 'just fine' is good enough for the MacKays?" Jacob wanted to know. It took only a few moments for me to agree. Jacob was right. *Just fine* wouldn't do. Everyone deserves more than *just fine* from life.

"Is it too breezy back there, Mumma?"

"It's good, Jewel," I say. "Everything is wonderful."

There's this woman in the Forties who wants to meet me. I just found out a few weeks ago. Her name is Sandra. She sounded quite friendly when we spoke. She asked how I was doing and mentioned a bit about the weather. We chatted about insignificant things for a few moments, the conversation stilted and a bit forced. I'm not one for chatting on the phone, and using the one out in the hallway made me feel exposed. Mrs. Zimmer has a phone on her side of the room, and she sometimes talks to her niece on Saturday afternoons but I've never had reason to use a phone, let alone to ask for one.

All the while we were talking, I kept wondering who this Sandra was and what she really wanted. When she asked me if I remembered her, I had to admit that I didn't. I'm afraid I went on to tell her about the treatments they gave me that swept my memory out from under me, and then I wondered what made me blurt all that out to someone I didn't even know. Suddenly frightened that my past was catching up with me, I asked her right out how she knew me.

"We are sisters," she said. "Half-sisters, actually." There came a long pause. Her words took a while to register. But then she ambushed me, and before I had time to think it through, I agreed to meet with her. Jewel said there had never been any mention of Sandra being my half-sister and that she could be making it up for all we know. Yet I wonder why she would have called in the first place if it wasn't true. I can't imagine anyone making such a claim for no good reason. She likely saw my story on the television last fall like a lot of other people, but what if Jewel's right? What if she *is* making it all up? I have no way of knowing. A few days after she phoned, I had a dream. I was in a cemetery filled with tombstones. There were other people there, and a coffin was being lowered into the ground. Flowers; there were so many flowers. And then I was screaming at someone. Even though I couldn't see her face, I knew it was this Sandra who wanted to meet me—this woman claiming to be my half-sister. The dream left me shaken.

"I remember Sandra Peterson from when we lived in the Forties," Jewel said. "Her son was an ass." I know there was more she wanted to add, but she stopped. In time I'm sure she'll tell, but I've learned it's best not to push for answers. I wrote to this Sandra and told her I thought perhaps meeting at this time was not a good idea. Both Jacob and Jewel agreed.

Those small flickers of memory I've experienced in the past continue to catch up to me, and some days I wonder if they're not becoming more frequent. Still other days, I'm content enough that I don't bother looking for anything more. And I think maybe that's the best way to live. I've explained to Jewel and Jacob how all the electroshock treatments left me unable to recall so much of the past; a by-product of the treatment that was deemed acceptable by those who were supposed to know what they were doing. There are the letters—the ones Dylan's wife wrote. I've read and reread them, imagining the parts of the children's growing up that I missed. I would like to thank her for writing them but sense that wouldn't be a good idea. She was one of the ones who left me suspended in the past. She must have had her reasons, people usually do, and while the letters have been helpful, there's this bitterness inside me.

I'm watching the road ahead, and a slight stirring begins in the pit of my stomach as I see the churches appear.

"This is the Cross, where the three churches are," I say, perplexed as to how these words have found their way to my lips. "New Ross. We're in New Ross. Make a left turn right here," I add, confidence now growing inside me.

"We used to get groceries at that little store sometimes," says Jewel, pointing to her right. "I remember!"

"It's not far now," I say, moving toward the edge of my seat, at this new realization now tapping me on the shoulder.

"Does anything else look familiar?" Jacob asks, as we pass the sign for the Forties Settlement. I search my mind for some landmark, anything recognizable. We drive up one hill and down the next and still nothing catches my attention. A burst of sunlight shines through the windshield as we round the top of a hill. Jewel quickly pulls the sun visor down. Looking over her shoulder at me, her eyes and her voice are filled with expectation as she asks, "Anything?"

"I'm afraid not." For years I tried to get back some small part of the past, searching for something that was no longer there. Now, that need to get back what was lost seems senseless. Memories got scattered along the way. Things I thought I remembered with clarity have become dull and cloudy. I can no longer distinguish what is real and what are mere whispers from a mind that wants desperately to hang fast to something, anything. But I don't need that now. I have Jewel and Jacob and a future filled with hope. Just the other week we talked about the possibility of my getting an apartment, somewhere handy to where Jewel lives. At first, I thought they were joking; how could I possibly live on my own? But then I saw the sincerity in their eyes, the possibilities that suddenly said, "Maybe, just maybe."

"No," I say firmly from the back seat. "There's no need to do this. We can go back."

"What do you mean? Don't you want to go home?" asks Jacob looking at me in the rear-view mirror.

I smile then, knowing that home is not an actual place as I once thought. Home is knowing that you belong in someone's heart and they belong in yours.

Jewel

Dawn breaks. A golden glow is cast upon my bedroom
wall. I survey the room, the white lace curtains, the vanilla
walls. Pictures of a happy family are on the dresser beside
me, taken at a time when we lived in the Forties Settlement—
Mumma, Daddy, Jacob, and me. In the distance you can see
the barn, an apple tree at the edge of the pasture that bears
yellow fruit in late August. Farther still, almost invisible
to the eye, running at lightning speed, is a chestnut pony.
Jacob's head is turned slightly toward the sound of hooves
pummelling against the green grassland. Mumma is smiling, beautiful as always. We are all smiling except for Jacob,
who has thoughts on his mind besides having his picture
snapped.

There is no looking back. Only the reality of what is.

No thoughts of how it was.

No was.

Just is.

No longing for a chestnut pony that will never come into being.

There is peace, serenity, hope as I look ahead.

And now it might be.

All this might someday be.

Acknowledgements

My sincere gratitude to Patrick Murphy for seeing the larger picture and encouraging me to create a novel around what originally began as a collection of linked stories. Had it not been for your suggestion, I'm certain this novel would never have been written. My thanks to *Transition* magazine and *The Nashwaak Review* for publishing three of the original short stories I built upon when writing this book: "Mad Money," "There's This Thing about Leaving," and "Balloon Man." Thanks to Jan Coates for reading my original story collection and assuring me that there was indeed a novel hidden in there.

My thanks to Nimbus Publishing and Vagrant Press, most especially Whitney Moran, for making my long-held dream a reality. Thanks to my editor, Penelope Jackson, for your enthusiasm and your gentle way of nudging me into discovering a better alternative.

To Sherry and Gail for lending me your names in one of the scenes; enjoy your second of fame. To Syr for your faith in my writing ability and for always believing this day would come.

My thanks to the people who get me where I need to go: Brian, Matthew, Michelle, and Alicia. Thanks also to Darlene and George for your hospitality and the most delicious lasagna I've ever tasted.

To all my family and friends, your love and support keeps me writing.